The Author

Raymond Jones, a teacher for twenty-six years, draws on his experiences to write his first novel. This humorous account of school life will ring true with many teenage boys. Essential reading for all parents and teenagers!

Apart from the characters Biggs and his adversary Christopher Bird, who are based on real people, all characters in this book are fictional.

Thanks to Christian
- the inspiration for this book.

"Come on, Sir. Stop frigging about ... Let's get airborne"

THE
GORDON BENNETT
CHRONICLES

RAYMOND JONES

TIGER

A TIGER Paperback

Published in Great Britain 2001
by
Raymond Jones
2 Laura Drive
Hextable, Swanley. Kent BR8 7RX

This book is sold subject to the condition that
it shall not, by way of trade or otherwise, be lent,
resold, hired out, or otherwise circulated without the
publisher's prior consent in any form of binding or cover
other than that in which it is published and without a
similar condition including this condition being
being imposed on the subsequent purchaser.

Copyright © Raymond Jones 2001

TIGER
is an imprint of Raymond Jones

ISBN 0-9540603-0-X

Printed by Gullpine Printers, Welham Green, Herts AL9 7DX. 01707 262506

To my sister, Vi.

WHO'S WHO AT

THE STAFF

MR MARTIN
HEADMASTER
(HIS MAJESTY)

DON ROYSTON
2ND DEPUTY

LYNN HARMON
(LYNN-THE-GRIN)
DRAGONESS

MALCOLM ROWE
SENIOR YEAR HEAD (U/S)

UPPER

LOWER

HARRY LANGTON
1ST DEPUTY
(ROVER)

LAURA CLAYTON
SECRETARY
(THE HEADMISTRESS)

IAN McTAGGART
HEAD OF FIRST YEAR
(CHIEF ANKLEBITER)
DON'T ASK!

RAY SMITH
SENIOR YEAR HEAD (L/S)
(BIGGS)
MR. NICE GUY

BRENDA HICKMAN
ENGLISH TEACHER
(A MATYR TO PMT)

PAUL SCOBIE
(RESIDENT HIPPY)

PETER PARTRIDGE
(TOKEN GAY)

PLUS THE

GORDON BENNETT

THE KIDS

ANDREW BOLTON
5TH YEAR LOUT
(I.Q. OF A DAFFODIL)

SCHOOL
SCHOOL

→ ADVERSARIES ←
BECOME
(GOOD FRIENDS)

THE ELITE THIRD YEAR MATHEMATICIANS

CHRISTOPHER BIRD
(SMART-ARSE)

ALAN LANE
(WOBBLE-GOB)

TONY ROBERTS
(CB'S BEST FRIEND)

MANY OTHERS

PAUL SMITH
(LAZY GIT)

STEVEN BIRD
ANKLEBITER
(CB'S PAIN-IN-THE-BUTT BROTHER)

ALSO RANS

"No Sir. It wasn't what she didn't say that bothered us.... it was more.... the way she didn't say it!"

"But, Sir, it's Friday! It's our chat-day! You know you enjoy listening to us and we work better when were chatting!"
"Oh yes! And how does chatting help you to work better?"
"It lubricates our brains, Sir!"

"I don't believe it!" Biggs said. "You jammy sod, Chris! You couldn't repeat that in a month of Sundays."
"Easy-peasy..... and there's me thinking that you were a big hero! But there's nothing to this flying lark, is there? It's kid's stuff!"

PROLOGUE

Gordon Bennett was a small and not unpleasant Comprehensive school for boys somewhere in the South East of England. A couple of decades earlier our educational masters, in their infinite wisdom, had decided that the segregation of children at a tender age, according to their ability, was divisive. 'Big is beautiful' was the policy current at the time and enforced mergers were commonplace. Following an amalgamation, resulting from the sad demise of the local grammar school and a nearby secondary modern school, Gordon Bennett rose like a phoenix from their ashes. After a somewhat shaky start it quickly settled down to becoming a popular community school. Gordon Bennett in its turn was to suffer a further traumatic merger a couple of decades later. Meanwhile, blissfully ignorant of its own future demise, it enjoyed salad days.

The Upper School, accommodating the seniors, was located in a quiet middle class residential area. Half a mile away, near the local shopping centre was the Lower School annexe, housing the younger boys. The annexe was in the nominal charge of the First Deputy Head, Mr. Harry Langton, a tall Scotsman. A jovial will-o-the wisp character, Harry Langton had been given the nickname 'Rover.' It was bestowed on him by the Headmaster, on the one recorded occasion that he had been known to suffer a mild attack of humour. Being a bit of a poser, Rover usually carried a British Telecom radio pager slung low on his right hip, so that he could be contacted in an emergency, should his roving take him away from the school on urgent business. Harry Langton always seemed to have a lot of urgent business! Mobile phones for the masses had yet to make an appearance, so the sight of young adolescents walking to school with them glued to their ears, or teachers having to contend with multiple ringing in their classrooms, was a joy yet to come. The radio pager, being the next best thing, fell into the category, 'executive toy.' Rover liked executive toys. He also liked personalized car number plates for himself and Mrs. Rover..... and of course roving.

The day-to-day running of the Lower School was in the capable hands of the Senior Year Head, Mr. Ray Smith. Ray had been given the nickname 'Biggs' by boys and staff alike for reasons that will become apparent later. Mr. Langton's roving afforded him a quiet life and allowed him to run things his way. Although great rivals at almost everything, they were the best of friends and a bit of a double act in the Gordon Bennett annexe. The incidents portrayed in this book are the true recollections of Biggs; a teacher's eye view shall we say.

A central character in the life of the Lower School and the real power behind the throne, was that of Mrs. Laura Clayton, the school secretary and confidante to everyone. By nature a bit of a bossy-boots, Mrs. Clayton was known as 'The Headmistress.' She played an important part in the smooth running of the Gordon Bennet annexe. She alone knew Mr. Langton's radio page number and would divulge it to nobody, especially not to Biggs, knowing that he always had a yearning to try it out, with mischievous intent. Mrs. Clayton was a keen scuba diver and enjoyed writing magazine articles. She had little time for naughty boys and was decidedly cool towards awkward and over demanding members of staff.

Christopher Bird was an exceptionally bright, rather cheeky, but not unpleasant Third Year extrovert. Having survived his first two years in the school and having gained moderate success in most things, he regarded himself as a bit of an expert in the business of being educated. His razor-sharp wit and total mastery of repartee made him popular with his peers. Looking back on his own youth, Biggs always saw something of himself in him and they generally got on rather well. Christopher went on to join the Royal Navy after leaving school. A master in the art of sailing close to the wind, he interjects from time to time with a pupil's perspective.

Teachers being of a type, will inevitably see something of themselves or their colleagues in many of the characters portrayed. It must be made clear at this point that although they may based on real people, they are all fictitious. Most characters are an amalgam and names have been changed to protect the innocent...... and the not so innocent! Although Gordon Bennett is a fictitious school, the events and incidents described are for the most part true, or at least a very close approximation to the truth, so as to highlight the absurd and the funny.

Other characters are revealed as the story unfolds. The setting is the early nineteen-eighties.

CHAPTER 1

AUTUMN TERM - THE FIRST DAY BACK

"How can any sane person have the nerve to drive round in a monstrosity like this?" Harry Langton remarked, fiddling with everything within his reach.

"What's your problem," Biggs replied. "I see no problem!"

"You only see what you want to see...... that's your problem."

"That's not a problem...... that's an asset...... Anyway, you seem quite happy to be seen in the passenger seat, or do I detect a touch or jealousy?"

"Me jealous? Don't be so ridiculous! What have I got to be jealous about?"

It was the first day of the new school year. Only the new First Year intake came in on the morning of first day. Often referred to as anklebiters, they were due to arrive at 10.30 after the beginning of year staff meeting in the Upper School building. It was always a mundane affair, but thankfully short. The usual welcome-back address was delivered to the staff by HM (Headmaster, not His Majesty, although he always liked his staff to think of him in that light). All too dazed from the trauma of returning to school after the long summer holiday, his words largely passed over their heads.

Glancing round the room, Biggs viewed his colleagues with a mixture of suspicion and dismay. They were all there, the same old faces; the whingers and the whiners, the trouble makers and the back stabbers and of course, the eager beavers! Despite having been one himself a decade or so earlier, he disliked the eager beavers as much as the back stabbers. Their incessant beavering away simply served to highlight his own lack of enthusiasm..... and at least he knew where he stood with the back stabbers! He could count on one hand those that he could loosely regard as friends. He was not looking forward to the start of yet another school year and he wished that he could be somewhere else.... anywhere else! It was not that he didn't like his job, or that he didn't do it well. He knew that he did do it well and some bits he enjoyed very much. But much of the fun of his early days in teaching seemed to have disappeared and it had become an all too serious business. He was by no means old, in fact barely middle aged. He was just a sad case of been there and done that! Having read the book and seen the film many times over, he knew that he was a fast becoming a terminal case of deja-vu.

As His Majesty prattled on in his usual monotonous tone, Biggs' mind wandered back to the previous week. He reflected on how only a few days earlier, he had been lazing without a care in the world on the sun drenched shore of Lake Marianna in central Florida. Preferring the peace and quiet of the central lakes to the crowded beaches, he had been staying alone at a small hideaway resort situated on the banks of the lake. He spent much of his time in school dealing with the seemingly interminable problems of kids, colleagues and parents, so he made a point of getting away by himself at least once a year, in the forlorn hope of refreshing himself. It hadn't all been calm and serene though, he thought to himself and smiling inwardly, he remembered how he had been soaking up the sun in a small rowing boat in the centre of the lake. Drifting aimlessly without a care in the world, he had become aware of what he at first thought was a log, sliding with barely a ripple pass his port side. But why was it moving? He was on a lake and he wasn't moving, so he reasoned that the log shouldn't have been! He had then become somewhat alarmed to discover that the log had teeth and turned out to be an alligator! Having the presence of mind to stay calm and keep low in the boat, the danger eventually passed, but it had been a scary moment. Recounting the incident to the owner of the resort later in the day, he'd been told that they were a common sight, but that they were generally harmless and rarely came ashore when people were about. He had not been entirely convinced by the assurance so glibly given, since the previous day the local radio had reported that a group teenagers fishing in a nearby dyke, had been attacked by one of those harmless logs. Fortunately the lads managed to escape without harm, but they had been forced to sacrifice their fishing gear to the creature. There were always a few incidence each year of people attacked and occasionally killed by alligators and he'd had no wish to become one of their number. He thought of one or two of their own kids and several members of staff that he could have happily have watched being devoured by an alligator!

Biggs was awakened from his daydream by the moving of chairs and the shuffling of feet, as the meeting was brought to a close by the Headmaster, saying "I'm sure that Mr. Smith will be able to answer that question later."

But what question? He hadn't the foggiest idea and he suddenly realized that he could recall barely a word that had been said during the meeting! Never mind, he thought to himself, I'm sure that some bugger will enlighten me in due course, when they want their petty problem solved. It was 10 o'clock and after sundry last minute irrelevancies from the usual windbags, the meeting broke up and the Lower School staff returned to the annexe.

Being a bit of a fanatic at the time for American muscle cars, Biggs had earlier in the summer holiday purchased a magnificent black Trans Am. It had an enormous gold phoenix on the bonnet, real Smokey and the Bandit type. It was the second American car that he'd owned and he had traded in his bright yellow Camaro for it. The Camaro had been okay, but it hadn't been a Trans Am! There was something about a Trans Am which made it stand out from other American 'muscle' cars. Biggs liked American muscle cars; he liked the American way of life; in fact he liked all things American!

Harry Langton readily accepted a lift back to the Lower School. Having left his own car, a Rolls-Royce no less, at the annexe, he had earlier scrounged a lift to the Upper School. It was not often that Harry brought his Roller to school, his usual mode of transport being a small white van. He seemed quite impressed with Biggs' new acquisition, but he hated being out-posed and felt the need to deride it.

"What does this do?" Harry asked, opening the glove locker and before he could be stopped, pressing a hidden button.

A reply was unnecessary....... the boot lid flew open with a bang, just as they were passing the local bobby, PC Brian Stevens. He was the school liaison officer and recognized them at once. Raising both eyes to heaven, he shook his head in despair. Cringing a little, Harry sank low in his seat. Harry was prone to cringing when confronted with authority. Although a charismatic character who could be quite domineering at times, he was a sheep in wolf's clothing.

They arrived at the Lower School to find the place swarming with parents and their darling offspring. Many had been there since 9 o'clock, despite being clearly informed of a 10.30 start. After a few words of encouragement to several doting parents, their offspring were reluctantly left to fend for themselves. One or two parents seemed only too pleased to get shot of their little darlings and disappeared as soon as the staff arrived. The majority of the little darlings were certainly only too pleased to get shot of their parents! Nothing can be more embarrassing to an eleven year boy starting his new school, than having his mother standing beside him. However first things first, it was time for a sustaining cup of coffee. The coffee machine bubbled away merrily in the general office, inviting them to partake of a well earned cup of the delicious brew. Laura Clayton played mum. She had spent much of her summer holiday scuba diving in Jersey and had a gorgeous sun tan.

Just after half past ten, the new boys, resplendent in their new uniforms, were rounded up and taken to the hall for a welcoming address by Ian McTaggart, the Head of First Year. Known as the Chief Anklebiter, Mr. McTaggart sported a splendid proboscis in the form of a large roman nose, somewhat resembling a parrot's beak. It was the bane of his life and at times the subject of much merriment. He always took it in good part, however and usually gave as good as he got. He introduced Harry Langton, Biggs and

Gladys to the assembled multitude. Gladys was the nickname bestowed by boys and staff alike on Mr. Mike Gladstone, the Head of Second Year. He hated it, which naturally served to make everyone use it all the more!

Glancing round the hall, while Harry was saying a few words of encouragement to the new recruits, Biggs played his usual first day of the year game of 'spot the sibling.' Looking like miniature clones of their older brothers, picking them out was always easy. If only they could have stayed looking so smart and innocent, he thought to himself. Even the kid brothers of their more undesirable element seemed to have an air of innocence about them. But he had been in the game too long and his sixth sense enabled him to identified a few characters likely to end up on the wrong side of his desk before the week was out, as perpetrators of some wrongdoing or other.

Introductions over, the hierarchy returned to the office for another cup of coffee leaving Ian McTaggart and the new First Year tutors to continue with the assembly. Ian was grateful for their departure, since being newly appointed it was his first assembly and he preferred not to be watched over. He had to go solo sometime and there was no better time..... with the new innocents?

The rest of kids were not due in until the afternoon so there was little for the staff to do other than pretend to look busy, discuss their summer holidays and bemoan the fact that they were over. The lunch menu offered a choice of Shepherd's Pie or Bangers and Mash, good enough to tickle the taste buds of the new anklebiters. Generally speaking the food was not at all bad, although it was always fairly predictable; Wednesday was Curry-day and Friday was Fish-day. Biggs decided that he would go out for lunch and visit his sister.

In the afternoon the old hands returned. Biggs arrived back in time to meet a motley crowd of Third Year lads chatting outside the main gate. They were blocking the entrance to the car park, but parted on hearing the distinctive throb of the Trans Am's engine. Christopher Bird appeared out of nowhere and gave Biggs a friendly wave as he drove through the gates. He called out "Poser" and followed him to the car park, with his entourage on tow. They had not seen the Trans Am before and were obviously very impressed.

"Hello, Sir. Got a new motor?"

"Hello, Chris. Now where have I heard that remark before? Let me see now, was it on University Challenge?.... No, perhaps not!"

"How about Mastermind, Sir?" suggested Tony Roberts. Tony was Christopher's closest friend. They were practicably inseparable and went way-back.

"Mastermind? Yes, I do believe it was, Tony..... You should be on Mastermind, Chris. Yes, I can see it all now..... And the next contestant is, Christopher Bird..... And for his special subject...... the bleeding obvious!"

"Nice one, Sir. I see you haven't lost your razor-sharp wit over the holidays?"

"That's right. In fact I've been honing it, to keep up with you."

"Your not in the same league, Sir!"

Christopher insisted that the bonnet should raised, so that they could have a look at the engine; six point six litre of shear muscle. They were obviously very impressed. When they had drooled sufficiently and made enough cooing noises of approval to satisfy Biggs' ego, he sent them back to the playground. Not in the same league, eh, he thought to himself! He knew that there was an element of truth in what Christopher had said. He also knew that they would soon be gearing up for their regular bouts clever classroom banter and he was determined to give as good as he got. It was always good humoured and they both enjoyed the cut and thrust of repartee, but it was Christopher who had the razor-sharp wit and Biggs knew it! But he obviously had a great taste in cars, so he went up in his esteem.

The new recruits having been issued with their diaries and timetables, were beginning to settle in. Since they would be having some of their lessons in the Upper School they were taken there on a visit, marching crocodile fashion through the streets. The Upper School was a rambling old building full of nooks and crannies in which it was easy to get lost. Design Technology lessons were held there. It used to be called woodwork and metalwork in days gone by, but that's progress for you! During a tour of the building the new boys met Mr. Martin, the Headmaster and the Second Deputy Head, Mr. Don Royston. The Headmaster was an all too frequent visitor to the Lower School annexe, although he generally did not interfere with the day-to-day running. It was his custom to take a full assembly every other Friday.

Don Royston was also Director of Studies. By nature, a bit of a recluse, he endeavoured to keep a low profile at all times. Only on infrequent occasions was he known to visit the Lower School. He seemed to spend most of his time closeted in his office preparing a timetable for the following year. Harry Langton and Don Royston were like chalk and cheese, but they did have one thing in common; rarely were either to be found teaching in a classroom!

By three o'clock the new recruits had survived their first day and were allowed an early departure. Moving from room to room for different lessons with different teachers always came as a novelty and very different from the regime in their primary schools. Excited by the thought of their next five years, many had already made new friends. Some of course were still a little apprehensive, but they always quickly settled in, their primary schools soon becoming distant memories.

Having got through the first day without too much trauma, Biggs was in two minds, whether to go to G19 for a nogging or go for a nice relaxing sauna at the local sports centre. G19 was the public hostelry and solace at times of crisis next to the annexe. Rather like a golf course, so named because the end room on the ground floor of the annexe was G18. It was not the most salubrious of places, but they did a very nice cauliflower cheese at lunch time and it made a welcome retreat at the end of the day. He didn't relish hanging around for them to open so he opted for the sauna. It was nice to unwind after a grueling week's teaching and it had become his custom to go for a sauna on Fridays. He had managed to wangle a timetable without a teaching commitment on Friday afternoons. He had contrived a similar situation the previous year, his argument being that since he was responsible for the day-to-day running of the Lower School, he needed to be free at the end of the week to tie up any loose ends. In fact there rarely were any loose ends and he usually sneaked away fifteen minutes before the end of the day. Harry Langton, aware of his early departure, turned a blind eye. Bearing in mind his own illicit roving, he always needed to keep Biggs sweet! Of course, being the first day of term, it wasn't a Friday..... but Biggs just thought, What the hell?

CHAPTER 2

THE TERM CONTINUES. Having got through their first afternoon, the old hands were beginning to settle into their normal routine and the new boys were rapidly on their way to becoming old hands themselves!

The Third Year 'Express' Maths set were destined to take their public examination a year early. GCSE exams had yet to make an appearance, so they were due to take their GCE O level at the end of the following year. It was Biggs' pleasure to take them for their first lesson. They were bright! In fact, they were very bright and they knew it! One or two, including Christopher Bird were too clever for their own good, but on the whole they were a great bunch of kids. He arrived a little late for the lesson, to find them chatting quietly outside the classroom. Letting them in, he became aware of a strong aroma, reminiscent of cheap afteshave, percolating the room.

"Come on then. Who's wearing the scent?"

The class giggled and Alan Lane piped up from the back of the room, "That's not scent, Sir. It's Tony Robert's aftershave!"

"Is that right, Tony?"

"Yes, Sir," Tony replied, defensively. He was sitting next to his mate Christopher, who was holding his nose. They sat immediately in front of Biggs, in knuckle-rapping range. Biggs liked to have them in knuckle-rapping range and he kept a ruler handy for the purpose!

"Did you shave first?" he asked, hoping to further embarrass Tony.

"He doesn't have to shave, Sir," Christopher chipped in. "He's only just got through puberty and he's only got a bit of bum-fluff."

The class giggled and Christopher ended up on the receiving end of a hefty thump on the arm. Feigning to cringe a little, he accepted his friend's reprimand without complaint, obviously regarding it as fair payment for his remark.

Mathematics was the only subject with an Express set from the Third Year upwards. In fact, the very idea of fast-tracking was a complete anathema to quite a few of the staff. However, some of the more enlightened staff had argued that a great deal of time was spent helping the less-able pupils, so it was only reasonable that the brighter kids should be allowed a fair crack of the whip. Biggs was one of the prime movers in fast-tracking and the retention of ability sets. Somewhat of an elitist, he made no secret of the fact that in his opinion, it was no bad thing for a school to be inclined towards a meritocracy.

There were twenty-five boys in the group. Selected from the thirty boys in the top Maths set the previous year, they were deemed to be the most able mathematicians in the Third Year and probably in the school. They worked hard and as a group they got on extremely well. Of course that didn't prevent them from slagging each other off, which they did at the drop of a hat. In fact, they enjoyed slagging each other off! It was expected of them. And without giving it a second thought, they would happily grass on each other, over the slightest thing, if it enabled them to put one over on their classmates. But it was all a game and they knew that any punishment meted out by Biggs as a result of grassing, would be quite minor and designed to embarrass rather than punish. But then they liked embarrassing each other! Having taken them the previous year, he knew them all well..... too well in fact and a certain familiarity had crept into their relationship...... a familiarity that was sometimes resented by certain members of staff. At other times Biggs was a strict disciplinarian and these teachers resented the special relationship he seemed to have with his *elite*. Mostly on the far left of the political spectrum and advocates of mixed ability teaching, the very idea of an elite was totally alien to many of them.

Much of their first lesson was given to the distribution of text books and new exercise books and not a lot of work was done. But feeling the need to lay down the ground rules for the year, Biggs explained that they would be getting homework without fail every lesson. He added that he would consider it a personal insult if any boy failed to complete it. They all knew the rules from their previous year in Set One, but that didn't stop a general mumble of disapproval.

"It's no good you mumbling away like that," Biggs said. "This is......"

"That means five times a week," Tony queried, interrupting him. "We have Maths every day. What about our homework timetable? We're only meant to have Maths homework twice a week." But he already knew what Biggs' answer would be. He had heard it many times before, but he smiled on hearing it yet again.

"If you can't stand the heat, get out of the kitchen. Homework timetables are for wimps! This is the Express set and you're here on my terms and that means homework every lesson. I'll be expecting great things from you this year. I don't have to tell you that you've all got ability. You already know that, but......"

"Yeah. We're the dog's bollocks," Christopher said ..... then wondering if he'd rather overstepped the mark, he gave himself a slap on the wrist and added, "Sorry, Sir."

"I don't think that I would have put it quite as crudely as that, Christopher. I hardly think that comparing yourselves to canine genitalia does you justice."

A giggle went round the room.

"What he meant to say, Sir, was that we're the creme-de-la-creme," suggested Tony. "...... You know, like in that film the Prime of Miss Jean Brodie."

"Yes, Sir. That's what I meant," Christopher confirmed.

"I see ...... well so long as you don't see me in the roll of Miss Jean Brodie."

"No, and we're not your 'Gals' either," said Alan Lane.

The class giggled again.

"No...... We're your lads, aren't we, Sir?" Christopher said.

Alan was a pleasant enough lad, with a cheerful disposition, but he was a chatterbox. He was the class motor-mouth and often referred to by the other boys as 'wobble-gob,' or just plain 'wobble.' A tragic case of rabbit, rabbit, chat, chat....... he had more bunny than Sainsbury's. Raising the matter of his nonstop chatter one parent's evening, Biggs had been told by his mother, 'He hardly says a word at home!' He was able to assure her that he certainly made up for it in school. In fact, Alan regarded himself as a bit of a Jack-the-lad and sometimes tried to emulate Christopher in his banter with Biggs, but Biggs would rarely play ball. It wasn't Alan who was the personification of Jack. It was Christopher, with his razor-sharp wit and his sophisticated sense of humour. Christopher could expertly parry a put-down and rarely took offence. But these were the very qualities which Alan lacked. Christopher always reserved his own put-downs, witticisms and cutting remarks for his friends and those that he knew would not take offence. They were never directed at the quieter, less exuberant members of the class. To them he was always friendly and courteous. But Alan was less discriminate and sometimes caused offence! Alan's problem was that he was his own biggest fan! But he was no match for Christopher and he knew it.

Setting their first homework caused howls of anguish!

"You must be joking, Sir." Tony complained. "I thought you meant we'd start the homework next lesson. It's only our first lesson! Have a heart, Sir."

"I'm full of heart. Tony, but let's start as we mean to go on, shall we. It's 'O' Levels next year. I'm just being cruel to be kind."

A general mumble of acquiescence went round the class. They had known at the end of the previous year what they would be letting themselves in for by joining the Express set and they had all been willing participants.

"Teachers are all sadists," Christopher said, determined that Tony should not to be fobbed off with a platitude. "I bet you enjoy making us slave!"

"I bet he does too," Tony agreed. Biggs just smiled at them.

"Well, do you, Sir? Christopher asked, trying to elicit a response.

"You can bet your life on it, Chris! I had to do it when I was your age, so I don't see why you could get away with it. Anyway, it's not a proper homework. I just want you to prepare yourselves for a table test tomorrow."

"A table test!" Alan queried. "You must be joking, Sir. That's kids stuff."

"Then you won't have any problem sailing through it, will you, Alan? I agree, it is kid's stuff, but I expect you to know them off pat. We're meant to be doing advanced work this year and I don't expect you to be wasting valuable time using a calculator to work out simple things that should be in your heads. In fact, I am not going to permit the use of calculators in the lesson until you can prove to me that you don't need them."

"I know my tables," Christopher said. "I'll sail through the test."

One or two of the others didn't seem quite so sure!

"Okay, Chris. Since you're so confidant, let's make it a bit more interesting shall we and have a bet on the side. Any answer you get wrong, you can do that number of press-ups."

"What sort of bet is that?" Christopher demanded. "What do I get if I win?"

"Good point...... Okay, how about five tuck shop vouchers?"

"That's worth a pound," Tony whispered to Christopher.

"You're on, Sir..... No problem."

"You seem very confidant, Chris! But just reflect on how many you would have to do if you got twelve times twelve wrong!"

"What? You mean I'd have to do a hundred and forty-four?" Biggs nodded. "I didn't think you meant it like that, Sir. I thought it would just mean doing twelve." He was beginning to have second thoughts about the bet!

"You can't back out now," Tony said, chuckling to himself.

Not wanting to lose face and resigned to his commitment, Christopher nodded and said, "I bet you don't know what six times nine are, Sir."

Biggs thought about it for a moment; it was obviously a trick question! He then remembered that earlier outside the classroom, he had overheard them talking about 'The Hitch Hiker's Guide to the Galaxy,' which Christopher had been reading over the holiday. Having read the book himself, he knew the answer. "Don't Panic," he said. "I'm in deep thought! Oh, yes ..... I do believe, it's forty-two ..... but I wouldn't advise you to give that answer tomorrow. That's how many press-ups you'd have to do!"

Christopher smiled. "And I suppose that means you know the answer to the meaning of life, the universe and everything."

"Yes I do," Biggs confirmed. "Again, it's forty-two."

When the new intake of anklebiters arrived each year, he expected them to know their tables. He also expected them to be able to read and write! After all, it was the job of primary schools to see that their kids could read and write before graduating to the secondary level. But especially, he expected them to know their tables. He had a thing about tables! In fact, he expected them to know them so well that they should be able to correctly answer rapid fire questions without having time to think. They should know them as well as they knew their own names and door numbers. Unfortunately, learning tables by rote was no longer in fashion in certain educational circles and one or two of their feeder primary schools didn't teach them. He considered that these schools were doing their kids a great disservice.

The Trans Am, although Biggs pride and joy, was a bit too ostentatious for every day use, so the following day his arrival was unceremonious in an aging mini, much to the derision of Bird and his mates. Christopher made some remark about it having faded and shrunk in the car wash. It was a typical Bird twitter and did not warrant a reply. However, Biggs made a mental note to get even with him during games that afternoon. Christopher had elected squash for his games option, but was unaware that Biggs would be taking him. A science teacher, turned to teaching maths, he looked forward to taking games once a week. He always thought that the games staff had it easy and saw no reason why he shouldn't get a piece of the action himself. It got him out of the school and provided a welcome digression. Of course he wasn't prepared to go as far as taking a team activity on the games field, such as a football. After all, that would possibly mean getting cold and wet if the weather was inclement and he didn't particularly like football anyway. Football was for the games staff! It was their job to take football and getting cold and wet was part of their remit. But indoor court games such as badminton or squash, well that was different. He had never been a team player, much preferring one-on-one and he had elected to take the squash group during his Third Year games session on Wednesdays. The school did not possess its own squash courts, so they had to make use of the local sports centre, located a short distance from the school. The sports centre was situated adjacent to the local girls finishing school. It had a notorious reputation and contained the most unladylike collection of young ladies it was possible to imagine. The school was known locally as St. Trinian's! By comparison Gordon Bennett was a paragon of virtue! The boys normally made their own way to the centre after lunch. It shared a common entrance with the school, so they were forced to run a gauntlet of obscenities, obscene gestures and sexual innuendo from the young ladies. Burly Forth and Fifth Year boys would cringe at the very sight of them. It was enough to put them off sex for the rest of their lives!

Later that morning, during his second lesson with his Express group, Biggs gave them their promised table test.

"Rough books out. Number 1 to 20 down the side. You've got twenty rapid fire questions and no time to think...... Everyone ready?" He rattled off the twenty questions, with no more than a three second pause between them. "Okay, change books..... Standby for the answers?"

After marking each other's books and changing back again, they each called out their marks out of twenty as their names were called. Christopher's name was third on the list and pausing before calling it, Biggs looked with anticipation in his direction. Christopher feigned a look of total dejection, until he observed the first glimmer of a smile on Biggs' face. Dejection instantly changed to delight.

"TWENTY," he said, throwing his fist upwards into the air. "That'll be five tuck shop vouchers please, Sir."

"Okay, Chris. You win..... See me after the lesson."

"You'd better check their answers," Alan Lane said. "Chris and Tony might have cheated and given each other full marks. I reckon they might be planning to share the vouchers." It was a typical wobble-gob remark and Alan's attempt at being witty, but it only served to irk Christopher and Tony, who both reacted indignantly to his suggestion. Although they got on well enough with Alan, they knew that he could be a bit of stirrer and they sometimes regarded him as a pain in the butt!

"Who rattled your cage?" Christopher said. "How many did you get right?"

Alan was not forthcoming, but they were placated when Biggs said that he had no need to check their answers, since he regarded them both as *honorable* men who wouldn't dream of cheating. He continued recording their scores in his mark book, this time pausing before calling Alan's name.

"Eighteen," Alan whispered barely audibly, his head buried in his textbook.

The class giggled and Christopher and Tony fell about laughing. "Speak up, Alan," Christopher said. "Did you say EIGHTEEN?"

"Eighteen," Alan confirmed with forced smile, clearly having lost his former exuberance.

When Biggs had completed recording their marks, he said, "Okay. Only those boys who got all twenty correct are permitted to use calculators in class from now on. The rest must not use them until they've been re-tested. When you think you're ready for a re-test, let me know." He felt sure in his own mind there would be no elicit use of calculators by those boys who had failed to get twenty correct answers, because he knew that they would immediately be grassed upon by the rest of the class.

The results of the test were quite pleasing. Only five boys out of twenty-five failed to get a perfect score and with just one exception, no boy got more than two wrong.

Biggs knew that if he had given them slightly more time between each question, they would probably have all got a perfect score. The exception was Paul Smith, who got six wrong. Although very bright, Paul was rather lazy and seemed to be in a permanent state of detachment from reality. He was in grave danger of being demoted before he'd even started. He accused Biggs of picking on him, when told to buck up his ideas.

"Don't give me that," Biggs said, tetchily. "In the 'getting picked on' stakes you come nowhere, but if you're not careful I'll be more than happy to oblige."

"Sir's right," Christopher said, trying to ingratiate himself and turning round to Paul. "Stop whingeing. You're the last one to get picked on.... I'm always first."

"That's right Christopher comes first..... with Tony a close second," Biggs confirmed, looking in the direction of Tony Roberts. Bird and Roberts both nodded their agreement. Thankful as he was for their support he told them to be quiet..... or rather, he told Tony to be quiet. He told Bird to stop twittering and perch to the front. The class giggled.

"Nice one, Sir," Christopher said, giving a thumbs-up. "Of course it's hardly original, or on the cutting edge of witticism, but a nice one just the same."

Biggs could not think of a suitably apt reply, so shaking his head he just smiled benignly at him.

It would normally be regarded as unprofessional to be constantly making fun of a boy's name, as Biggs did with Christopher's. He was always being told to 'stop twittering,' to 'perch this way,' or to 'stop ruffling his feathers.' They had a mutual understanding, however. Christopher didn't object and in return, he was allowed a latitude in repartee not normally allowed to other boys. If he overstepped the mark he would be jumped on much harder than would have otherwise been the case. The arrangement worked well and had the tacit agreement of the rest of the class, except that Alan wished he'd been in on the act. In fact the other boys regarded them as a bit of a double act, their banter and often humourous exchanges serving to lighten the atmosphere. Christopher usually knew where to draw the line, but always took great pleasure in getting as close to it as he could. Outside the classroom, he was always polite and friendly towards Biggs. In fact they got on well and enjoyed each other's company. When his own friends were not to hand, Christopher would sometimes seek out Biggs' company in preference to that of his peers and they would enjoy chatting informally together, sometimes over a cup of coffee in Biggs' office. Biggs knew that he should not openly display favouritism towards him and the banter in the classroom, or when other boys were around, was just done for effect.

That afternoon Christopher had to run the gauntlet of St. Trinian's to join the squash group at the sports centre. He seemed genuinely pleased to discover that Biggs would be taking the group. Christopher looked to be quite a promising player and when the session was over, they both stayed on and played two games together. Biggs passed close to Christopher's house on his way home, so he gave him a lift in his aging mini.

"I always thought that you were a bit of a poser, Sir. What's with the mini? You might have brought the Trans Am!"

"You must be joking! Leave my beautiful Tranny in the car park, with St. Trinian's turning out! I think, not!"

"Good point. I should have thought of that.... They're disgusting, aren't they? I would have been molested on my way here if I hadn't run the last hundred yards."

"You should be so lucky!"

CHAPTER 3

HARRY'S OFFICE. Harry Langton was of the opinion that the decor of an office reflected it's owner. He spent a great deal of time endeavouring to make sure that his office reflected the image that he wanted to project...... that of a suave debonair executive! He'd read somewhere that an ounce of image was worth a pound of performance, so he generally concentrated on improving his image rather than raising his performance, since this involved considerably less effort.

It was a very large office, tastefully decorated, with a chaise longue by the window and three very comfortable armchairs, which always seemed to completely engulf the sitter. Harry was quite partial to a bit of greenery, a large rubber plant standing in the corner near his door. A baby Swiss-cheese plant stood on one side of his chaise longue, while on the other side stood an enormous yucca. The mummy Swiss-cheese plant which he called his Triffid, stood in another corner of the room. Having been allowed to grown to monster proportions, this Monstera Deliciosa certainly lived up to its name! It had completely taken over and practically covered the entire wall behind his desk. It was Laura's task to keep the plants fed and watered. It was not a task that she relished, since if ever a leaf dared to turn brown or fall off, it would become the subject of a major enquiry. Harry would show great concern and without actually saying as much, give her the impression that he held her personally responsible. The room was festooned with numerous mobiles and executive toys, designed to impress kids, staff and parents alike. A small pair of brass scales, meant to symbolize justice, hung by a fine thread from the ceiling over the front edge of his very large desk. The scales hung in such a position that they were directly between him and anyone sitting or standing in front of him and were designed to giving the impression that he was the fountain of all justice. A nice touch, except that with Harry justice usually played second fiddle to expediency! Inclined to punish first and ask questions afterwards, a hanging sword would have been more appropriate! Under the scales, he kept a small dish of sweeties. He would offer one to any boy with a pleasing disposition, not before him for a reprimand.

An adjoining door led to a large walk-in cupboard, in which Harry kept his drinks. Now most heads have a hospitality cabinet in which they keep the odd bottle of sherry to offer important guests, but Harry's *walk-in* almost defied belief. It would certainly have done justice to any self-respecting off licence. Lagers, mixers and soft drinks came stacked in crates on the floor, while the array of wines and spirits adorning the shelves had to be seen to be believed. Whatever may have been Harry's shortcomings, and some thought they were legion, he certainly could not be accused of a lack of generosity. If fact, he had a very generous disposition and was never short on hospitality. If in a good mood at the end of the day, he would sometimes offer a glass of wine or sherry to his closest associates. Biggs was very partial to a glass of sherry and if Harry was around he would often pop in to see him on some pretext, hoping to scrounge a glass. Laura was also partial to the odd glass and would sometimes join them.

By comparison Biggs office was relatively small and functional, although it did have a few creature comforts. He originally had an office much the same size as Harry's when he was Head of Third year, but it was in a far flung corner of the building. Since his promotion to Senior Year Head, in addition to his continuing responsibility for the Third Year, he was additionally responsible for the day-to-day running of the Lower School annexe. He needed to be near the centre of things and he had given up his spacious office to be next to Laura in the general office. It had the additional advantage of being next to a regular supply of coffee which could be passed to him through a connecting hatch. He usually commandeered Harry's office if he wanted to hold a meeting or see a parent. It was generally accepted that the best way to give parents a feeling of inferiority was to seat them on a hard chair on the wrong side of a huge desk in a large office! The hanging scales were of course a bonus.

One morning Harry, resting after a hard day's roving, found Biggs' educational diary, which he had earlier misplaced, stuffed under the cushion of his chaise longue. He accused him of lying on the chaise longue when he was out! Biggs was not allowed to lie on it...... not since he had been caught the previous term, in the fashion of a Roman emperor, being fed grapes by Laura. He vehemently denied the accusation and told Harry not to be so petty. He was however, grateful for the return of the diary, since its loss had niggled him. There was nothing of any consequence in it, but he had spent some time carefully marking in the school holiday dates, information of vital importance and always the first to be entered.

THE HIPPY.   Looking out from his office window one morning, the 'pips' having sounded some ten minutes earlier, Harry Langton spotted Mr. Paul Scobie trying to sneak in without being seen. Paul Scobie was a lapsed Physical Education and Games teacher, all that physical exertion apparently having been too much for him. It was the third time since the beginning of term that Paul Scobie had been caught coming in late and Harry had already spoken to him twice on the matter.

"Scobie's late again," he snorted to Biggs, who happened to be standing by Harry's connecting door to the general office. "I've just about had enough of him and the term's barely started! I'm likely to blow my top if I speak to him again, so will you deal with him for me?"

"No!" said Biggs, with a defiance that rather took Harry aback. "You've already spoken to him about his lateness. It's *you* he's defying and giving the run-around, so it's *you* that will have to deal with him."

"Huh! And I suppose that if you had spoken to him about being late and he'd taken no notice, you would have referred him to me?"

Biggs could see that Harry was getting annoyed, but having made his position clear, he had no intention of backing down. "Of course, that's what you're here for. The buck stops with you, so you can't go passing it back down the line. It's your problem. You deal with it."

Christopher Bird was standing in the doorway to the general office, about to return his class register. He had obviously overheard the heated words between Harry and Biggs and not wishing to end up on the receiving end of

Harry's wrath, he was clearly reluctant to enter. He gestured to Biggs, indicating that he would like him to take the register. Biggs took it, giving him a wink.

Unfortunately Harry witnessed Christopher's beckoning gesture and Biggs' wink and stormed, "Oh, I see you seem quite willing to do *his* bidding. What's his name?.... Bird, but you're not prepared to do *mine*."

"That's right. But don't take it out on Christopher. He's just doing his job. It's not his fault you're in a bad mood."

"Me in a bad mood, huh? The grief I get around here, it's not surprising, is it? Well, since the two of you seem so buddy-buddies, perhaps you wouldn't mind asking him to ask Mr. Scobie to come to see me during morning break." Then, glaring at Christopher, he added, ".... that's if your little friend's not too busy, of course."

Biggs nodded and Christopher wisely resisted the temptation to make a witty response to Harry's sarcasm. Biggs took him through to his own office.

"Take no notice of Mr. Grumpy, Chris. He must have got out of bed the wrong side this morning." He wrote a hastily written note to Mr. Scobie and gave it to Christopher. "Would you mind, Chris?"

"For you, Sir.... anything."

Paul Scobie had to be seen to be believed. A hippy, fast approaching middle age, he was the spitting image of John Lennon. His long red hair fell well below his shoulders and small gold rimmed spectacles perched on the end of his nose. From one ear hung a gold ear ring with an enormous *sun* motif; from the other ear hung *the moon*. He was frequently in trouble for wearing unsuitable clothing. Following a reprimand from His Majesty during the first week of term, for wearing a black T-shirt and scruffy jeans, he had been sent home to change into something more suitable...... He did look a bit of a scruff. He returned a short while later wearing a track suit, the top half of which did not match the bottom. The trouble with people like Paul Scobie is that they always go over the top and make it worst for the rest. In the first weekly staff bulletin of the term an edict appeared banning 'dark tops and jeans.'

Complementing his extraordinary appearance, was his colourful language, almost every other word beginning with an 'f......' and ending with an '......ing.' Mr. Scobie taught English! He seemed able to turn his colourful language on and off at will, fortunately turning it off in the classroom. At parents' evenings it was usual to put him in a dimly lit corner, where he was least likely to be seen. Fortunately the boys in Mr. Scobie's tutor group took their example regarding tardiness and general appearance elsewhere. On more than one occasion, they had been known to mark their own register in pencil and then pack themselves off to their first lesson before he arrived. The three times that Harry Langton had caught him coming in late had been probably just the tip of the iceberg!

Golf was the only form of physical activity undertaken by Paul Scobie, since switching from Physical Education to teaching English. He apparently played a fair game, but not being a member of any club, he had never acquired an official handicap. Of course many would have said that his general appearance and uncouth behaviour, made him his own worst handicap and that it was inconceivable that any club would have been prepared to accept him as a member! In fact Paul Scobie regarded golf clubs as elitist and always played on courses that were open to the general public. His thirteen year old son also played a fair game of golf and had entered a Junior Tournament, organized by the local golf club. Having proved his worth in the tournament, the lad had been offered a year's free Junior membership. On hearing of this, Paul decided that if his son was good enough to be a member, it was only fitting that he should also be allowed membership. Somehow he managed to get two existing members, who had obviously taken leave of their senses, to support his application. His application went before the club committee and he was promptly blackballed! The club had been unaware that Scobie Junior was Paul Scobie's son. Ashamed of his father's extraordinary hippie appearance and not wishing the sins of his father to be visited on him, the lad had apparently gone to great lengths to keep the information from them. He had entered the tournament under his mother's maiden name!

A new History teacher, Andrew Jones, had been taken on at the start of the term. Out of college a couple of years, Andrew had been looking for a new post to widen his experience. Andrew's first encounter with Paul Scobie came on his second or third day. Mr. Scobie had apparently taken exception to Andrew marking a set of books in the staff room. Unceremoniously, he picked up the books and threw them out of the window, saying in a loud voice, 'No marking in the staff room.' There was a staff workroom adjoining and there was an unwritten rule that books should not to be marked in the main staff room. It had not occurred to anyone to brief Andrew on the matter so, needless to say, he was left somewhat gob-smacked by his experience. Paul Scobie's actions, however, were entirely without justification. But lacking in any consideration towards a new member of staff, it was just typical of his total lack of decorum.

Andrew, although taken on mainly to teach History, rather fancied trying his hand at special needs teaching and, as it happened, Gordon Bennett was looking for some extra help in this field. They was going through a phase when some of the new intake were rather lacking in basic literacy. This was due largely to new and undesirable teaching methods, current at the time and employed by a number of feeder primary schools. Ray Dennard, in charge of special needs, wanted some extra help and Andrew, although primary trained, seemed eminently suitable. The fact that he was Biggs' nephew had nothing to do with his appointment and any suggestions from the staff of nepotism were almost entirely without foundation. The boys were generally unaware of their family connection. Of course with names like Smith and Jones, the connection was by no means obvious!

At the end of the day, Christopher went looking for Biggs and found him in his office enjoying a refreshing cup of China tea. He liked a cup of China tea at the end of the day and so did Ray Dennard, who would sometime pop in for a cup. In fact the two Rays got on rather well and they would sometimes go out for lunch together on Fridays to a pub a mile or so from the school.

"Can I come in, Sir?" Christopher asked, giving a cursory tap on the door.

Biggs nodded. "Yes, come in, Chris. What can I do for you?"

"What's that you're drinking, Sir? It's got a strange smell!"

"China tea. Lapsang Souchong. Want to try some?"

"I'll give it a go."

Biggs poured him a cup. "It's a bit of an acquired taste."

Christopher sniffed the cup before taking a hesitant sip, washing the brew round in his mouth before swallowing, as if tasting wine. He then took a bigger sip. "It's not bad, Sir. I think I could get to like it."

"Good. Is this a social call, or did you come for any particular reason? We had Maths only an hour ago. Surely you can't be pining for me already?"

"No, Sir. I just wanted to let you know that I passed Mr. Langton in the corridor this afternoon, after we'd left you and he apologized for taking it out on me this morning."

"Good. I'm very pleased to hear it. We can't have him going round upsetting a sensitive young man like you, can we, Chris?"

"No, Sir, but it's not like him to apologize for anything and I was a bit surprised.... I wondered if you'd had anything to do with it?"

Biggs just gave him a wink! "Finish you tea."

CHAPTER 4

DRESS. Now the dress of the majority of staff at Gordon Bennett was never very formal and over a period of time, Harry Langton and Biggs had gradually fallen in with this informality. Taking games once a week was justification enough in Biggs' eyes for him to wear a track suit much of the time. The Hippie apart, casual but smart was the order of the day. This did not please His Majesty, who liked to see his staff dressed in suit and tie. It particularly niggled him to have his two senior teachers in the Lower School failing to follow his example. It was obvious that sooner or later the matter would be brought to a head.

Following a morning assembly moan to the boys about their uniform, which was always very good making the subject quite unnecessary, he decided to have it out with Biggs and Harry Langton. They listened attentively while Mr. Martin attempted to lay down the law concerning staff dress and setting an example to others, but said nothing. They both knew from past experience that once he had the bit between his teeth, counter argument was pointless. Having said his piece, His Majesty returned to the Upper School, leaving Harry and Biggs to considered the implications of his sermon. After much deliberation, they decided that if the Headmaster wanted a pair of dandies running the Lower School he would get them, but with a vengeance!

The next time that Mr. Martin was due to take morning assembly they arrived early to prepare themselves. They were both wearing their best dark suits, dress shirts and colourful waistcoats. To their waistcoats they each attached a gold watch and chain. Some time was spent practicing the art of swinging the watches in a circle on the ends of the chains and then catching them in their waistcoat pockets. The trick was soon perfected. Laura had arranged to provide them with carnations and dutifully pinned them to their lapels.

His Majesty arrived! Seeing them both and obviously recollecting his earlier comments, his face dropped and a glint of anger appeared in his eyes. He closed them for a moment and then, as if they no longer existed, turned to Laura and wished her good morning.

"Good morning Mr. Martin," Laura replied, trying to look nonchalant.

Harry Langton, also attempting to look nonchalant, tried to keep a straight face. Biggs thought that it was a good time to make himself scarce and quickly came up with an excuse for leaving.

"I'm just going to the hall, Harry, to supervise the assembly," he said.

"Cowered," Harry whispered under his breath, knowing that he would be left alone to deal with the Headmaster's wrath.

The boys had great difficulty in believing their eyes as they entered the assembly hall and started muttering under their breath. They were even more surprised when Harry appeared on the stage alongside Biggs. They rarely saw either of them wearing suits, let alone gold watches, chains and carnations.

"When's the wedding?" some wag called out from the middle of the hall. "Which one is the best man?"

The remark was ignored and after a few minutes, the assembled multitude rose to their feet as the Headmaster made his usual dramatic entrance. Harry and Biggs stood behind him, one on either side, while he delivered his sermon...... something about charity and fund raising. Hardly the most enthralling topic for an assembly, delivered by one of the least charismatic of Headmasters, the kids were clearly being bored out of their minds. One or two started shuffling their feet.

When he had gone on long enough, on Harry's cue and with very deliberate actions, they took out their watches, opened them and glanced momentarily at the time. Then after closing their watches in unison, they swung them in circles, catching them in the left hand pockets of their waistcoats. It went like a dream. The assembled multitude, boys and staff alike were reduced to hysterics.

The Headmaster turned slowly round, smiled wryly at them and took his leave without saying another word. Laura could be seen peeping through the swing doors at the back of the hall, unable to contain her mirth. The subject of staff dress was never mentioned again!

Biggs vividly recalled the first assembly taken by Mr. Martin in the Upper School, shortly after his appointment as Headmaster and before Harry Langton had been appointed as First Deputy. He had decided to wear his gown for morning assembly, despite being advised that the boys were not used to seeing members of staff wearing them. Academic gowns were usually reserved for speech day and other special occasions and then usually only by senior staff. A few years earlier, there had been one old-timer who had always insisted on wearing his mortar board as well as his gown and hood to speech day, but he had always been regarded as a bit of an eccentric. The everyday wearing of academic gowns has since become a rarity, outside the public school sector and some of the better grammar schools. Ignoring the advice, Mr. Martin flounced into hall adjusting the shoulder of his gown to take his first assembly, only to be met by a chorus of boys from the Forth Year who sang out aloud, "Dah-Dah, Dah-Dah, Dah-Dah, Dah-Dah..... BATMAN." The assembly was reduced to hysterics even before it started. Needless to say, Mr. Martin managed to lose all credulity with the boys on his first morning! Biggs always suspected that they had been tipped the wink by their Form Tutor. That was the first and last time that the Headmaster wore his gown to assembly!

CHAPTER 5

Laura had been asked to write a magazine article about Christmas and she was looking for ideas for an original theme. Her articles usually turned out to be a joint effort between everyone in the office and they all said that they would give it some thought.

A couple of days later Laura, still trying to think of an original theme, gave everyone an ear-bashing for not coming up with some suggestions. At the rate she was going she was unlikely to have the article ready for Easter, Ian McTaggart observed. Mike Gladstone suggested something about the discovery of the Christmas Islands. Penny Passmore, their new office assistant, had an idea about the Apollo mission which circled the moon at Christmas a few years earlier.

"Why not combine the two," Harry Langton suggested. "They must have been just about a century apart."

A glint appeared in Laura's eyes. Her problem had been solved.

The Lower school office were in need some extra help and Penny Passmore had moved from the Upper School that morning. She had been overwhelmed earlier, when presented with a bunch of flowers and a box of chocolates as a welcoming gift. Many of the female teaching staff would have regarded this as a sexist act, but Penny was not in the least adverse to such a gesture. Apart from helping Laura in the office, her duties included lunchtime dinner assistant, running the tuck shop during morning break and tending to the first aid needs of the boys and staff; in other words being 'mum.'

Tom Bane popped his head round the office door, looking for Penny! Tom taught Chemistry and General Science in the Upper School and it was rare for him to visit the annexe. Gordon Bennett was Tom's first teaching appointment after leaving college and he had been with the school for seven years. That's a long time for a first appointment; in fact far too long! Most new teachers out of college expect to spend two or three years at most in their first post, before looking elsewhere to widen their experience or to gain promotion. Tom was by no means lethargic, but he had got himself into a rut and found it easier to stay put rather than go through he hassle of moving on. Although in his late twenties, he was one of those people who, whether by looks or bent of personality, appeared much older than their years.

Covering a second year class for an absent teacher a couple of years earlier, no set work having been prepared, Harry Langton had written the names of twenty staff on the blackboard. Mindful of his own self image and being somewhat conscious of his own age, he'd asked the class to rearrange the list in age order, putting the youngest first and oldest last. Now bearing in mind that young adolescents generally regard anyone over thirty as having one foot in the grave, they could hardly be regarded as the best judges in such matters, but the results proved to be quite revealing. The three oldest were deemed to be Bob Griffin, the Forth Year Head, in his late thirties, Alan Howlett, a bearded and rather rotund maths teacher and Tom Bane, both in their twenties! Needless to say the boys put Harry Langton near the top of the list, but their judgement was probably clouded by the fact that he had been standing over them at the time. On seeing the results Biggs had been quite uplifted by coming immediately after Harry on the list.

Although a very dependable member of staff, in fact one of the stalwarts, on a charismatic scale from one to ten, Tom would have scored two at the most.

"Hello," he said. "I'm on the scrounge."

"A member of the Upper School staff on the scrounge?" Laura said, smiling. "Now there's a thing."

"I'm afraid so. I was hoping Penny could to do some copying for me."

"You must be joking," Laura said vehemently, her smile instantly changing to a scowl. The 'Headmistress' was on the warpath. "Penny has only just joined us and you're chasing after her with Upper School work on her first day here. What's wrong with your own office staff?

"They say that they are too busy and can't manage a rush job," said Tom rather cowed by Laura's onslaught.

"There shouldn't be a need for a rush job," Laura observed, then relenting a little when Penny said that she would be happy to oblige, just this once, she said, "You're too easy with them, Penny..... Well, all right. But it must be the first and last time."

Ian McTaggart entered the office, having just come from the Upper School after taking one of his examination classes. "Guess what," he said. "On my way back, I passed the Headmaster in the corridor.... and he actually acknowledged my existence."

"You should be so lucky," said Tom. "Outside the classroom, I've yet to have a boy acknowledge my existence!"

Apart from being a very useful and reliable member of staff, Tom was an accomplished piano player, although he steadfastly refused to play in morning assembly. Unable to read music, he played entirely by ear. Tom insisted that he played from memory and not by ear, but nobody really knew the difference.

Tom's only other claim to fame was his uncanny ability to speak backslang! Without thought or hesitation, he was able to repeat anything said to him as though it read with the first and last letters of each word interchanged, making a jumble of very amusing, but totally incomprehensible sounds. 'Hello, how are you,' for example translates to 'Oellh woh era uoy.' A dubious talent, but he always found it useful when answering inane questions from foolish boys. He leant the skill from his father, who apparently developed it for use when talking to like minded acquaintances. A bit like Cockney backslang designed to fool the Old Bill, it was used when they didn't want their womenfolk to know what they were saying. Tom came from the West Country..... they must be a funny lot down there!

"Doog eby," he said.

"Doog eby," Laura replied smiling, regretting her earlier onslaught on Tom.

"You're a hard woman, Laura," Ian said, after Tom was out of earshot.

"Hard! I need to be around here. If I didn't, everyone would just take advantage."

"Now I know why they call you, The Headmistress!"

CHAPTER 6

BIRD JUNIOR. The remnant of the bad weekend weather was still hanging on. The rain had stopped, but the wind was still very gusty. That was bad news and often indicated a troublesome day ahead. It is a little known fact outside the teaching profession, that there is a strong correlation between the wind strength and the state of mind of adolescent boys. The law governing this strange phenomenon states:-

'Rowdiness is directly proportional to the square of the wind velocity.'

In other words, if the wind speed doubles the kids become four times rowdier than they were before. The law holds true for all ages up to fourteen, but it is particularly applicable to the eleven to thirteen age group. This is probably because most of them are far too rowdy at the best of times, in nil-wind conditions. Come their Third Year, most boys have begun to calm down a little and by the end of their Forth Year, the majority have become positively lethargic! Of course outside the classroom and games field, many teachers would regard lethargy as a positive attribute to be encouraged!

Patrolling the building during break morning, Biggs came across a group of anklebiters stampeding along the top floor corridor, screaming at the tops of their voices. Apart from the noise they were all exceeding the Lower School speed limit of four miles per hour by a huge margin. At intervals along the corridors and on the stairs there were little red circles with the number four inside to act as a reminder to the kids, rather like the speed limit signs displayed on the roads. They were rather taken aback when stopped and given an on-the-spot fine for their misdemeanour.

"Speeding and ungentlemanly conduct. Twenty press-ups on each count."

"That's forty, Sir," complained one of the boys, obviously good at maths. "I can't do that many. It will kill me."

The boy looked familiar, but Biggs couldn't place him? He looked a bit like Christopher, but somehow different. He had the same hair colour, cut the same way, but his face was a totally different shape. His nose was more squat, but the eyes..... there was something about the eyes! Could it be? he wondered.

"Name?"

"Steven Bird, Sir."

I should have guessed, he thought to himself; it *was* Christopher's brother and he began to recognized the family resemblance. His plea for clemency was rejected out of hand. The boys did their press-ups with much gusto and rather to Biggs' surprise, they managed to complete them, albeit flagging a little towards the end. Steven was obviously very fit and, despite his protestations, completed all forty without rest. He was told that he was very lucky not to get an extra ten for whingeing.

Teachers each have their own way of dealing with miscreants. Biggs always favoured the short sharp shock whenever applicable. This was also Harry Langton's preferred method. It had the advantage of getting the matter dealt with there and then and was generally preferred by the wrongdoers as well. Most boys hate having a punishment hanging over them. They would much rather get it over as soon as possible.

Bob Griffin, the Head of Forth Year, always favoured reasoning with miscreants and talking them through their wrongdoing. Noted for his very slow and deliberate speech which droned on and on, he had on more than one occasion had boys fall asleep in his lesson. On Tom Bane's charismatic scale from one to ten, he would have achieved a negative score! But he was a very caring Year Head and his approach was not entirely without success. In the end he usually managed to bore the kids into submission! In fact, some would have said that he could have bored for his country!

The following day, Steven was caught making a derogatory remark about a member of staff to a group of his friends, who could hardly contain their mirth. Steven was clearly under the impression that it was his remarks that they found amusing, which only served to encourage him to continue with his degradation of the master. But it wasn't his *remarks* that caused their amusement. It was the fact that Steven hadn't realized that Biggs was standing directly behind him at the time. On discovering the fact, he became somewhat embarrassed.

"Would you like to repeat that, young man?"

"I'd rather not, Sir," Steven replied, head bowed

Since Steven appeared to be so accomplished at press-ups, Biggs thought that he would try another form of reprimand, so gave his elbow a tweak, causing him to collapse helplessly on the floor like a lump of jelly, much to the further amusement of the other boys.

"How do you do that, Sir?" Steven demanded, after getting up from the floor. "My brother told me about how you sometimes tweaked his elbow when he got too cheeky, but I didn't believe him."

"Then I suggest that you believe him in future. As for how I do it, that's my secret and I strongly suggest that you don't cross my path again this week young man..... that is of course, unless you want to discover what other torturous reprimands I keep up my sleeve..... all designed to inflict agony and anguish."

"Yes, Sir..... I mean no, Sir."

Meeting Christopher in the corridor shortly afterwards, stuffing a chocolate biscuit into his mouth, Biggs remarked, "I've just had dealings with your brother..... for the second time this week. He's a bit of a scamp, isn't he?"

"You can say that again, Sir. He can be a right pain in the butt. He's just the same at home. He winds me up all the time and I usually end up giving him a thump.... Only a gentle one of course..... You know I'm not a violent person."

"Well you can give him one for me."

"Okay, Sir, but I have to watch him though. He goes to self-defence classes and he can be quite handy with his fists."

"Self-defence, eh! What sort?"

"Origami! He's got a black belt, you know!" Biggs smiled. "No, not really.... He does judo once a week."

"But that shouldn't bother you, should it? He's only small. Surely you can defend yourself...... I thought you told me last year that you went to judo classes."

"I did, but it's not much use to me at home!"

"How do you mean?"

"When he tries it out on me and I complain to mum, she just says that he's only practicing and that I should encourage him. But if I attempt to use it on him in self-defence when he bugs me, he goes running to mum saying that I'm bulling him and I end up getting it in the neck."

"Well..... that's kid brothers for you!"

"Don't I know it!..... Did you have a kid brother, Sir?

"Have one? No...... I was one."

"Really?..... I bet you led your brother a right dance?" Biggs smiled, but did not reply. "I was never that bad in my first year here, was I, Sir?"

"No, I don't believe you were. But you could be a sarcastic little sod at times and you still can..... but you were never a bully and never gave grief. You were much more subtle. In fact a master of innuendo and repartee...... And a master in the art of being cheeky, but somehow, without being offensive."

"Gee, thanks, Sir. That's the nicest thing you've said to me for ages!..... Have a chocolate biscuit."

"Thanks.... Want a coffee?"

"Yes please, Sir. Better still, can I try that Lapsang Souchong again?"

"No, I'm afraid you can't. I only brew it at the end of the day."

"Okay, coffee's fine."

They both adjourned to Biggs' office to chew the cud.

Sliding open his connecting hatch to the general office, Biggs said brightly, "Two coffees, please Laura,"

"What do you think this is?" Laura demanded. "Fred's cafe?"

"No. Laura's," Biggs said jokingly. But then seeing that Laura was busy typing and clearly in no mood for his quips, he added. "Oh, never mind. I can see your busy."

"I'll get them," said Harry Langton, who had been pouring out a cup for himself. He poured out two coffees and passed them to Biggs through the hatch, thinking that he might be interviewing a parent. But as Biggs took the coffees from him, Harry spotted Christopher sprawled on one of the armchairs. "Do you mean I've just poured out a coffee for that scalawag?" he demanded.

Christopher smiled benignly at him and, resisting the temptation for sarcasm simply said, "Thanks, Sir."

Closing the hatch door, Harry snorted, "Huh, so that's what I'm reduced to, is it?.... A bleeding waiter for the kids!"

Smiling at each other, both amused at Harry's remark, Christopher offered Biggs another chocolate biscuit, which he readily accepted. For a few moments, neither spoke. Christopher was clearly contemplating some weighty matter! He slowly sipped his coffee.

"Sir?"

"Yes, Christopher?"

"Has Mrs. Hickman said anything to you...... about Tony and me?"

Brenda Hickman was their Form Tutor and English teacher.

"No. Why?.... Should she have done?"

"I don't know. It's just that she's been very offhand with us this last couple of days and we don't know why!"

"Maybe she just considers you a pain in the neck. Why don't you ask her?"

"We did, but she just glared at us!"

"She didn't say anything?"

"No, Sir..... but it wasn't what she didn't say that bothered us..... it was more.... the way she didn't say it!"

Biggs smiled. Nobody says nothing quite as loudly as Mrs. Hickman he thought to himself. He had come across her haughty attitude before. It was probably her time of the month, but he thought he'd better not say that to Christopher! "I wouldn't worry about it, Chris," he said, unable to stop himself from chuckling. "I'm sure she'll get over it."

Christopher did not reply, but stared hard into Biggs eyes, his own eyes slightly screwed, wondering what he found so amusing. It wasn't an offensive stare. It was an inquisitive stare, a stare attempting to probe the depths of his mind. Then, imperceptibly at first, his expression slowly changed to that of a knowing look and the glimmer of a grin appeared as he said, "Got it! ...... time of the month! Why didn't I think of that?"

"Chris! How did you *do* that? You must be bloody telepathic...... But I didn't say a thing.... and neither must you. Okay! Not even to Tony."

"Telepathic eh! Well, we must both be, Sir. If you don't transmit, I can't receive! And you manage to read my mind easily enough at times." Then drawing an imaginary zipper across his mouth, he added, "Don't worry, my lips are sealed."

They chatted away amicably about nothing in particular until the pips sounded, indicating the end morning of break. After Christopher had gone, Biggs remembered his first encounter with him, when he had been in the First Year. The First Year boys were not set in ability groups for Maths, so he hadn't actually started teaching him until he'd entered the Second Year and had been put in Set One. He'd heard his name mentioned many times in the staff room, as a likely character who would need bringing down a peg or two! But he hadn't actually come across him and it was some weeks after the start of the year before he had been able to put a face to the name. Passing a group of anklebiters in the corridor, he'd heard one of them address another as Chris! Stopping by the group, Biggs had looked at the lad in an enquiring manner.

"Hello, Sir. How are you today?" Christopher had said, taking the initiative and smiling at him.

Biggs had instinctively known who he was, but thought he'd better just confirm the fact. "Is your name Christopher Bird, young man?" he'd asked, expecting a simple yes or no answer.

"I do have that privilege, Sir," Christopher had replied, causing Biggs to burst out laughing.

Another teacher might have taken offence, but Biggs liked boys who made him laugh. There was little enough to laugh about the way things seemed to be going in education, so he was all for anyone who could lighten the atmosphere. It was from that first encounter that both had instinctively known that they were going to get on and that they were on the same wavelength! Biggs remembered how pleased he had been when Christopher had shown himself to be an able mathematician and had joined his Set One in the Second Year and how he had been delighted when he had proved himself to be worthy of the elite Third Year Express set.

Elbow tweaking was a skill that Biggs had acquired and perfected over the years. It necessitated catching the funny bone in just the right place and usually resulted in the recipient being reduced to lump of jelly. He could sometimes send former recipients into a frenzy of anticipation by simply holding his finger and thumb either side of their elbow without even tweaking. It was all quite harmless, but proved very useful as a mild rebuke when boys overstepped the mark and formed part of his repertoire short sharp shocks!

CHAPTER 7

Laura, had finished her magazine article over the weekend and was about to send it off. Having made a modest input himself, Biggs thought that it would be nice to read it, so he asked her if he could.

"Certainly not," was her curt reply. "Buy the magazine."

Laura was clearly not in a happy mood and was playing the roll of Headmistress again. She had been checking through the registers to collate attendance details for the previous week. Now one of the boring tasks that had to be completed at the end of each week by form tutors, was to work out the percentage attendance for the week using daily totals and half-day absences, gleaned from their registers; a simple enough task, not requiring any great mathematical dexterity. A task however, seemingly beyond the capabilities of a number of form tutors. A significant number each week, either through lack of dexterity with figures or more often due to shear carelessness, managed to get it wrong. A school register is a legal document which has to be accurate and since Laura had no way of knowing which teachers would get their calculations wrong, she was forced to check them all. Monday morning was not her favourite time of the week!

Laura had also started one of her regular diets, her lunch consisting of a dry biscuit. When Laura dieted everyone suffered and frequently got the sharp end of her tongue. She accused Harry and Biggs of being overweight, a suggestion to which they both reacted indignantly. Harry said that he went running most evenings and Biggs reminded her that he played squash every week and that during games last term, he regularly raced with the boys on the nearby cycle track.

"That was last term," she retorted, quite unimpressed.

The outcome was that they both agreed to cycle to school the following morning, weather permitting. They did it for a spell the previous term, but it hadn't take long for the novelty to wear off. They'd both quite enjoyed cycling to school in the morning, but neither of them had been keen on the long ride home at the end of an exhausting day.

The next day, true to their word they both arrived independently on their bicycles, much to the amusement of the kids. The usual array of predictable and pathetic comments greeted them entered the playground. The boys knew that in the long run they would have to pay for their remarks, but most of them reckoned that it was worth it.

Harry Langton was the first to arrive and he parked his bike in the staff loo. Ian McTaggart knocked it over when going to spend a penny and pulled a muscle in his back when bending over to pick it up. He complained to Harry that he shouldn't keep the damn thing in there since, apart from being a health hazard, it took up a great deal of space. But Harry was unmoved by Ian's whingeing. The previous term, he had insisted on parking his bike in the loo, despite numerous protestations from the staff. The annoying thing was that Harry didn't use the staff loo. He had his own *executive* loo next his office, with scented soap and pale blue toilet paper to match the decor. Biggs used to have a key to it, but the lock had to be changed a few months earlier, after a break-in. Why anybody would want to break into Harry's loo, nobody knew? Biggs kept asking for a replacement key and Harry kept promising, but that's as far as they got. There was no real need for him to have access, since the staff loo was only next door. But it had become a matter of principle, his argument being that since Harry did so much roving, he was all too frequently left in charge of the building. It was therefore only right that he should have access to the executive loo. He knew that his argument was a frivolous one, but that did not stop him from pursuing it at every opportunity.

Having been given the brush-off by Harry, Ian was not in a happy mood, but he was determined to bring the matter of Harry's bicycle parking to a head. He discussed the matter with a couple of the other staff in the staff room and together they hatched a plot! Later in the day, when everyone knew that Harry was in his office, Mr. Hermon Hardcastle went to the general office seeking a first-aid plaster for a graze on his shin. Penny Passmore attended to his needs.

"That's quite a graze," she remarked. "How on earth did you do that?"

"I went to the staff loo and knocked that damn bike over," Hermon said quite loudly, intending Harry to hear through his connecting door to the general office. "The sharp edge on one of the pedals caught me on the shin. It shouldn't be in there. It's a health hazard. Who's bike is it, anyway?"

"I believe it's Mr. Langton's," Penny said, almost apologetically.

"Well, he should know better. I shall have to have a word with the Union's Health and Safety representative. I might be able to get some compensation."

The adjoining door to Harry's office was wide open and Harry was inside sitting at his desk, reading a book on executive stress! His ears had pricked up when he'd heard his bicycle mentioned. They doubly pricked up at the mention of compensation and Union Reps. The outer door of his office could be heard opening!

"Would you like me to put the plaster on for you?" Penny asked Mr. Hardcastle.

"No thank you," he said. "I can manage." He took the plaster from Penny and returned to the staff room.

A few minutes later Harry wheeled his bike into his office and parked it against the wall! Meanwhile, in the staff room there was much merriment!

"That'll teach the sod," Ian McTaggart said...... as he watched Hermon removing the red biro marks from his shin with a damp cloth!

Most schools have one...... a teacher who should never be let loose with more than one child at a time, for fear of the ensuing commotion or riot. Mr. Hermon Hardcastle was that one! Heading a department of one, he taught Music at Gordon Bennett. He was a brilliant musician and extremely knowledgeable in many fields. An actor for a time, he had the sort of voice that carried, even without being raised. He frequently did raise it, however and was prone to flying into a tirade of verbal abuse directed at the kids when they misbehaved. Having spent some time out in the Far East, he spoke fluent Chinese.

Very useful one might think, in a school with a small but regular intake of boys from Hong Kong. Nobody really knew why they got so many Chinese lads, but since they were hard working and always extremely well behaved, they were generally regarded as an asset. And of course Gordon Bennett always liked to play its part in keeping the local Chinese restaurants fully staffed. Although these boys had been taught English in their former Hong Kong schools, they often had a minimal command of the language when they first arrived. Their native dialect was Cantonese and since this was generally spoken at home, they had little chance to practice the spoken word. Unfortunately Hermon spoke Mandarin and his skill was next to useless. Apparently, despite a common written language, the spoken Chinese dialects are very different.

During break one morning whilst on his way to the general office, Biggs was accosted in the corridor by a group of Third Year boys led by Christopher Bird and his mate Tony, complaining that Hermon had referred to them in class as 'a load of swines.' They're not usually that sensitive about being called names, he thought to himself? He called them names all the time and they never reacted indignantly! Somewhat bemused by their complaint, he asked "Were you?"

They thought about it for a moment, getting a general consensus before committing themselves. "Yes, I suppose we were," Christopher said. "But you can't say *'Swines.'* We tried politely to correct him, but he just threw a wobbly! Now he's given us a detention."

Their complaint was not that Hermon had referred to them as swines. It was that he had used the wrong plural! Apparently an attempt by the swine to correct his bad grammar had resulted in a further tirade of verbal abuse that they should have expected.

"I know we rattled him a bit, Sir and we may have deserved being call names," Tony said. "But he should at least have the courtesy to use the correct grammar. We have to!"

To the adage, 'Those who can, do; those who can't, teach,' most teachers would add the rider, 'Those who can't teach, inspect, or advise others on how to teach.' But it doesn't always ring true. Failing teachers are often brilliant in their field, but simply unable to get their message across. Almost everything they do manages to antagonize the kids. They spend much of their time ranting and raving, trying to get the attention of the class and must dread coming to school each morning. Young teachers, with support, usually overcome their difficulties, but once the mould is set, it is often very difficult to break. To make matters worse, older teachers often resent any attempt at help from younger, but more senior staff. Hermon had no such hang-ups, however and he would frequently send wrongdoers to be dealt with elsewhere. He didn't really care to whom he sent them, so long as they were out of his hair. They usually ended up in front of Biggs' desk! This did not best please him, since dealing with the disciplinary shortcomings of others was the part of his job that he hated most. He was quite prepared to give every assistance possible to teachers new to the school, until they got established, or to young teachers just out of college. But he usually resented having to come to the aid of experienced teachers, who after some years standing should have got their act together. In some cases he seriously considered counseling them to consider if they were in the right job! But not wishing to appear unfeeling, or become the subject of resentment, he never did!

CHAPTER 8

THE AUTUMN FAIR. This was the first event of any consequence in the school calendar. It was usually held on the first Saturday of half-term, at the Lower School. It was organized by the Parent Teachers Association in conjunction with several members of staff on a joint committee. Quite a few boys involved themselves in running stalls and side shows and there were always plenty of staff willing to give up a Saturday to lend a hand. Biggs usually kept a low profile and took little part in its organization.

Harry Langton and Brenda Hickman were meant to be helping the PTA organize the event that year. Brenda was a Third Year tutor and taught English. Harry and Brenda had always been on friendly terms, spending a great deal of time together. They were both married, although not to each other and for some time they had been giving cause for tongues to wag! They may have been on friendly terms, but knowing Harry of old, Biggs assumed that Brenda would be left to do most of the organizing. They had been trying to get him involved for sometime, but he would have none of it.

On the day of the Fair, the weather was kind; a nice bright autumn day. It was a bit chilly, but the sun was shining brightly and the forecast indicated that it would soon warm up. Biggs arrived in his *posemobile* just after midday to find that things seemed to be well in hand, with parents and boys scurrying busily about. Few staff were evident, but it was lunch time, so he guessed that they would be in G19, having a quick nogging and a bite to eat. The playground and staff car park were taken up with stalls, so the Trans Am had to parked in the street. He didn't like parking it in the street, since it was likely to become a target for sticky fingers or possibly scratches from someone with a grudge. He parked in a side road well away from the school and walked round to G19. The saloon bar had been taken over by the Gordon Bennett staff. The landlord always regarded them as the mainstay of his business and they certainly did him justice that Saturday. There must have been at least twenty of the staff propping up the bar or sitting at tables.

Harry Langton was seated at a table near the window, with Laura and Brenda, drinking what looked to Biggs to be a very large scotch.

"I thought that you were meant to be organizing things?" Biggs said.

"It's all under control," Harry confirmed. " Sit down and have a drink."

Laura and Brenda Hickman disappeared to the little girl's room to powder their noses, or to do whatever women do in the little girl's room.

Meanwhile, attention was drawn to a noisy group in one corner of the bar. It was the Hippy, 'f.....ing' away like a good'un and spouting forth some socialist claptrap to several of the left wing trendies. The pub had been open for less than hour, but he was already slurring his words.

Some ten minutes later Brenda and Laura returned from the little girl's room! It had always been constant source of wonder to Biggs, what women find to do for so long in their inner sanctum. If two men spent a similar amount of time in the little boy's room, tongues would most certainly start wagging. They both declined the offer of another drink.

"I must keep a clear head," Laura said. "I should be getting back to my stall. I've got a lot of things to unwrap."

Laura had volunteered to run the white elephant stall. She was keen on that sort of thing and went to a jumble sale or boot sale most weekends. She usually managed to acquired some fantastic bargain.

Brenda and Harry decided to take the hint and after quickly finishing their drinks, got up to return to school. They might well have been having second thoughts about everything being under control, Biggs thought to himself.

"Oh! Not leaving are you?" he said, getting up to return with them "Just as it was my round too."

Harry just smiled benignly, but it was obvious that he'd made a mental note of the. omission with a view bringing it up at an appropriate juncture. Over the years Biggs had somehow managed to acquire a reputation for being frugal with money, a reputation that was quite unjustified in his eyes. He always considered himself to have a generous nature, although he didn't like being put upon and would react unsympathetically to unsolicited demands for money, no matter how good the cause. In the staff sweepstakes for the Derby or Grand National he always seemed to end up with a ticket for the no-hope outsider, so in the end he stopped buying tickets! This of course only served to enhance his reputation for frugality.

It was not yet two o'clock, but the place was swarming with people and most activities seemed to have started. The Morris Dancers were in full dress, but were not due to give their performance until three o'clock, by which time Biggs hoped to be long gone. Peter Johnson, a chemistry teacher based in the Upper School, was 'Foreman' of the troop and carried a sort of 'tickling stick' with which he struck the other members of the troop. He always was a bit of an exhibitionist, but it must have taken some nerve to dress up in costume and prance around with hoards of kids watching; kids that he might well have been taking for Chemistry earlier in the week!

Malcolm Rowe, the Senior Year Head from the Upper School, was running his usual secondhand book stall. Malcolm always maintained that he would like the option of early retirement and to open a small bookshop in a country town somewhere. The option of early retirement was no more than a pipe-dream at the time, but was to become a welcome reality several years down the line, for both Malcolm and Biggs. Complementing the books were several piles of comics which were selling for 10p and 20p each; all confiscated no doubt!

Biggs looked in at Penny Passmore's second hand clothes stall. She has a very odd assortment of unisex garments. Paul Scobie, no doubt ejected from the pub for his bad language, was rummaging through them. He picked out a couple of T-shirts, one pink and one...... a sort of fluorescent 'yuck.' He haggled over the price and Penny let him have them for 50p each. Everyone wondered who his tailor was? He had been spoken to many times by Harry Langton and by the Headmaster about his dress, but it was always to no avail. There was usually an improvement for a short period, but he was never long before lapsing back to his normal hippie state.

Christopher Bird was running a 'Throwing a Wet Sponge' stall with Tony Roberts and a couple of his other mates. He was wearing a plastic cycling cape to keep the worst off, but he still looked pretty wet. His kid brother, Steven, wanted to have a go at throwing the sponge at him, but Christopher would have none of it. He threatened Steven with dire consequences, should he so much as look at a sponge, let alone throw one!

'Three Throws for 20p' was just too good to miss, so Biggs handed over his money and took aim with the first sponge. It missed, but the second one just caught his left ear, spraying him with water.

"Go easy, Sir," he said. "I'll let you win at squash next time we play."

"Right Christopher! That does it. I don't need you to let me win."

The third sponge, guided by sheer determination, hit him squarely on the nose, drenching him with water, much to the amusement of the crowd and his younger brother. Biggs took out 20p for another go, but Christopher pleaded with him not to. "It's only meant for kids, not nasty teachers hell bent on revenge."

Biggs took pity on him...... and gave the sponge to his brother, who had been standing beside him, watching with glee. Before Christopher realized what was happening, Steven seized his opportunity and hurled the wet sponge with all his strength, hitting him squarely in the face...... and then ran. Throwing off his cape, Christopher leapt from his chair, picked up the sponge and chased after his brother, hurling abuse. Steven cleverly foiled him by standing next to the Headmaster while he was engaged in conversation with the Chairman of the PTA.. He had gained a temporary reprieve, but it was not for long. A short time afterwards, Steven was seen with his head held firmly under Christopher's arm while his mate Tony squeezed a wet sponged down the inside of his trousers, making him look as though he had wet himself.

Having set the cat amongst the pigeons, Biggs thought that it was time for him to take his leave. He managed to slip away unnoticed. With no more school for a whole week, it was the start of half-term!

CHAPTER 9

One of the major headaches shared by kids and teachers alike, is constantly having to return to school between the holidays! The weather during half-term break had been quite pleasant, with a touch of Indian summer. It made for a pleasant break, but the leaden sky which greeted them on the Monday morning was not in the least inspiring.

Christopher Bird attempted to stop Biggs at the gate as he drove into the school grounds. Slowing to a walking pace, he continued towards the staff car park with Christopher jogging alongside and tapping on the window of the Trans Am. He obviously wanted it to be lowered it, so Biggs conceded three inches to him.

"Christopher, get your dirty paws of my clean window."

"Are we still playing squash, Sir?" Christopher asked, ignoring the remark.

"I suppose so. Why do you ask? Games options are changed at the end of term, not after half-term. You should know that."

"I know, Sir. I was just checking. I've been practicing over the half-term and I owe you one for getting me wet at the Autumn fair, so I won't be going easy on you like I did before."

His personality had obviously taken a dive for the worst over the half-term. Biggs closed his electric window, trapping Christopher's hand and continued towards the car park, his speed increasing to a slow trot.

"Been dreaming again have you, Chris. You'd better make sure that it doesn't turn into a nightmare then, hadn't you,".

They had been playing each week since the start of term and Christopher's game had improved considerably during that time. Graciously, he'd even admitted to having a good coach! The squash group was quite small, there being only four courts available at the sports centre. The group consisted of just twelve boys, three boys sharing each court and playing each other in rotation. Biggs was never a brilliant player, but then he didn't consider it necessary to be good to teach newcomers to the game. He always enjoyed playing Christopher and, since one or two of the group were sometimes absent, they usually managed to get in at a couple games each session. If the court was not booked, they would sometimes stay on after the official session was over, playing in unofficial time. A good natured lad, always cheerful and totally without malice, he had always been popular with his peers. But because of his quick wit and total mastery of repartee, he was sometimes less than popular with some members of staff, who generally regarded him as rather cheeky and a bit of a smart-arse. But these were the very qualities which endeared him to Biggs and the reason that they got on so well! He passed Christopher's house on his way home, so after games he usually gave him a lift.

During their last games session before half-term, Christopher had managed to win one of the two games that they played and since he won the second game, with no time for a decider, he misguidedly thought that put him on top! Biggs had to resort to tweaking his elbow when he was accused of being past it.

The needle match took place later that week during their Wednesday games session. There were no absentees from the group that day, so not wishing to deprive another boy of a game, it meant remaining behind to play in unofficial time. They started with their usual five minute warm-up knockabout to get the ball bouncing nicely, but without really exerting themselves.

"Spin for service, Sir?" Christopher called, eager to get started.

Biggs nodded and called, "Smooth." The racket landed rough side up.

"Best of three," he suggested, tongue in cheek.

"Knickers," said Christopher. "It's my service."

Biggs ignored the knickers and conceded the service. They started playing in earnest and managed a couple of good rallies. One of Biggs' points came from a blatant obstruction and Christopher complained that they should play the point again. It was then Biggs turn to say, "Knickers," a mild degree of cheating always taking place. In fact they both regarded cheating as gamesmanship. It was accepted as part of the game and adding to the fun. It was a close game, but Biggs eventually managed to beat Christopher 9 - 7.

In the second game, despite having been playing nonstop for over an hour, Christopher got his second wind. Obviously much the fitter of the two, he clearly enjoyed giving Biggs the run around and this time, despite numerous further deliberate and quite blatant obstructions, he won 9 - 7. He shrieked with delight as he smashed the final ace service into the bottom left hand corner of the court. It was again one game all and once again, with no time for a decider. Christopher pleaded for another game, feeling sure that he would win, but there was a knock on the court door indicating that it had been booked and that their time was up.

"I bet you were pleased to hear that knock, Sir," he said, as they shook hands. "I would have won a decider, you know."

"Dream on, my son!"

"How about a game of snooker, Sir?"

"Snooker!" Biggs, queried. He knew that Christopher sometimes played after school in the snooker hall opposite the Lower School, but he had never before been invited to play. He liked watching it on television and occasionally played himself, but he wasn't particularly good at it.

"I don't know, Chris! Are you any good at it?"

"No, I'm useless," Christopher said, totally unconvincingly.

"Thanks for the offer, but another time perhaps."

Biggs drove Christopher home as usual and as they pulled up outside his house, he asked, "Want to come in for a cuppa, Sir?"

"A cuppa?" Another first, Biggs thought to himself! He had taken him home after games many times, but he had never before been asked in! "Are you sure, Chris? Won't you mother think it a bit odd?"

"No, she won't be back for ages yet. She won't mind anyway."

"What about your brother? I'm not exactly flavour of the month with him?"

"Oh, don't worry about him. Anyway, he won't be home. He always stays behind for football training on Wednesdays. Come on, Sir."

"Okay. Thanks Chris. I'd love to."

Christopher showed Biggs into his living room. "Have a pew," he said. "Tea or coffee?"

"Tea will be fine, thanks."

As Christopher disappeared to the kitchen, Biggs sank low into the most comfortable looking armchair and looked round the room. It was tastefully decorated and spotless. On the mantelpiece there were a number of family photographs, including one of a baby lying naked on a rug. After a few minutes, Christopher brought in a tray from the kitchen with two cups of tea and a plate of biscuits."

I'm afraid its not Lapsang, Sir. Just plain old Indian. Help yourself to sugar and dig into the biscuits."

"Thanks, Chris.... Who's the baby in the photograph?"

"Trust you to spot that, Sir. It's me! I suppose now, you'll be telling all the lads back at school that you've seen a photograph of me in the nude."

"Chris, would I do a thing like that?.... I might tell Tony, though!"

"Tony's already seen it..... Have another biscuit."

"Thanks. Don't worry, I won't say anything."

"I've just joined the sea cadets, Sir."

"I'm very pleased to hear it, Chris. They might instill some discipline and knock some of the crap out of you!"

"Really, Sir! Such language!"

"Oh, I'm sorry if I offended your sensitive nature. I was forgetting what a delicate bloom you are! And me a guest in your house too!"

"Only joking, Sir."

"Seriously though, if you are still intending to join the Royal Navy when you leave school, it's a good move. I know it's not quite the same as the real thing, but at least it will give you an insight into Navy life."

"That's what I thought, Sir."

They chatted away happily for nearly half an hour, the topics discussed being many and varied. Eventually, not wishing to be there when Christopher's younger brother, Steven arrived home, Biggs decided that it was time to take his leave.

"Anyway, Chris, I'd better be making a move. Thanks again for the tea."

"No problem, Sir. I really enjoyed our little chat. We must do it again sometime.... In fact, since you always give me a lift home after games on Wednesdays, if you like, we could make it a regular thing?"

Biggs looked hard at Christopher and realized at once that he was making a serious suggestion. Although he had many friends and was popular with the other lads at school, Biggs knew that he also liked the company of adults. He could be quite frivolous at times, but he also had a serious side and liked a discussion. He also knew him well enough to know that his invitation had no ulterior motive and that he would not expect any favours for his hospitality. Back in school, he would expect to be treated the same as always and the same as any other member of his Express Set.

"Okay Chris, you're on!"

CHAPTER 10

It was raining heavily one Friday morning. There had been a spectacular display of thunder and lightning in the early hours and the roads were very wet with large pools of water everywhere. Driving down a fairly narrow road on his way to school Harry Langton had been forced towards the gutter by oncoming traffic. Not known for his sedate driving manner, he had been traveling at a fair turn of speed. Becoming aware of a boy walking along the pavement near to the edge of the road where there was a large pool of water, he attempted to slow down to avoid splashing the lad. Unfortunately he was not able to slow sufficiently to avoid driving through the pool still at a fair old lick. A huge mountain of water forced up by his near-side wheels, completely drenched the boy from head to toe. Feeling very guilty Harry came to a stop, with the good intention of going to the lad's assistance. However, he caught sight of the boy in his rear view mirror making threatening gestures at him with his fists. In a rage to end all rages, he was stamping his feet and had completely lost his composure! Harry instantly recognized the boy as being Ronnie Day, one of Gordon Bennett's former pupils. He would have been a Third year boy, that is if he hadn't been expelled two terms earlier for being an out-and-out little sod. The bane of everyone's life, Ronnie had subsequently been sent to a school for maladjusted boys. Thinking it prudent to be elsewhere at that moment in time, Harry drove off at speed leaving Ronnie to continue with his rage alone. Relating the incident to everyone in the general office when he finally reached school, it became the subject of much merriment.

"Yippee," cried Ian McTaggart, thrusting his right arm in the air, in the fashion of a footballer who had just scored a blinding goal. "One back for the teachers! It's about time that little sod got his comeuppance."

The school doctor was due to do a BCG skin test that morning and needed to use the hall. She wanted to start at 9.30 so the assembly had to be cancelled and Harry Langton put up a notice to this effect in the staff room. Howls of anguish followed from the Form Tutors.

"What are we supposed to do with the kids for over an hour," complained Alan Howlett, the somewhat laterally challenged Second Year tutor.

"Pastoral care," Harry ventured, tongue in cheek. "You could try having a discussion or possibly talking to them about your experiences in Jamaica. Failing that, set some maths."

Alan was not amused. He had just returned to Gordon Bennett after spending a year in Jamaica on an exchange visit. On the whole, he had enjoyed the experience, but he'd unwisely spent too much time looking at holiday brochures before going. He went expecting a life of ease on sun-drenched beaches and was rather taken aback by reality. Not only was he expected to do some teaching, but his first class had fifty-two children in it. This was apparently the norm and set the standard for the rest of the year. A beautiful young Jamaican lady teacher had replaced Alan as part of the exchange deal. Everyone was sorry to see her leave when she had to return to Jamaica at the end of the Summer term.

Returning to his office, Harry passed a small and very worried looking First year boy, who attempted to stop him in the corridor.

"Will the injection hurt, Sir?" the lad asked, nervously.

"You bet!" said Harry, without stopping.

The lad looked with pleading eyes at Biggs, who had been standing nearby.

"Don't worry," he assured him. "Take no notice of that nasty Mr. Langton. It's only a skin test. It won't hurt."

The lad looked relieved. "Oh! Thanks, Sir..... I hate injections and I was worried there for a minute."

Biggs polished his halo, his good deed for the day having been done.

His Majesty arrived to take the assembly! Nobody had remembered to tell him about the skin tests and that the assembly had been cancelled. They each blamed each other for the omission. The Headmaster was not pleased and accused everyone of wasting his valuable time. He obviously intended gunning for someone and since everyone was a viable target, they all tried to look busy. Laura typed away madly and Penny busied herself counting the tuck shop money, for the second time. Gladys adopted the old army dodge of walking around with a list of names in his hand. Biggs just returned to his office, leaving Harry to deal with the Headmaster. He may not have been able to take the assembly, but Mr. Martin clearly intended to make his presence felt by wasting everyone else's valuable time. He decided to go walkabout! That meant wandering round the school, with Harry Langton in tow, looking into every nook and cranny, trying to find something amiss. He visited each classroom briefly, while the Form Tutors were looking after their tutor groups, the assembly having been cancelled. The tutors must have been doing their stuff, since he found nothing untoward. If the truth were known, that in itself probably displeased him..... finding nothing to criticize. Clearly not a happy little bunny, he eventually returned to the Upper School, in a foul mood. Harry thought of phoning the Upper School office to warn them that he was on the warpath, but having second thoughts, he changed his mind. "What have they ever done for us?" he said. "Let them find out for themselves."

It was still raining heavily and the forecast for what it was worth, indicated that it wouldn't stop until late morning. That meant a 'wet-break' and the boys would have to remain in the building, with more staff on duty to control the rabble. They were normally allowed in on fine days, but most chose to go outside and there was rarely a problem.

More staff on duty, usually turned out to mean Biggs, Ian and Gladys. Harry Langton invariably contrived to be elsewhere during wet-breaks. His usual excuse was that he had to go to the Upper School to see the Headmaster on some urgent matter. He hadn't yet realized that Biggs sometimes checked up on him by phoning the Headmaster or his secretary on some pretext, at the same time casually enquiring if he was there. He never was! Harry wasn't able to use his usual excuse that day however, having just had a belly full of His Majesty. He would clearly have to think up some other plausible excuse!

Sure enough, just before the pips were due to sound for morning break, Harry popped his head round the connecting door to his office and after surveying an unusually busy scene said, "Hello Girls."

Penny, preparing to open the tuck shop, was counting some loose change, while Laura was taking down in shorthand a letter that Biggs was attempting to dictate. Ian daydreamed by the window as he sipped an early coffee, that generally being regarded as quite busy for him. Harry attempted further to elicit a response, his greeting having been virtually ignored.

"It's still raining," he said. "Wet-break today?"

Biggs nodded agreement, without interrupting his dictation.

Realizing that his presence had failed to make a major impact, Harry continued, "Good, there shouldn't be a problem...... should there?"

They all continued with their various tasks, without looking up. Deliberately ignoring him, they waited in anticipation for his excuse for not being around during the wet-break. It was not long in coming.

"Right then," he added. "I'm just nipping along to the Upper School to see Mr. Royston on an urgent matter. I'll be back after break."

He had never used that excuse before, going to see their low profile and very elusive Second Deputy! Stopping what they were doing, they all looked up and stared knowingly at him, oozing disbelief, but saying nothing.

"I'll be back after break," he repeated, indignantly. "I'm teaching fourth period."

Now there really was cause to disbelieved him! Ian, so far only vaguely aware of what had been going on, was stunned out of his daydream.

"TEACHING!" he exclaimed.

"Yes, that's what I said, Mr. McTaggart..... TEACHING!..... That's when you stand in front of a class and talk to them and try to get information into their thick sculls!"

"*I* know what it is.... I'm just surprised that *you* still remember!"

"Very funny, I don't think.... Anyway I'm covering Jenny Miller. She has to go to the dentist after break and she says it's an emergency."

"What? You mean you actually put yourself down to cover a lesson? That's not like you. Are you sure that you are not sickening for something," Ian continued, rather pushing his luck.

Harry was not amused. He stormed out of the office and, adopting the broad Scots accent he reserved for occasions when sarcasm seemed appropriate, made a parting shot at Ian. "Just be sure to check the cover list very carefully on Monday morning, Mr. McTaggart. I wouldn't want you to miss anything of interest that might concern you."

The trouble with Ian was that he didn't know when to keep his big mouth shut. He returned to his daydream and Biggs continued with his somewhat hesitant dictation of his letter. Although Laura was an expert at shorthand, it was not often that he availed himself of her skill. The problem was that she wrote her funny little squiggles faster than he could dictate and she ended up spending much of the time twiddling her thumbs. Dictating letters to be taken down in shorthand requires clear thinking and is a skill that has to be acquired with practice. Biggs never got enough practice, so he usually ended up roughing his letters out in draft form, using his own version of shorthand that only Laura could read. Really important letters, he would write in red ink, so that they would be given priority. On the odd occasion when he did not have a red pen to hand, he would write in black, but preface the letter with 'This is a red letter.'

The following Monday morning, Ian checked to cover list and discovered that he had been put down to cover two lessons. He was not amused!

CHAPTER 11

THE RUNNING-IN SAGA. Harry Langton had continued cycling to school once or twice each week. Biggs did it just the once and was not allowed to forget it. Harry was never one to pass up on an opportunity to be 'holier than thou.' After a while he decided that he would give up cycling to school in the morning. He announced that in future he was going to *run* in the four miles from his home to school! He even went as far as to buy a brand new designer tracksuit.

Biggs arrived one morning to find him in a state of exhaustion, prostrate on his chaise longue. Brenda Hickman was patting his brow with her handkerchief and offering him soothing words of comfort. Laura entered the room, bearing a large cup of coffee and looked at him with disdain.

"Coffee, Mr. Langton," she said, managing to spill half of it in the saucer, as she plonked it down on the small table beside his chaise longue. She clearly had little sympathy for his foolhardiness. "I take it that you won't be going across the road this morning for your usual?"

By going across the road, Laura meant going to the greasy spoon opposite the school with Brenda for breakfast. Biggs used to pop in himself on the odd occasion, if he had skipped breakfast at home, or he would ask them to bring him back a crusty cheese roll.

"I don't think so," Harry replied, clearly in no fit state to consume a fried breakfast. It was at this point that Harry noticed that Biggs had entered his office.

"Good morning, Mr. Smith," he said, barely able to get the words out. "I had a great run in...... a very invigorating. I feel great.... Why don't you try it? It will do you a power of good and rid you of a few pounds."

Biggs viewed him with dismay! "I don't think so. If that's your idea of feeling great, I'd hate to see you when you're not feeling too good," he said, with more than a modicum of sarcasm. ".....and if I want to loose a few pounds, I'll get in touch with Oxfam."

The trouble with Harry was that, whatever he did, it was usually all or nothing, rarely the happy medium. He usually gave up on most things after a while and Biggs guessed that his idea of running in to keep fit would go the same way. He recalled how Harry had bought an expensive set of golf equipment the previous year. He'd spent over a thousand pounds on clubs, an expensive trolley and on clothing, only to find that he couldn't play and that he didn't particularly like the game anyway! He kept a low profile throughout the rest of the morning and disappeared completely in the afternoon. Laura pinned a notice on his door, 'GONE ROVING.'

A few days later and much to everyone's surprise, Harry no longer appeared to be suffering from the effects of his morning run-in and it was looking a bit suspicious to Biggs. He found him seated at his desk one morning, wearing a track suit with a towel rapped round his neck. Not a drop of perspiration was to be seen? A few days earlier he had almost collapsed with exhaustion after running in! Now we can all put on track suits and rap towels round our necks, Biggs thought to himself and he had his doubts that Harry did actually run in the four miles from his home! Of course, he could have got in earlier than normal, giving himself time to recover, but Biggs decided to register his doubts with him on the matter. Now Harry's reaction when his propriety was challenged could be unpredictable and at times spiteful. He became quite indignant and embarked on a verbal tirade to the effect that he most certainly did run in and that anyone who even thought of doubting him had one hell of a nerve. Biggs decided that it would be prudent to let the matter rest for the time being.

The following day, Biggs was sitting in his office during morning break, contemplating nothing in particular, when Christopher Bird popped his head round his door, grinning like a Cheshire cat.

"I know something that you don't," he bragged.

He came out with these inane statements from time to time. Deciding not to take the bait, Biggs leaned back in his chair and closed his eyes, in the forlorn hope that when he opened them again Christopher would have gone. No such luck!

Undaunted he continued, "You really would like to know, Sir."

"Christopher, what piece of information could you possibly have that would be of the slightest interest to me?"

"Ah, that's for me to know and for you to find out, Sir."

They were obviously going to have one of their regular silly conversations. They often proved to be amusing, however and Biggs thought that he might as well play along with him.

"Okay, Chris. Give me a clue."

"It concerns Mr. Langton."

"Christopher, you're skating on thin ice! Now stop twittering and tell me." His interest had been aroused. Any low-down on Harry was always welcome!

"What's it worth, Sir?"

"Chris, you can be so boring and predictable at times. It's obvious that you're dying to tell me, so spit it out and if it's worth anything, I'll let you know."

"Okay, Sir. It's a deal.... Next time Mr. Langton runs to school in the morning, take a drive up the hill to the park."

"And what will I find?" Now Christopher really had got him interested!

"You know I'm not a grass, Sir, so I can't tell you directly. Just take a look up the hill and you will see something very interesting...... Trust me, I'm a pupil."

"Chris, you would grass on your grandmother if you thought it would help you to stir up trouble and as far as trusting you goes, I would rather trust my head in a lion's mouth."

The 'pips' sounded for the end of morning break, so their conversation had to be curtailed, just as it was getting interesting too.

"You'd better get along to your next lesson. We'll continue this conversation later. In the meantime, if I do find anything interesting, I'll let you know."

Christopher gave him a thumbs-up. "See you later, alligator."

"Not if I see you first...... and you'd better hope that I do find something interesting, or I'll be feeding you to the crocodiles."

"Nice one, Sir." he said, giving another thumbs-up. "By the way, you know we've not had our game of snooker yet?"

"Yes, I know. We will. But for now, scram."

Biggs could hazard a pretty good guess as to what he might find up the hill, but he decided to wait and confirm his suspicion before taking any action.

'Trust me, I'm a pupil,' was the 'in' phrase current at the time and was banded about by the kids whenever a teacher doubted their veracity. It had been hijacked from 'Trust me, I'm a Teacher,' a phrase that Harry Langton had taken to using whenever boys doubted something he said to them. Of course, originally it came from 'Trust me, I'm a Doctor.' As far as trusting Christopher was concerned, whatever else he may have been, Biggs considered him to be completely trustworthy. He could honestly say that he would have trusted him with his life. He did, in fact, a couple of years on, after Christopher left school, but more about that later.

It must have been a couple of days later, that Biggs arrived about half past eight to find Harry seated in Laura's chair in the general office, sipping his morning coffee and stuffing his face with a bacon roll from the greasy spoon.

"Good morning, Mr. Smith," he said cheerfully.

Once again he was wearing his track suit and had a towel rapped round his neck, with not a drop of perspiration to be seen. Christopher's words sprang instantly to mind!

"Good morning, Harry. Good run in?"

"Great," he replied, quite unaware that everyone was getting very suspicious. Harry could be quite naive at times!

Laura burst through the door, carrying an enormous bag, which she dumped on her desk in front of Harry, indicating that he was expected to move.

"Morning all," she chirped. "Good run in, Mr. Langton?"

"Great," Harry repeated, leaping out of Laura's chair.

"Black, with no sugar," she said, looking in Biggs' direction.

Thinking that he must have been just about the highest paid tea-boy...... or coffee-boy in the business, dutifully he performed his roll in life and handed Laura her coffee.

"Is it all right if I carry on with running the school now, Laura."

"Oh! That's what you do? We always wondered. Yes thank you Mr. Smith. Please feel free to carry on."

They went through that kind of banter from time to time. It helped to oil the wheels and relieve the tedium.

Biggs had a Maths lesson with a Second year group, the first two periods. The were a dozy lot at the best of times, but they seemed unusually subdued that morning and time dragged. Eventually the pips sounded for morning break and he hurried down to look for Christopher. He found him standing with a group of friends, eating a bag of crisps. He was rather taken aback when pulled by the scruff of the neck towards the staff car park.

"Come on, Chris. We're going for a drive."

Being quick on the uptake, he realized immediately where they were going.

"Did he run in today, Sir? I didn't come that way this morning."

"Show me," Biggs said.

Following Christopher's directions, they turned right out of the main gate and drove up the hill towards the park. After following the park road for just a short distance, they spotted it, barely half a mile from the school....... Harry Langton's white van! With the distinctive letters HAL on the number plate, there was no doubt that the van was his. The crafty sod, Biggs thought to himself. So much for his four mile run to school each morning. No wonder it's been having so little effect on him!

"Well done, Chris. I owe you one...... but remember *mum's* the word."

"Right, Sir. mum's the word," Christopher confirmed, giving his usual thumbs-up.

The problem which then posed itself, was what to do with that delightful piece of information? The situation called for tact and needed careful handling, to get the maximum mileage from it. It was no use confiding in Mike Gladstone; he could be a boring old fart at the best of times and tact was never his strong point. Biggs could have related his discovery to Laura, but he had a sneaking suspicion that she already knew more than she was letting on and she might have tipped the wink to Harry. After all, she was his personal assistant and she knew which side her bread was buttered. Ian McTaggart was the best bet, so after break, Biggs told him the story.

"The crafty sod," Ian exclaimed, echoing Biggs own reaction. "I knew something wasn't quite right, but I never dreamed that he would have tried to pull a fast one like that!"

"I would ...... but then I've known him much longer than you."

They put their heads together and quickly came up with a stratagem, ready for the next occasion that Harry would pretend to run in.

During the midday lunch break, Ian and Biggs wandered along to Harry's office, with a view to putting their ruse into operation. They found him seated at his desk, playing with his latest executive toy, a Newton's Cradle. His office door was open, so they wandered in.

"New toy?" Ian ventured.

"What do you want?" Harry said, rather acidly. "Can't you find anything better to do than make silly remarks. It's a piece of scientific apparatus."

"Of course it is," Ian said, tongue in cheek. "Perhaps you'd care explain the scientific principle it's meant to illustrate."

"Ask Mr. Smith. he's supposed to be the scientist...... he should know," Harry said, clearly trying to cover up his ignorance on the matter. "Anyway, what do you want? Can't you see I'm busy."

"Oh yes, so you are!" Ian said, with a grin. "Well..... we were just wondering if you intended running in tomorrow? The forecast seems quite good."

"I expect so," Harry replied, looking up rather suspiciously. "Why do you ask? What's it got to do with you?"

"Oh, it's just that we both thought that we might give it a try."

"So, I've finally shamed you into it," Harry bragged, taking the bait.

"You'll probably get in long before us," Ian said, buttering him up a little. "After all, you've been doing it for some time now and should be quite fit."

"I am, but that's all right. Don't worry about how long it takes. Just take it steady and try not to overdo it ...... Oh, but don't be late." Harry continued, still playing with his new toy.

"Try two balls," Biggs suggested, as they left Harry to continue playing with his Newton's Cradle. As soon as they were out of sight, they gave each other a thumbs-up.

Little did Harry know what was in store for him the following day!

Biggs let Christopher win at squash that afternoon and they also played their promised game of snooker! He won that too!

Ian and Biggs arranged to meet before school the following morning, driving to a spot not far from where Harry had parked his van the previous day. They were wearing track suits and had towels rapped round their necks! They drove cautiously, the final few hundred yards, as they approached the spot, in case he was still around. The van was there, parked in the same place, but there was no sign of Harry. It was looking good, so they parked their cars, one in front of the van and one behind, their bumpers almost touching. Well and truly boxed in, Harry Langton had no possibility of moving without first getting one of them to move.

Pushing themselves fairly hard, so as to get up a bit of a sweat, they ran the remaining half mile to school, arriving ten minutes before the pips were due to sound.

"You made it then," Harry said.

"Just about," Ian replied, flopping on to Harry's chaise longue and pretending to pant. "I'm knackered!"

Ian may have been pretending, but Biggs panting was for real. Clearly well out of condition, he flopped down beside Ian, pushing his legs out of the way.

"There, there," said Laura with a modicum or sympathy, tinged with a great deal of sarcasm. "Let me get you a nice cup of coffee."

"Laura! What are you doing?" Harry demanded. "They can get their own coffee. You'll be feeding them grapes next!"

Shaking his head with despair, he went to the staff room to pin up the cover list. At that moment Christopher Bird entered the general office to collect his class register. Seeing Harry's open door and being nosey by nature, he poked his head round.

"Nice one, Sir," he said. "I like it. Paul Smith came that way today and saw you parking your cars. He told me all about it."

"Chris, do you remember what I said about keeping mum?" Biggs said.

"Yes, Sir."

"Well, it's cancelled!"

Christopher thought for a moment, then smiling broadly, he gave his usual thumbs-up, saying "Right, Sir...... got it! It was a sure bet that it would be all round the school in next to no time.

Towards the end of the day, just before three o'clock, Harry Langton looked into the general office. Biggs was attempting to dictate another letter to Laura.

"I'm off now, Girls," he said. "I'm going to have a gentle jog home." They both looked up and made a point of looking at their watches, but before they had a chance to make a comment, Harry added, "Don't say any thing that I might remember when you want to leave early for a sauna, Mr. Smith...... or when you next want to meet someone at the airport, Mrs. Clayton."

The previous day Laura had taken the afternoon off, so that she could pick up her husband from the airport. He had been to Jersey on a business trip.

"Nothing was further from our minds," Laura assured him, heeding his advice, but adding with a wry smile, "As if we would!"

"He'll be back in ten minutes," Biggs said, after Harry had left.

"What makes you think that?"

"Oh well...... it's like this." Biggs told her about Harry's jogging fiasco and how his van had been had boxed in before school that morning.

"He'll be furious," she said, with a wry smile. "I wouldn't like to be in your shoes when he finds out."

Biggs hadn't thought of that aspect of it! He got the impression that Laura knew more than she was letting on, but said nothing.

Half an hour later, Harry had not returned and shortly after the pips sounded for the end of school, Ian burst into the general office.

"He's gone then! I saw him from my window, jogging up the hill."

"Yes, but that was half an hour ago and he hasn't returned yet!"

"That's very strange, I wonder what he's up to?"

"Give him another ten minutes," Laura suggested. "If he hasn't returned by then, you'll have to go and investigate."

Ten minutes later, Harry had still not returned, so Ian and Biggs began their jog up the hill to the spot where their cars had been parked. They arrived to find that their cars were still there, but that Harry's white van had gone! Careful investigation revealed that Ian's had been moved forwards a couple of feet. Somehow Harry had managed to unlock the door, push the car forward and then lock it again.

"The crafty sod has fooled us," Ian exclaimed.

"Not really," Biggs said. "He may have got away with it for the present, but he now knows that we know, he's been pulling a fast one. In any case a little Bird will have been squawking it all over the school by now."

"Brilliant, but what will Harry say in the morning?"

"I don't know....... I thing I'll be ill."

"Me too."

They weren't ill and the next day and Biggs arrived to find on his desk a small sports trophy, the sort that was normally awarded to boys on sports day. It was for running! Ian had one too, so they guessed that it was Harry's way of conceding defeat and that the 'running-in' saga was closed. It was never mentioned again.

CHAPTER 12

EXAMS AND REPORTS. It was customary for internal exams to be held twice a year. The major session always took place towards the end of the Autumn term and was combined with interim reports. Mock GCE exams for Fifth year pupils were held just before the Spring half-term, the senior boys not being required to sit the autumn exams. Mini exams were then held towards the end of the Summer term, together with full reports. Of course by this time, the GCE examinations had been completed and the senior boys who would be leaving school were allowed to depart early on an extended summer holiday. They were also allowed 'study leave' during the period of their public examinations and were only required to attend school to sit each exam. Not a lot was seen of them during this period! Of course it was open to speculation as to how much studying was done at home. It was generally accepted that those who needed to study most, usually studied least! On the plus side, teachers who would normally have taken the senior boys, suddenly found themselves with a lot more free time. Of course, they still bitched like hell when asked to cover for absent colleagues, but then that's the nature of the beast. As December approached everyone was busily preparing examination papers.

The preparation of exam papers can be a tedious task at he best of times and teachers have diverse ways of going about it. Harry Langton's method was quite simple. It usually consisted of searching through past papers, cutting out suitable questions and sticking them in a suitable format on plain A4 sheet.. The photocopier did the rest; simple, but effective.

Since it was usually Biggs' task to arrange the examination timetable for the whole school, he always arranged for the Maths exams to be held at the beginning of exam week. This meant that he was able to get his marking done, while the other exams were still going on. It was customary for several groups to be put together in the hall. This had a twofold effect. Firstly, it introduced a more formal atmosphere, preparing the kids for the time when they would have to sit their public examinations. Secondly, it freed a few staff to do more important things, such as sitting in the staff room drinking tea or coffee.

When the exams were over, there naturally followed the even more tedious task of marking scripts and writing reports. There always seemed to be an impossibly tight deadline for completing these tasks. Scripts had to be marked and reports completed by the end of the week following the exams. Of course, having contrived to get his maths marking completed while the other exams were still going on, Biggs always had a head start with his reports. He always maintained that he needed the extra time, however, since one of his other onerous tasks was having to read through the drivel, platitudes and banal comments written by other teachers in their reports. After signing them, the Lower School reports were then ready for presentation to the Headmaster. His Majesty always read each one thoroughly and took great pleasure in finding mistakes. In order to avoid getting it in the neck, it was always in Biggs interest to find the mistakes first and have them corrected before they reached him. A handful of reports always had to be returned to their originators for correction of spelling mistakes, or because unsuitable comments had been made.

It wasn't too bad that year, but one report had to be returned because the teacher had obviously got a pleasant mild-mannered boy confused with someone else, probably a mass murderer. He had made totally unsuitable comments and was somewhat perturbed at having to rewrite it. Another, written by the Head of PE and Games, had to be returned because the boy had been given quite a favourable report, the problem being that he was a persistent truant and hadn't attended a single PE or Games lesson the entire term! Yet another had to be returned because it looked as though it had been written by a drunken spider. It was covered with ink smudges and the writing was almost illegible. To add insult to injury, the text or the report referred to the boys scruffy presentation of his work. It was written by the Head of English!

The previous year at a staff meeting, the Headmaster had registered his displeasure at the poor standard of reporting and in an attempt to rectify the matter, he produced a compendium of suitable phrases that could be used. It had ridiculous words in it such as 'interface' and 'inappropriateness.' The use of 'could do better' was specifically forbidden, which came as a bit of a shock to the system for quite a number of teachers, since it was their favorite phrase. A copy was sent to each teacher, together with a list of the one hundred most commonly misspelled words. The list caused great merriment at the time, since it contained no fewer than four spelling mistakes! Of course His Majesty tried to blame the office staff, saying that it must have been a typing error. The office staff, their competence having been so cruelly affronted, produced several photocopies of his original handwritten list and carelessly left them lying around for all to see! Of course whether or not the errors in the original list *had* been spotted, but deliberately allowed to go through, was open to speculation!

Some wag had been busy that year! A large notice appeared on the staff room notice board alongside the Headmaster's compendium of suitable phrases. It read:

'The following phrases may prove invaluable when writing reports. For the benefit of colleagues new to the school, a translation is provided:

COMMENT	-	REAL MEANING
Has a lively personality.	-	Very disruptive.
Keeps a low profile.	-	I can never remember his name.
Underachieving.	-	Bone idle.
Doesn't find the work easy.	-	Can't write his name.
Now realizing his potential.	-	Can write his name.
Not without ability.	-	Can do joined-up writing.
An able pupil.	-	Can spell most four letter words.
A very helpful lad.	-	A creep.
Gets on well with his peers.	-	Gives them sweets.
Can be very informative.	-	A super-grass.
Behaviour has improved.	-	A credit to his probation officer.
Could do better.	-	Applicable to most boys and all teachers.

ANON.

Parents should note that there is more than a modicum of truth in the above list of euphemisms. Anon was probably Ian McTaggart?

CHAPTER 13

CHRISTMAS. Laura was in a bubbly mood! Her Christmas magazine article had just been published under the title 'Christmas Through The Ages.' It was by no means the first article that she'd had published, but that did not diminish the obvious pleasure she gained from seeing her work in print. Laura bought three copies of the magazine and was looking forward to receiving her next assignment.

Biggs couldn't say that he ever looked forward to the last week of the Autumn term. On one hand, the Christmas holiday was only a short week away, but on the other, it could quickly turn into a week of chaos and turmoil. That usually meant a headache for him and he always tried to keep a low profile and let others organize the festivities. Fortunately Harry Langton, always the showman, was good at organizing the festivities and Biggs usually let him get on with it. Of course he didn't actually do the work himself, so it would be truer, that he was good at delegating the organization of the festivities.

Each tutor group was responsible for decorating its own room, a prize being awarded for the best effort. There was always a full size red cardboard post box located outside the general office, for use by boys and staff alike. With a couple of boys acting as postmen, they were all able to send Christmas cards to each other. There was always great rivalry amongst the staff, to see who got the most cards. Biggs was usually quite happy if he managed to get half as many as many cards as Harry Langton. That was an awesome task, however, since Harry had been known to bribe the kids by offering sweets to each boy sending him a card. In an attempt to redress the balance a little, Biggs suggested to Christopher and his mate Tony, who had volunteered to act as postmen, that they might accidentally lose some of Harry's cards. Knowing which side their bread was buttered they readily agreed, but instead of losing the cards, they delivered them to Biggs, along with his. This left them with a clear conscience, but put Biggs in the invidious situation of having to decide what to do with them. In the end he did the right thing and delivered them to Harry himself.

It had been a long standing Lower School custom at Christmas, for boys to distribute fool parcels to the elderly and needy in the local area. Suitable tins and packets were collected by each tutor group and delivered one afternoon by small groups of boys. Names of suitable recipients were readily available from Age Concern or the Social Services. The biggest problem always, was getting the boys to bring in the goddies. However, they usually managed to get sufficient in the end for each group to make up four parcels.

One afternoon was always reserved for the distribution of the parcels. Each tutor group, having managed to bring in sufficient goddies, would spend half an hour or so wrapping them ready for delivery. A Christmas card was always enclosed with each parcel, once the names of the recipients had been obtained from Laura. The hoards were then let lose on the streets in groups of five or six, each bearing a parcel. There were always a few names in reserve, in case any of the old folk had moved to a higher (or lower) place since the list was complied.

One year, a group of Second Year boys returned with their parcel, the old lady apparently having shuffled off this mortal coil two days earlier. Very sad! The boys were obviously upset, but quickly regained their composure, when they were given another name from the reserve list. This time the elderly gentleman was very much alive and very grateful to receive his gift. The boys were invited in for tea and cakes.

Having reported back that their Christmas good deed had been completed, it was the custom to allow the boys to go home early.

The Upper School, although taking no part in the door-to-door distribution, did their bit by hosting a Christmas party and dinner for another group or old folk. They used to participate in the distribution of parcels, but since an occasion a couple of years earlier when one old aged pensioner called the police, thinking that he was about to be mugged, it was thought that hoards of burly Forth and Fifth boys knocking on the doors of the elderly was perhaps not a good idea!

The Christmas dinner, held on the penultimate day of term, consisting of Turkey, Christmas pudding and mince pies, was always supplemented by soft drinks and Christmas crackers. This was the one day of the year when the boys seated themselves and were served by the staff. Harry Langton usually dressed up as Santa Clause and it was always a great success. The afternoon was usually given over to a film, or to watching videos, each boy being able to choose one of several available. It kept them quiet and allowed the staff to have a quiet doze.

In the evening the Upper School would hold their Old Folk's Party and dinner. This time the Headmaster would dress up as Father Christmas. It was always a lively affair, with singing and old time dancing. It was not Biggs' scene, but he always looked in for a while, just to show his face.

Short of volunteers that year, Upper School had to appeal to the Lower School for assistance. Christopher Bird and his mate, Tony had volunteered to act as waiters. Smartly dressed in white shirts, black bow ties and colourful waistcoats, they really looked the part. Having done his duty by showing his face, Biggs was about to sneak away, when the waiters sidled up to him.

"Who's that gorgeous bird.... er.... I mean young lady dancing with Mr. Rowe?" Christopher asked, in his usual familiar manner.

A traditionalist of the 'old school,' Malcolm Rowe taught English. He was Biggs opposite number in the Upper School. He was very well spoken and could at times be quite punctilious. In many respects he was very different from Biggs, but since they were equally contemptuous of new fangled ideas in education, they got on rather well.

In all honesty, Biggs was able to say in the true time-honoured fashion, "That's no young lady...... That's his wife."

"You're joking, Sir. She can't be more than eighteen and Mr. Rowe must be turned sixty!"

Christopher was a bit amiss on their ages. The young lady was a former pupil of Malcolm's from his previous school. She was in her early twenties and Malcolm had only just turned fifty. Biggs fully understood Christopher's reaction, however, so he just repeated, "That's no young lady, Chris..... That's his wife.

"Coor!!"

Biggs took his leave, leaving Christopher and Tony to carry on with their waiting.

The last day of term was always a bit of an anticlimax. It was given over to mundane things such as taking down the decorations and clearing up the mess from the previous day. Not a lot of teaching was ever done! After lunch and a final assembly, the boys went home.

Christopher and Tony dropped in on Biggs to wish him a Happy Christmas.

"Can't stay too long, Sir, but we've got you a present," Christopher said, producing a small carefully wrapped box.

"Thanks lads. That's very nice of you."

Biggs unwrapped to box to reveal a key-ring, with a small rubber pineapple attached to it.

"Don't take it the wrong way, Sir, but try squeezing the pineapple."

Biggs squeezed the pineapple and out popped a small rubber plonker. He burst out laughing. "That's disgusting.... but I like it. Thanks lads."

"Got to go, Sir. See you next term."

"Okay. Have a nice Christmas."

Most of the staff adjourned to G19 for a final nogging. Biggs joined them for a while, but happy to see the end of a busy term, he soon headed for home. Nearly three weeks with no school..... now that can't be bad, he thought to himself.

CHAPTER 14

SPRING TERM

It was the first week of the Spring term and Harry Langton and Mike Gladstone were preparing to set off for Italy on the Friday, with the skiing party. Biggs was due to lose four of his Express set to them, including Christopher and Tony. Not wanting them to miss any new work, he had planned a week of revision for the rest of the set. Jimmy Bunting, the number two in the PE department was going with them. Gladys was still a novice when it came to skiing, but Jimmy was quite proficient and Harry certainly fancied himself on the piste. Jimmy had a very loud and booming voice which, when he forgot to tone it down a little, somewhat resembled a ship's foghorn. At times, listening to him could be quite painful, but no doubt he was going to prove quite useful for attracting the attention of the kids on the slopes. Of course there was always the possibility of starting an avalanche, but that was a risk they seemed prepared to take. They were due to be away for the whole of the following week, leaving Biggs to run the Lower School alone. In other words it was to be business as usual! Ian McTaggart would still be around of course, but Biggs always regarded him as a be a bit of a liability at the best of times. The Headmaster said that he would look in from time to time, but that was the last thing Biggs wanted.

Harry had forbidden any major changes during his absence. This was not really a problem for Biggs, since he hadn't planned making any major changes...... just subtle little ones. He had been allowed the use of Harry's office for the week and the key to his executive loo. He did of course have unlimited use to the chaise longue...... he remembered thinking at the time that he should ask Laura to get in some grapes!

Harry spent most of that week fussing about, making final arrangements for his trip. He could be quite elusive at the best of times, but that week he was particularly difficult to track down.

"What about your office key?" Biggs asked, finally cornering him in the corridor on the Wednesday afternoon before they were due to leave.

"What about it?"

"You said that I could have it while you were away."

"What's the hurry? I haven't gone yet," he said, evasively. "I still need it."

"Leave it unlocked....... Nobody's going to steal anything."

Harry started to remove the key from his bunch, but stopped when Biggs added, as an afterthought, "and your loo key?"

"You can't wait to get your feet behind my bloody desk, can you?" Harry said. "You can have them both tomorrow....... Coming to see us off on Friday morning, are you?"

"WHAT!.....at 6.30. You must be joking."

"You really ought to, you know." The boys would expect it."

"I don't think so. Nothing will be further from their minds. By the way, what about the key to your drinks cupboard...... I might want to do some entertaining while you're away."

"Knickers. You keep your hands off my bloody drinks. It stays locked."

Harry must have been taking lessons from Christopher, Biggs thought to himself. But then perhaps not! Harry didn't understand Christopher, as he did and he was sometimes openly hostile towards him! He wondered if Christopher and Tony would lead him a merry dance? He hoped not and he had taken the precaution of warning them to watch what they said to Harry!

At the end of the following day, Biggs went along to Harry's office to collect the keys. Harry was discussing the final arrangements for his trip with Mike Gladstone and Jimmy Bunting. Biggs wished them a nice holiday.

"HOLIDAY!" Gladys exclaimed, indignantly. We'll be working. It's a big responsibility taking thirty kids skiing, you know. "You're the one who goes swanning off to Wales each year in the mini-bus...... on holiday with five kids and two teachers."

"Five kids....... FIFTEEN, if you don't mind!"

"Oh, I beg your pardon..... Fifteen....... I make that seven and a half each!" Gladys said, exercising his prowess at maths. "In fact as I recall, last year you even had the help of a student teacher as well, so that made it just FIVE kids each!"

"You've only got TEN each!" Biggs retorted. "Anyway, I don't see what your moaning about? You know that I'm giving it a miss this year."

"Only because the Headmaster found you out and put a stop to it."

"That's not true..... I'm just giving it a miss."

Gladys was referring to Biggs annual camping expedition to the Welsh mountains, towards the end of the Summer term with a group of hand picked boys. He was the first to admit that it was a bit of a skive, but then he always regarded it as his reward for a year's hard work! Teachers don't get many perks, he reasoned! There had been an element of truth in Mike Gladstone's remark about His Majesty having found him out. He had not exactly put a stop to the trips, but the previous year he *had* questioned the cost-effectiveness of the expedition and he *had* queried the manner of selection of boys. The trip had always been oversubscribed and Biggs had been able to select those that he thought would most benefit, at least that was his story. His Majesty had not been entirely convinced by that argument and registered his doubts on the matter. In the end he attempted to impose unacceptable conditions and in a fit of peak Biggs had said that he didn't like having his propriety questioned and in any case, he intended giving it a miss the following year. He had been thinking of giving it a miss anyway, because Harry Knight who always accompanied him on the trip was expecting to undergo a minor operation about the time that they would have gone.

After collecting Harry's keys, he wished them a final good-bye and made a mental note to have a duplicate made of the loo key.

Needless to say, Biggs didn't arrive at 6.30 to see the boys off. Getting in early when you had to was bad enough, so getting in at a ridiculously early hour to see someone else go on holiday was clearly a nonstarter.

Having completed the first task of the day, putting on the coffee machine, by 8.30 he was ensconced behind Harry's desk, working on the cover list. It was a thankless task at the best of times, but controlling the daily destiny of others did give a feeling of power. Harry always regarded the cover list as an excellent instrument for settling old scores, often resulting in ill-feeling when members of staff thought that they were being asked to do more than their fair share. Biggs usually tried to avoid seeing it in that light, but it could be sorely tempting at times and he did on occasion give in to temptation. The list always needed constant amendment between 8.30 and 9 o'clock, as teachers phoned in their excuses. In the end it turned out to be not too bad. Only two teachers were absent, apart from Harry and Gladys and Harry certainly didn't need much covering! The PE department always arranged their own cover, unless they were all off sick, so there was no need to cover Jimmy Bunting. David Reed, their permanent supply teacher was available to do much of the cover work. Biggs had also arranged on the quiet for him to cover some of his own classes that week, while he was in charge.

The coffee machine next door in the general office started bubbling away and there were sounds of someone moving about. The aroma of coffee infiltrated the room and a moment later Laura, in a very bubbly mood burst in bearing a cup of the delicious brew.

"Good morning, Mr. Smith. I've made you a nice cup of coffee."

"Good morning Laura. Very formal today, aren't we?

"Well, I thought that you might like a little deferential treatment now that you're in charge," Laura said, with a grin.

"No, I don't think so....... just remember to get in some grapes."

The pips sounded for the start of morning school, so Biggs had to hurry to the staff room to pin up the cover list. As always, hoards of bodies descended on the notice board. Several mutterings and sighs of relief could be heard as he made a quick retreat back to Harry's office to finish his coffee.

His Majesty arrive to take the morning assembly. Biggs had forgotten that he was coming and had intended taking it himself. Ian, trying to ingratiate himself, poured him a cup of coffee.

"Thank you, Mr. McTaggart, said the Headmaster, taking his coffee through to Harry Langton's office. Biggs was seated at Harry's desk, trying to look busy.

"Good morning, Mr. Smith. Uneasy lies the head that wears the crown! Got everything in hand, have you?"

"Good morning, Mr. Martin. Yes, everything's under control and my head lies comfortably, thank you ..... it's only a little crown, you know!"

"Is it now? By the way, I'll be taking the assembly solo today."

"Right you are! Any particular reason?"

"Yes...... any particular reason," His Majesty replied, in a vain attempt at being funny.

Git! Biggs thought to himself.

Ian wandered through from the general office. "Would you like me to supervise the boys assemble, Mr. Martin?" Ian asked, still trying to ingratiate himself.

"Yes please, Mr. McTaggart. That's very nice of you."

It was not like Ian to volunteer his services, Biggs thought...... at least not without an ulterior motive. He must be sickening for something!

Feeling like a spare prick at a wedding and having nothing better to do while the assembly was going on, Biggs decided to investigate Harry's executive loo. He discovered that the old skinflint had removed his monogrammed towels and luxury scented soap. Fortunately he'd had the foresight to bring in his own, so there was no problem. Rummaging through Harry's desk draws and filing cabinet, in the forlorn hope that he might find the key to his walk-in off licence, he came across his supply of soap. But there was no sign of the key, much to his frustration. He did, however, come across something of great interest...... Harry's old passport, with the top corner cut off! Biggs knew that he had only recently renewed it and presumably he had remembered to take his new one with him. He thumbed through the pages, noting the countries that Harry had visited, hoping to find a 'Deported - Undesirable Alien' stamp somewhere, but there were none. He looked at the photograph, thinking that Harry looked much younger, but then it was taken ten years earlier! His eyes wandered across to the page showing place and date of birth. A glimmer of a smile appeared! The glimmer changed to a broad grin and his eyes began to sparkle, as he did a quick mental calculation. "The crafty sod," he said quietly to himself. "..... I knew it...... I bloody well knew it!" Harry was very sensitive about his age and he had led everyone to believe that he was thirty-seven. He had said as much the previous year, when angling for a birthday present. Harry wasn't known for his subtlety at such times and he had been dropping hints for several days before the event.

"I bloody well knew!" Biggs said again, this time out loud....... Harry's old passport showed him to be forty-five! "Look what I've found, Laura." he said, still smiling, as he went through to the general office, waving Harry's passport above his head. He handed Laura the passport.

Missing the point completely, Laura looked at the photograph, saying, "It doesn't do him justice, does it?"

"Doesn't do him justice! You must be joking...... look at his date of birth. Considering his age, I think it does him bloody proud."

Laura looked at the date of birth and did a quick mental calculation. "Well, I never....... and he said he was only thirty-seven!"

The patter of feet could be heard, indicating that the assembly was being dismissed. Biggs grabbed the first boy that he came across in the corridor and gave him a hastily written note. The boy's name was Kevin Bartlett, a very small, rather cheeky, but good natured Second Year boy.

"Give this to Mr. McTaggart please, Kevin."

Kevin smiled as he looked the note which read, 'Who's a pretty boy, then?'

"He'll kill me, Sir," Kevin protested, obviously aware that the note referred to Ian's large Roman proboscis.

"No he won't, Kevin. Just tell him that the note is from me..... and scarper before he gets a chance to read it."

Returning to the general office and looking out of the window, Biggs was surprised to see the Headmaster getting into his car, obviously returning to the Upper School after taking the assembly.

"Well that is a surprise! I thought he would be hanging around to see what we get up to while Harry's away."

"He said he's got a parent coming to see him," Laura said. "Just be thankful for small mercies. While the cat's away........"

"Not while I'm in charge, they won't," said Biggs, tongue in cheek, interrupting Laura before she had a chance to finish. "I intend running a tight ship this week, so there will be no slacking!"

Laura just grinned inwardly to herself and resisted the temptation to make a witty retort.

A few moments later, Ian McTaggart entered the office, still clutching the note. "I suppose you think that's very funny," he said, clearly not amused "That little sod, Kevin Bartlett ran off before I had a chance to grab him."

"I told him to! Now don't be an old fart and stop whingeing and feast your eyes on this." He showed him Harry's passport.

"Well, what about it? It's his old passport!"

"Der! Is it now?.... For goodness sake, Ian, do you have any grey matter between your ears?..... Look at his date of birth."

Ian looked at the date of birth and attempted to do a quick calculation, but mental arithmetic was clearly not his strong point. "That makes him ....thirty ...er ....no....forty....er." .

"Forty-five," Laura suggested, tired of waiting for Ian to complete his mathematical mentathlon.

"The crafty sod!" Ian exclaimed. "He told us that he was thirty-something?"

"Thirty-seven," Laura confirmed. "Well, at least we know what to get him for his next birthday..... a certain preparation for fortifying the over forties!

The rest of the day passed quietly with nothing untoward happening. An unscheduled bout of conscientiousness, however, prevented Biggs from leaving before 3.30 for his relaxing weekly sauna.

It had been quite a mild winter, but it turned very cold over the weekend and the forecast, for what it was worth, indicated the possibility of snow. Now snow is all right in it's place, such as on the piste, but school is most definitely not the place. Virgin snow is not too bad, but with so many trampling feet about, it quickly turns into slush and gets carried all over the school. Even virgin snow has it's hazards, in the guise of nasty schoolboys ambushing nice teachers with snowballs. No doubt the skiing party would have welcomed a smattering of overnight snow, but Biggs was not enthralled by the possibility. The sky was very dark and threatening, but Monday morning arrived with the snow yet to make an appearance.

Cover wasn't too bad that day; only Paul Scobie phoned in with a hangover. It always amazed everyone that he didn't phone in more often. After all, considering the amount of alcohol that he managed to consume each week, it must have been difficult for him to know when one hangover finished and the next one started.

The following day must have been a record! No one was absent! Harry didn't need cover and Gladys would normally have spent most of the day in the Upper school, so his cover was their problem.

Shortly after morning break, there was a timid knock on Biggs' door. A sheepish looking Kevin Bartlett entered with a note from Mrs. Manning, his English teacher. It read:

'This boy should wash his mouth out with soap. He used foul language to me......... signed Janet Manning.'

"Kevin, would you care to repeat what you said to Mr. Manning?"

"I can't, Sir," Kevin protested.

"Why not?"

"I don't like to."

"Why not?"

"I'm too ashamed."

"Give me a clue."

"It began with an F....."

"Say no more. Have you read the note?"

"Yes, Sir."

"Do you thank that Mr. Manning's suggestion in fair?"

"Yes, Sir," Kevin replied, head bowed.

Reaching into the bottom draw of the filing cabinet, where he had earlier discovered Harry's soap, Biggs produced a virgin bar and wrote in red on the bottom of the note:

'Agreed. I think two licks should do the trick!'

Kevin read the note. "Your joking, Sir. You can't be serious."

"Dead serious! Off you go, before I think up something far worse."

The young offender was sent back to his class with note and soap. A few minutes later raucous laughter could be heard from a classroom at the end of the corridor....... Justice had been seen to be done!

On Wednesday morning six staff phoned in to say that they would be absent. The excuses ranged from a gippy tummy (too much beer the previous night) to a severe migraine (too much beer the previous night). These were of course in addition to Harry and Gladys. Gladys would normally have had a full day and even Harry needed covering three periods.

"Three periods," Ian exclaimed. "I didn't think that he taught more than three periods in the entire week."

"Not many more," Biggs replied. "Six actually.... It's just that three of those periods happen to be on Wednesdays."

The cover took ages to complete and it was only just finished as the first pips sounded for the start of school. Dying for a cup of coffee, Biggs asked Ian to pin the list on the staff room notice board for him.

"You must be joking!....... with that much cover, I'll get lynched," he exclaimed. "Pin it up yourself."

"Coward. What are you Ian, a man or a mouse?"

"Eeek, eeek." Ian replied, scampering from the room.

Biggs pinned up the cover himself. Much whining and gnashing of teeth could be heard coming from the staff room as he made a hasty retreat to the general office.

Later that morning a postcard arrived from Harry. Gladys, it seemed, was hobbling around on crutches with one foot bandaged! He apparently took a tumble on his first day on the piste and sprained his ankle. Biggs also got a postcard addressed to him personally from Christopher and Tony, telling the same story and saying how much they were missing their maths lessons!

"It couldn't have happened to a nicer chap," Laura said, barely able to contain her mirth. For some reason, unbeknown to Biggs, Laura and Mike Gladstone had never got on. They rarely saw eye-to-eye on any matter and they were often at each others throats!

"Now don't be catty," Ian rebuked her, with a broad grin. "Pin it on the staff room notice board. We might as well give everyone a laugh." It did!

THE BOUQUET.   Shortly after lunch the following day, as Laura and Biggs were sipping their coffee in the general office, there was a cursory knock on the door, which opened to reveal a large portly gentleman bearing an enormous bouquet of roses.

"Interflora..... Special delivery," he said, abruptly. "Sign here please."

"Oh, thank you," Laura said, thinking that they might be for her.

Laura signed the receipt and the portly gentleman left as unceremoniously as he had arrived. A card attached to the bouquet was addressed to Brenda Hickman, 'From a secret admirer.'   They both instantly recognized the writing..... it was Harry's.

"Well I never," said Laura, raising an eyebrow.

"A bit of a risky thing to do!" Biggs ventured.

"You can say that again. What will people say?"

A quick telephone call to the staff room brought Brenda to the office.

"Oh, how lovely," she exclaimed, with obvious delight.

"You know who there from, do you?" Laura asked.

"Of course...... There from Harry."

Brenda returned to the staff room with her flowers, either indifferent or quite oblivious to any inferences that might have been drawn. One thing was certain; tongues would soon start wagging.

The next day was Friday and Harry and the skiing party were due to return from Italy. It was therefore Biggs last day in the hot seat. It had been nice playing God for the week, but the novelty was beginning to wear a bit thin. Not for the first time, he was beginning to realize that second-in-charge was a much easier and a far less stressful number. He wondered how Harry always seemed to shoulder the burden so well? He cheered himself up by reasoning that Harry always had him to do most of the donkey work, while he had nobody. Mike Gladstone was away with Harry and Ian McTaggart had been as much use as a fart in a colander, so he had really been doing the work of three people!

Mid-morning a second bouquet arrived, delivered courtesy of Interflora and addressed to Brenda Hickman! Now Brenda had phoned in sick that morning, with a migraine, so being a Friday, she wouldn't have received them until the following Monday. The label was only loosely attached and fell off as Laura accepted it from the same portly gentleman who had called the day before. This time they both raised an eyebrow. Laura suggested removing the label completely to prevent further wagging of tongues.

"Good thinking, Laura," Biggs said. "Has Harry gone completely off his rocker?"

"I don't know, but he's certainly sailing very close to the wind. I think we'd better put them in his office."

Laura slipped the card into her desk draw and took the bouquet through, laying it carefully on the top of Harry's bookcase. Nothing more was said on the matter.

Just after two o'clock they got a phone call from Harry calling from Dover, confirming their arrival time of 4.30 that afternoon. Gladys apparently was still hobbling about with a stick. Laura spent the rest of the afternoon taking telephone calls from parents wishing to confirm the arrival time of their little darlings. She took her leave at 3.30, leaving Biggs to answer the remaining enquiries. By four o'clock, most of the boys had departed and the playground had begun to fill with parent's cars.

The coach arrived just after half past four and Biggs went down to meet them. He arrived as Christopher and Tony were collecting their bags from the luggage compartment.

"Hello, Sir," Christopher said. "Did you get our card?"

"Yes thanks. Did you have a good time?"

"It was great, thanks. I suppose we've got lots of maths to catch up?"

"No, not really. We did mostly revision, so you didn't miss much."

"Thank god for that," Tony said.

"I trust you behaved yourselves, gentlemen?"

"Little angles, that was us!.... We did sneak into Mr. Langton's room, though and give him an apple-pie bed! He never did discovered who was responsible. You won't tell him it was us, will you, Sir?"

"Of course not. Trust me, I'm a teacher."

"Got to go now, Sir. Tony's dad's here to pick us up.... See you, Monday."

After many happy reunions, the playground soon emptied of cars and kids. Harry Langton was in a bubbly mood and had acquired nice sun tan.

"Good trip, Harry?" Biggs asked. "Where are Jimmy Bunting and Gladys?"

"Great," he replied. "Jimmy's wife met him off the boat. They're going to stay with some friends just outside Dover for the weekend."

"And Gladys?"

"Oh, we did a slight detour and dropped him off at his home to save him having to walk." Harry said. "He's still using a stick."

"Oh dear. What a pity. I was looking forward to seeing him hobbling around with a stick. Now I'll have to wait till Monday. Never mind....... Coffee?"

"Just what I need. I hope that you've kept everything back here shipshape and haven't tried to change things."

Biggs ignored his last remark, hoping that it was rhetorical as they repaired to the general office. After pouring himself a cup of coffee, Harry wandered through into what had just become Biggs ex-office. Looking somewhat mystified, he picked up Brenda's bouquet.

"Didn't Brenda get these?" he asked.

"No, she was away today. She phoned in sick this morning, with a migraine. She got the first lot, though."

"I was hoping that they would have arrived before today, Harry said. "Never mind, I'll drop them into her on my way home."

"Is that wise?" Biggs asked. "Terry might be at home."....... Terry was Brenda's husband!

"Good thinking," Harry said, giving a sly wink and still holding the bouquet.

At that moment, the door burst open and Harry's wife, Helen poked her head round, smiling broadly.

"Hello, Harry," she said. "Good trip?"

Her smile quickly changed to a look of puzzlement, as she spotted the bouquet that Harry was holding. She was obviously not used to receiving flowers from him! There was a deathly silence for what seemed an eternity, but in reality could have been little more than a second, as Harry stood holding Brenda's bouquet. For that brief moment, time seemed to stand still! Harry was obviously thinking, 'God, how do I get out of this?'....... Then, quick as flash, he turned to Helen, saying, "Oh, Hello dear..... Yes the trip was great....... Look, I've brought you some flowers." He handed Brenda's bouquet to his wife, at the same time giving Biggs another sly wink.

"Oh, they're lovely...... Thanks Harry........ I'll just leave them here while I pop along to the little girls room......back in a minute." Helen put the bouquet on top of Harry's coffee table and went next door to use his executive loo.

Harry gave a sigh of relief as she left the room. The sigh quickly turned into a mad panic, as he suddenly remembered the card, addressed to Brenda and covered with love and kisses..... from a secret admirer. He dived on the bouquet, scattering the blooms in all directions, searching madly for the card.

When Biggs thought that he had panicked sufficiently to at least partially pay for his indiscretion he said, with a broad grin, "Don't worry Harry. The card fell off. Laura put it in her desk draw."

Harry gave another sigh of relief. "Thank God for that. I owe you one," he said, making a pig's ear out of trying to rearrange the blooms.

'The luck of the devil,' Biggs thought to himself...... The crafty sod's got away with it!

The following Monday Harry got in early and Biggs arrived to find him seated behind his desk, in the chair that he had occupied the previous week. In fact Biggs was quite happy to return to his own smaller office and his roll as second-in-charge. The crown hadn't been in the least heavy, but he'd come to realize that being in charge could at times be a pain in the butt!

"Good morning Harry," he said. "Recovered yet?"

Harry's response was far from what Biggs had expected. He had clearly forgotten that he owed him one!

"You've got one hell of a nerve," Harry said. "How is it that my loo has your towels hanging on the rail and there is some foul smelling soap in my dish?"

"There's plenty of room for two sets of towels," Biggs ventured. "and I can't see how you can complain about the soap..... it's yours. It came from the bottom draw of your filing cabinet."

"What makes you think that I'm going to allow you to carry on using it anyway?" I want my key back," he said aggressively.

"No problem. Here you are...... I had one of my own cut."

"You've got a dammed cheek doing that."

"I had my own key before the break-in. Really Harry, you can be so petty at times."

"Me...... PETTY?" Harry fumed.

His ears started to twitch, a sure sign that he was getting really annoyed. God..... he must have got out of bed the wrong side that morning, Biggs thought to himself...... or perhaps Helen had put two and two together over her bouquet and had given him some stick..... Now that was a thought! One thing was clear..... it was an excellent time to be somewhere else, so he discontinued the conversation and made a quick exit.

"Anyway, I've got to go...... I've got some boys coming to see me."

A white lie, but it got him out of Harry's office.

CHAPTER 15

THE ROUNDS. The following day they arrived to find everything covered with a white blanket. It had been bitterly cold the night before and it had snowed heavily. The playground soon became a barbaric battlefield, as groups of opposing teams hurled snowballs at each other, with great relish. Although everyone was a viable target, teachers were particularly singled out and small groups of boys would ambush them as they entered the school grounds. Biggs took the precaution of keeping his windows tightly closed, as he drove through the school gates and endured a barrage of snowballs. He was followed to the car park by Christopher and Tony, a snowball in each hand. They stood a few feet away, smiling and with their hands behind their backs as he reversed into his parking space. Making no secret of their intentions, they waited for him to get out. With no means of escape, Biggs made a quick dash for the door with his head down, as he ran the gauntlet of their onslaught.

Harry Langton had earlier not been so lucky, having failed to take the precaution of keeping his window tightly closed. Christopher had caught him squarely in the face, covering him with the white powder. It did not put him happy mood and he threatened Christopher with retribution later.

"That sod Bird covered me with snow," he complained to Biggs.

"You and me both."

"He's too full of himself. He needs bringing down a peg or two."

"Lighten up, Harry. It's the first snow of the year. What did you expect, for God's sake?"

"Never mind about that. Ask him to come to see me, will you."

"Don't make it personal. I'll deal with him, okay."

"All right, but see that you put him in his place."

Harry, now having been out of the hot seat for over a week and having somewhat lost touch with reality, decided to take hold of the reins again. He clearly felt the need to make his presence known around the school. Without knocking and still in a grumpy mood, he burst into Biggs' office a short while after the end of morning break.

"We'll do the rounds," he said, briskly.

Biggs had been drafting a letter to a parent and was not pleased with the interruption. Glancing up, he thought of saying that it was not a convenient moment, but seeing the look of determination on Harry's face, he just nodded.

By *doing the rounds* Harry meant having an unscheduled wander round the school to check that everything was shipshape and Bristol fashion. Biggs usually did the rounds unaccompanied, when he had nothing better to do. Occasionally however, Harry would decide to wander round with him. Classes with anything untoward going on warranted a visit, as did those due for a check on class work. The staff were divided in their reaction to unscheduled visits. Most welcomed a show of interest, but others with a closed door, this is my domain mentality, resented the intrusion.

"We'll start on the top floor and work our way down to the gym," Harry said, making his major command decision of the day and in all probability his only one! As a general rule Harry preferred to let others make the decisions! He would then either openly support them, but with reservations, or he would oppose them, but with reservations! That way he gave himself a let-out clause should things go wrong. He was always able to say, 'I told you I had my reservations, but you wouldn't listen, would you?' Of course he was on a fairly safe bet here!

Harry Langton's long legs propelled him up the stairs to the top floor in double quick time, while Biggs' somewhat shorter legs had to work in treble quick time to keep up! Sitting on the floor outside the music room they encountered a disgruntled looking Fifth year boy, named Andrew Bolton. Tall and very muscular, Andrew was the sort of character that you wouldn't want to meet on a dark night, if you didn't know him, that is. In fact he was quite docile and generally regarded as harmless. A gentle giant, a couple of sandwiches short of a picnic, he boasted an IQ that would have done grave injustice to a daffodil! He frequently landed himself in trouble for saying the wrong thing at the wrong time. It was not because of any mischievous or disruptive intent. It was simply that he didn't always comprehend the finer points of what was said to him.

"Are you quite comfortable?" Harry asked.

"Not really, Sir," Andrew confessed.

"Would you like me to get you a chair?" Harry continued, sarcastically.

It was a silly observation, sarcasm being the one thing that was wasted on Andrew. He invariably failed to recognize it!

"Oh, yes please, Sir," he replied, thinking in all innocence, that the offer was genuine.

"Are you trying to be funny, boy?" Harry fumed. "STAND UP. What are you doing here, anyway? Why aren't you in the Upper School?"

Now it was difficult enough getting Andrew to answer one question coherently, so three questions fired in rapid succession were certainly more than he could handle. He clambered to his feet, saying, "No."

"What do you mean, NO?" Harry demanded. "What kind of answer is that?"

A puzzled look appeared on Andrew's face, but after a moment, a glimmer of light dawned and he said, "No, Sir."

Now Harry was confused. "NO?" he said, obviously trying to stifle a bout of apoplexy. "But that doesn't answer my question! What are you doing here?"

It was obviously time for Biggs to come to their aid.

"I think you'll find that Andrew comes to the Lower School each week for his music lesson, with Mr. Hardcastle."

"I see," Harry said, and then turning his attention to Andrew again, ".....and I suppose that you were sent out for misbehaving?"

"I don't know, Sir," Andrew replied, somewhat bemused by all the attention so cruelly lavished on him out of the blue. He had been quite happy sitting on the floor and rather resented being subjected to an inquisition.

"Give me strength," Harry pleaded, eyes towards Heaven. "The boy's a fool...... What are you?"

"A fool, Sir."

He got that right at least. Shaking his head with despair and muttering under his breath, Harry just wandered off in the direction of his office, leaving Biggs to deal with Andrew. There seemed little to be gained from continuing the discussion, so he just gave the lad a wink and returned to the his office.

Peering round Harry's door a few minutes later, he found him lounging on his chaise longue, sustaining himself with a cup of coffee.

Seeing him, Harry said, rather abruptly, "You sorted him out, then?"

The question was obviously rhetorical, so he just asked, "How about the rounds?"

"Sod the rounds...... You do them!"

Biggs went back to his own office and returned to the letter he had been drafting, before he'd been so rudely interrupted by Harry. When he finished, he took it through to the general office for Laura to type. After noting that it wasn't a *red* letter, she put in her pending tray and returned to her typing. She was clearly busy, so Biggs poured himself a cup of coffee and returned to his own office. He went to the window and looked down at his magnificent black and gold Trans Am in the staff car park. His mind wandered back to his own school days. He remembered his old English teacher, L.I. Jones, a quiet well-spoken gentleman in his late fifties, in fact a veritable ancient! He had always been known as L.I., but no boy had ever managed discovered what his initials stood for? He drove to school each morning in a lovingly cared for black Morris Minor. Biggs recalled that when he was in the Fifth Year, L.I. had replaced it with a green one, a most audacious move on his part! He was a teacher of the old school, kindly but with strict Victorian values and in some ways, not unlike Malcolm Rowe. Everyone imagined him to live in an old Victorian house, with crystal chandeliers and books festooning every wall of his living room! That was until one day when Biggs was in the Upper Sixth, he arrived to school in a brand new open-topped white Triumph TR2 sports car! Everybody's image of him, boys and staff alike, had been instantly shattered!

Biggs wondered what the boys thought of *him*? He had done a similar thing to L.I., when he'd first arrived at Gordon Bennett in his bright yellow Camaro, his previous mode of transport being a Mini! Had their image of him been shattered? He wasn't sure. And what about the Trans Am? What were their views on his latest acquisition. He new that Christopher had been impressed with it, but as for the rest, again he wasn't sure?

Biggs was awakened from his trip down memory lane by a knock on his door. It was Ray Dennard.

"Got any plans for lunch?" Ray enquired, looking rather harassed

"No, not really. What did you have in mind?"

"I've had one hell of a morning and I need to get out of this place for a bit."

"Tell me about it!"

"I know it's not Friday, but I thought about going for a pub lunch. Do you fancy it?"

"Do I just? Let's go."

That afternoon, during Maths with his Express set, Biggs remembered Harry's words to him about the snowball incident that morning. He asked Christopher and Tony to see him at the end of the day in his office. They arrived shortly after the final pips.

"Let's talk snowballs," Biggs said.

"Snowballs!..... Surely you didn't take offence, Sir," Christopher said.

"Me take offence? No, of course not. But Mr. Langton wasn't very happy. I understand that you caught him in the face."

"Yes, Sir. But we thought he could take a joke. I didn't mean to hit him in the face, though. I'm obviously a better shot than I thought."

"Well, as I said, he wasn't very happy. He was going to deal with you himself, but I said that I would deal with you both."

"But Tony didn't do anything, Sir, Christopher protested. "It was just me. He shouldn't be punished."

"All right, Chris. Don't get your knickers in a twist. I'm not going to punish either of you, but I've got something for you." Biggs opened the bottom draw of his filing cabinet and took out two bags of crisps. "Cup of Lapsang, gentlemen?"

"Cheers, Sir."

"If Mr. Langton asks you about this morning, Chris.... you'd better say that I gave you some extra maths homework as a punishment."

"Okay, Sir," Christopher said, smiling and giving a thumbs-up. He then fell about laughing, as Tony grimaced at his first taste of China tea. "The boy's got no taste, Sir! That's his problem."

"No Chris," Tony retorted. "My problem is, that I have!"

CHAPTER 16

MALE CHAUVINISTS. Feeling rather bored one morning and having nothing in particular to do, Biggs decided to take a drive to the Upper School to catch up on any gossip that he might have missed. The general office was the best place to get an update, very little of the goings-on at Gordon Bennett managing to escape their grapevine.

On arrival Biggs encountered Malcolm Rowe, their Senior Year Head, remonstrating with a rather unpleasant looking Fifth year boy. A gesticulation from Malcolm indicated that he would like a word, so Biggs waited just within earshot, for him to finish. It would seem that the boy had been caught smoking in the toilet, when he should have been in class. Biggs didn't know the boy, so he guessed that he must have joined the school only recently, probably another school's expellee. By the look of him, a surly character if ever there was one, the toilet seemed an eminently suitable place to locate him and certainly preferable to a classroom, where he would probably have been a source of disruption. His teacher was most probably highly delighted by his absence.

Remonstration over, Malcolm said, "Just the man..... one of your dozy Lower School boys left his bag outside our staff room this morning. Would you like to take it back with you?"

Biggs didn't like! He hadn't come to the Upper School to collect bags for absent-minded boys, but he felt the need to oblige, so he said that he would return it to its rightful owner.

"Whose bag is it and anyway, what was he doing here?" he asked.

"The name on the bag is Paul Smith," Malcolm confirmed. "He apparently dropped in before school to see one of the Games staff. The bag is in the staff room."

"Paul Smith! Dozy is the right word...... and lazy," Biggs said.

"But I thought he was one of your elite mathematicians."

"He is...... He's very bright, but that doesn't stop him from being dozy. He seems to think that he can get by on ability alone. Though I must admit, he has started to buck his ideas up recently, so perhaps I'm doing him an injustice."

They wandered along to the staff room and arrived in the midst of a heated argument. Entering the room just as a female member of staff was leaving, Malcolm did the gentlemanly thing and held the door open for her.

He was rather taken aback when she snarled at him, "You don't have to hold the door open just because I'm a lady.......We're all women anyway, not ladies!"

"Evidently, Madam," Malcolm retorted, always quick with the repartee. "but then I wasn't holding it open because you're a lady...... I was holding it open because *I'm* a gentleman."

A couple of the male staff sniggered with amusement, which only served to aggravate the situation.

"CHAUVINISTS," she snorted at them, as she disappeared down the corridor, pushing aside an inoffensive Forth Year boy who had the audacity to be in her way.

"Absolutely, Madam," Malcolm called after her, somewhat bemused, but getting the last word as always.

The ladies name was Miss...... or rather Ms. Lynn Harmon. She had been dubbed, 'The Grin' by the boys, on account of the permanent scowl she sported! A regular sourpuss, who had never been known to crack her face, she lacked even the slightest excuse for a sense of humour! Lynn-the-grin was about as popular with the boys as she was with her male colleagues. Very much into women's rights, anti-sexism, political correctness and the castration of all chauvinist males, she did rather take things to extreme! The notion that Malcolm would have held the door open for another male member of staff, clearly seemed to have eluded her. According to Malcolm, it was her second frenzy of the week! A couple of days earlier, one of the male members of staff had made some seemingly innocuous remark, which for reasons known only to her, she had taken to be sexist. It had been along the lines that, while it was all right for primary children to be taught mainly by women, adolescent boys in a single-sex school needed to be taught mainly by men, who would act as their role models. She'd called him a Male Chauvinist Pig and in retaliation he'd called her a Female Chauvinist Cow, who wouldn't know one end of a penis from the other!

The current argument apparently started the previous day, when several of the male staff had complained that the female staff were being sexist, by insisting that they should have soft tinted toilet paper in their loo. The men apparently had to contend with hard shiny toilet rolls! To reinforce their point, one of the male staff had nipped into the ladies loo, presumably unoccupied at the time and replaced all the soft toilet rolls with hard shiny ones. The ladies in general and Ms. Harmon in particular, had taken exception to this violation of their inner sanctum and the whole thing had got out of hand.

Of course at the time, current thinking on political correctness and anti-sexism was still in its infancy. With the exception of Peter Partridge, defender of Gay Rights and Paul Scobie, the resident hippie, most of the men thought it was all a big joke. In fact Peter and Paul were just about the two only male members of staff that Lynn-the-Grin had time for, but then she probably regarded them as *honorary women*! And of course it was with them, that the argument about male role models rather fell down! The Inspectorate however, following the directions of their political masters, were latching on to political correctness in a big way. The Headmaster, whatever his own feelings on the matter, naturally had to tow the line in order to avoid being in trouble with them. He would always err on the side of caution, when making any decision that might have political overtones.

Of course, in the Lower School they were much more civilized, all the staff loos having soft toilet paper, albeit white. Only Harry Langton's executive loo had tinted paper. Hard shiny paper was of course reserved for the boy's toilets.

Biggs took his leave and, after picking up Paul Smith's bag, wandered along to the general office. He related the incident to the office staff, all women of course, but they seemed not in the least surprised. Most of them regarded Ms. Harmon, as much a pain in the nether regions as did most of the men.

The 'pips' sounded, indicating lunch time and time for Biggs to return to the Lower School. On his way back he spotted several of the young trendy members of staff going to G19 for lunch. No doubt the trendies were about to pass round the 'ready rubbed!'

At a staff meeting following the incident with the loo rolls, Ms. Harmon raised a question regarding the formation of a Women's Group to combat anti-sexism in the school! Several of the male members of staff derided the idea, but it got vigorous support from Peter Partridge and Paul Scobie, which was only to be expected. The suggestion also got unexpected prima-facie support from Harry Langton! However, knowing Harry of old, an arch-chauvinist if ever there was one, everyone assumed that his support was very much tongue-in-cheek. His Majesty didn't seem too keen on the idea.

"Surely the formation of such a group would itself be a sexist act," he mused.

"The men could be allowed to attend as observers," Ian McTaggart suggested, with a grin and very much tongue-in-cheek.

Ms. Harmon, who Ian normally avoided like the plague, was not amused and registered her disapproval by glaring at him!

"Not even a token man?" he ventured, meekly.

The glare intensified! However, Ms. Harmon apart, most of the female staff seemed in favour of allowing a 'token man' to attend meetings, so the Headmaster reluctantly agreed to the formation of the group.

The following week there was an announcement in the staff bulletin, that the Women's group had been formed and that Ms. Harmon had been elected Chairperson, which was of course a surprise to nobody! Why they couldn't have had a chairwoman, considering that all the members were women, Biggs had no idea. He just supposed that it was another example of political correctness taken to extreme! No 'token man' ever had the nerve to show his face at one of their meetings.

CHAPTER 17

MORE BIRD. Biggs had been taking a new group of Third year boys for games at the Sports Centre. Only a couple had played squash before and he'd spend some time going over the rules and basic skills. One or two looked quite promising including Christopher's mate Tony Roberts. Tony had tried to get into the squash group the previous term along with Christopher, but it had been oversubscribed.

The boys normally changed their games options each term, so Christopher was no longer in the group. This meant that he wasn't able to have his regular weekly game with Biggs, which they both regarded as a great pity. They had always looked forward to their needle matches and neither got the same satisfaction out of beating the other boys. It also meant that Biggs no longer gave him a lift home after Games and that he was no longer able to pop in for afternoon tea. Christopher had his two games choices rejected, because he'd put down swimming for both of them. The games staff, obviously regarding him as a bit of a smart-arse, had assigned him to the football group. He hated football! Of course he had never really been flavour of the month with them since the previous summer, when he had being experiencing the joys of cricket. A wide range of games options existed from the Third Year upwards, the

First and Second Year boys alternating between cricket, athletics and tennis during the summer term. Although Christopher played a fair game of cricket, he wasn't keen on the game and had never played for the school team. But one particular Saturday they had been short of players and Christopher had been asked if he would like to make up the numbers, to which he had replied, "I'd rather watch paint dry!"

During morning break one day, Christopher invited himself into Biggs' office, after giving a cursory knock on the open door.

"Christopher...... Fill free to wander in. Have a seat."

It was a silly observation and Biggs knew it as soon as he'd said it! Being thick skinned, sarcasm was always wasted on him and he invariably managed to turn it to his own advantage. He plonked himself down in an armchair. "Thanks, Sir."

"Chris, you're cruising for a bruising."

"Nice one, Sir...... I like it. Trans Am spoken here, I see! Did you ever go on the Chelsea cruise, Sir?"

"Yes once, in the Camaro."

"What a poser?"

"How did you know about the Chelsea Cruise?"

"I saw a programme about it on TV, some while back. There were all these posers driving round in their flash American cars. I didn't see yours though."

"I only went the once.... Anyway, what do you want?"

"I just looked in for a chat, Sir."

It was by no means the first time that he had been known to look in for a chat, usually hoping to scrounge a cup of tea or coffee. He sometimes came with his mate

Tony and it was beginning to become a regular thing. They would proffer a packet of crisps or some chocolate biscuits in exchange for liquid refreshment. However this time Biggs realized that he had come with a purpose They could always see through each other!

"What do you really want, Chris?"

"Well..... I was wondering if you have any more room in the squash group?"

"No, it's full. You know that."

"Come on, Sir. Surely you can squeeze one more in," Christopher pleaded. "You know there's usually someone away."

"That's as maybe, but you're meant to be doing football for games this term. You didn't even choose squash as a second option."

"I know, Sir. We're supposed to choose a different games option each term..... You know that, so I chose swimming."

"Twice!"

"I know, Sir. I thought that it would assure me a place, but they put me in the football group. But I don't like football. I've got two left feet and I'm no good at it.

"Two left feet!.... How come you managed to play squash, with two left feet?"

"You don't kick a squash ball with your feet!"

"True! But you play football at break sometimes? I've seen you."

"Not often and when I do it's only a kick-about. We don't play seriously. I'm no good at football. In fact I don't really care for any team game, except basket ball, that is. I much prefer individual sports, where it's one-on-one ..... like squash, say!"

"What you really mean is that you don't like getting yourself dirty on a cold muddy field in the middle of winter."

"Okay, Sir. You've sussed me, but surely you can fit one more in..... You'd be able to pop in for a cuppa again.... and I'll help you coach the new group."

"You coach! That would be a classic case of the blind leading the blind."

"I'm nearly as good as you," Christopher said. Then realizing that was not the best remark that he could have made designed to achieving his aim, he added, "But of course I had a great coach, Sir!"

"Flatterer! But I don't choose the games groups. The games staff do. You know that."

"I know, but you could have a word with Mr. Bunting," Christopher suggested eagerly, leaning forward in his chair, as if to emphasize the point.

"I could, except that he's ill and will be away for a couple of days. Anyway, give me one good reason why I should."

"Because I'm your favourite pupil, Sir," Christopher said with a grin, then adding in all seriousness, but playing what he thought was his trump card, "... and because we're mates."

"Mates! I'll say one think for you Chris..... You've certainly got some gall," Biggs said, unable to contain a smirk. He looked hard at Christopher and realized that it wasn't just a glib remark on his part, trying to be clever. He'd actually meant what he'd said! Of course they weren't mates in the ordinary sense, like Christopher and Tony were mates. But then he hadn't meant that! He'd meant that he recognized that an understanding existed between them, that transcended the normal relationship between teacher and pupil! "I'll think about it, Chris. Okay."

"Good on you, Sir," Christopher said gratefully, obviously thinking himself in with a chance.

"I said I'll THINK about it. Now scram."

"What about the chat, Sir?"

"Don't push your luck, Chris. In any case, you're a bit late. It's nearly time for the pips to go."

"Okay, Sir..... I'm gone."

Biggs understood Christopher's attitude to football and team games. He much preferred one-on-one himself and had never been a lover of team games. He had never played for any staff football team at Gordon Bennett and he hated cricket. Thinking back to when he was a schoolboy, he remembered how he had detested being made to play rugby. He fully sympathized with Christopher and began to realize why they got on so well and how much alike they were! He was mischievous without being naughty and he was cheeky without being offensive! He always knew where to draw the line and would back away from a confrontation. In fact if Christopher could have been transported back in time to his own school, in terms of temperament, behaviour and attitude to authority, they would have been dead-ringers for each other! There were usually one of two of the squash group off sick and they did enjoy their matches, so Biggs felt the need to oblige him. Changing his games option was a simple matter, but it was important that Christopher shouldn't think that he was twisting him round his little finger. He was, of course...... they both knew that he was..... but it was important that they should go through the pretence of him not thinking that!

A word with Jimmy Bunting when he returned ensured that Christopher was able to rejoin the squash group, but Biggs didn't tell him immediately. He had to sweat a little first!

A couple of days later, Christopher asked, "Have you had a word with Mr. Bunting yet, Sir?"

"What about?"

"You know, Sir...... about me rejoining the squash group."

"Oh that...... Yes, I had a word with him, but he's not very keen on boys changing groups in the middle of the term."

"Come on, Sir," Christopher pleaded. "Pull rank on him."

"I'm working on it. I'll let you know tomorrow." He did like making him sweat.

"That's no good, Sir. I need to know today. We've got games tomorrow and I need to know what kit to bring."

"All right, Chris. You can rejoin the squash group tomorrow. I was only stringing you along. Now what do you say?"

"Good on you, Sir. I knew you'd come up trumps..... I'll buy you a packet of crisps."

"Prawn cocktail, please. I suppose that you'll be expecting a cup of coffee in return?"

"Yes please, Sir...... Two sugars."

True to his word, he returned a couple minutes latter from the tuck shop with the crisps and with his mate Tony in tow. "Is it all right if Tony comes in, Sir?"

Biggs nodded. Christopher's coffee was waiting for him.

"Do I get one, Sir?" Tony asked.

"What do you think this is? Ray's cafe! I'm afraid your out of luck. The coffee machine in the office has run out. Chris had the last cup and I'm not asking Mrs. Clayton to recharge it just for you..... I didn't even get a second cup myself."

"That's okay, Sir. Doesn't matter..... Is that right you've let Chris rejoin our squash group?" Biggs nodded. "He's twisting you round his little finger, Sir. You let him get away with too much."

Biggs smiled and nodded again. "I think you might be right, Tony...... In fact, you are right!" Christopher smiled, but said nothing. "Anyway, changing the subject. Where's your brother, Chris? Mr. McTaggart said that he's been away for a couple of days."

"Steven? Oh, he's got the lurgy, Sir."

"The dreaded lurgy, eh." Biggs smiled to himself. He was thinking back to his own school days again. Any boy or teacher absent through illness was attributed to having caught the dreaded lurgy. It was either that, or a serious case of one of the other two fictional diseases prevalent at the time, namely The Galloping Nadgers or the Screaming Hab-Dabs. While Tony and Christopher chatted to each other, his mind wandered over other aspects of his school days. He remembered the 'Goons,' who were at their zenith when he was in the Sixth Form. Repeating their weird noises and their silly phrases and sayings was rife at the time and provided a welcome digression from their studies. He recalled the characters they portrayed with unlikely names like Neddie Segoon, Eccles, Bluebottle, Colonel Bloodnok, Minie Banister and Henry Crun. Prefects all and supposedly the school's elite, they would go round mimicking them and saying things like, 'Needle-Nardle-Noo,' 'You have deaded me' and singing the Ying-Tong song. Despite their zany behaviour, as prefects they had a deal of authority invested in them by the Headmaster; an authority not invested in many prefects of today. Miscreants would be given lines, detentions and even on the odd occasion, made to take a cold shower. They would dream up absurd punishments for juniors, such as hopping on one foot, or walking backwards round the school quadrangle. Apart from a small lapel badge, their symbol of authority which they themselves adopted, was the furled umbrella. Come rain or shine, they would carry it with them round the school. Held in awe by the younger boys, who would step aside as they approached, they were shown a respect not shown to many of their teachers. Happy days, he thought to himself.

"What's amusing, Sir?"

"Oh!..... The dreaded lurgy.... I haven't heard that expression in a long while. You know where it comes from, do you?"

"Yes, of course I do. It's from the Goons."

"How do you know about them? They were long before your time. In fact they were all the rage when I was at school, in the Six Form."

"God! That is a long time."

"Don't push your luck, Chris.... How did you know about them?"

"Only joking, Sir, I know you're not that old.... are you?" Biggs raised an eyebrow! "Tony's dad's got some old tapes of their shows and he let me listen to them." Tony nodded. "They made a film too. I remember seeing it some years ago. I was only young, but I guess it must have been a repeat...... Something to do with the army, I believe? I remember Harry Secombe as a private and Peter Sellers as an officer."

"Colonel Bloodnok."

"That's it, Sir..... Colonel Bloodnok. They were a bit zany, weren't they?"

"Peoples taste in humour changes. When I was at school, they were the bee's knees."

Tony was looking out of the window. "Bundle, Sir.... I think."

"What?"

"I may be wrong, but there are a couple of anklebiters gesticulating at each other and they don't look too happy!"

"Gesticulating, eh! Sounds painful," Christopher said, leaping to the window.

"It will be now," Tony confirmed. "One of them has just struck the first punch..... right in the mouth."

Biggs went to the window to witness two anklebiters going hammer and tongs at each other. A crowd of boys quickly gathered round, egging them on. After a few moments Brenda Hickman appeared on the scene. She was on duty in the playground and attempted to separate the combatants. After a struggle and after receiving a stray blow to her arm, she managed to separate them and dragged them off towards the staff room, holding one by the hair and one by the scruff of the neck..

"Damn! Mr. McTaggart has gone out for lunch. She'll be expecting me to deal with the little sods," Biggs said.

"Can't Mrs. Hickman deal with them until Mr. McTaggart gets back from G19? Christopher asked.

"She could, but I bet she won't..... Give her ten to get to the staff room, five to discover that Mr. McTaggart is out and five more to get to the phone."

"That makes twenty," Christopher confirmed.

"Start counting, Chris."

"One, two, three, four...........eighteen, nineteen, twenty, twen....."

The phone rang, right on cue!

"Am I a genius, or am I a genius?"

"Your a genius, Sir..... but what about the phone?"

"Just ignore it..... I'm not here. Let someone else deal with the little sods."

"Suppose she brings them up? She'll wonder why you didn't answer it."

"Good point, Tony. Right, if she does..... I just nipped out to the loo when it rang and you didn't like to answer it....... Okay."

"Okay, Sir," Christopher and Tony confirmed, grinning.

"You're all right, Sir," Tony said. "Mr. McTaggart is just coming back from G19. He's walking across the playground now."

"Thank god for that..... By the way, how do you know about G19?"

"We've told you before, Sir," Christopher said. "We're pupils...... it's our job to know these things."

Biggs smiled, shaking his head. "Not much gets past you, does it?..... Anyway the pips will be going soon, so you'd better finish up."

"Thanks about the squash, Sir..... I won't be too hard on you tomorrow." Christopher said, between finishing his coffee and stuffing the last of his crisps into his mouth. "See you later."

The following day, they played two games and the sod won them both! Christopher, sensibly deciding that it would be prudent to quit whilst ahead, said that he was too knackered to play the best of five! As a consolation, Biggs did managed to win the one game that he played with Tony. Deciding that it would also be prudent for him to quit whilst ahead and despite Tony's pleading, he refused to play the best of three games, saying that he also was too knackered! They adjourned for afternoon tea at Christopher's house.

CHAPTER 18

IDE! Sounds of a heated discussion came from the staff room one morning as Biggs passed on his way to the general office after a grueling double period with a load of mathematically challenged kids from the Second Year. Curiosity forced him to investigate and he discovered several of the Left-wing trendies, philosophizing on matters, educational. Peter Partridge had the floor and was pontificating to the others about anti-sexism and equal opportunities in schools. These were the buzzwords current at the time! They were banded about whenever an inspector or school governor was likely to be within earshot. Peter's argument was being reinforced by cooing noises of approval from Lynn-the-Grin, Harman and interjections from Paul Scobie, in his usual articulate manner. They were spouting the biggest load of garbage that Biggs had heard for some time...... and that was some garbage, since an awful lot of it was spoken at Gordon Bennett. As always, their arguments were politically motivated and had little to do with reality, let alone education. The fact that they taught in an all boys school, seemed to nullify most of what they were saying to Biggs way of thinking, but then he never pretended to be an intellectual. He wondered what the female dragon, Ms. Harmon was doing in the Lower School staff room. She only taught the senior boys and the last thing they needed was her coming down spreading her sexist propaganda. The dragoness should stay where she belonged! However, having witnessed her spitting fire in the Upper School over the loo roll incident, he certainly wasn't going to ask her to explain her presence.

The school did in fact pay lip-service to equal opportunities at the end of Third year, when the boys chose their optional examination subjects for their final years in the school. One of the options offered to them was Home Economics and Cookery. Only a couple of boys would take up the option each year and they were always farmed-off to the local Technical College on a half-day course. Admittedly they didn't offer Needlework or Crochet or any other of the girlie things, but then the uptake on these would have been zilch. They did offer an after school course in car mechanics, which in the true spirit of equal opportunities, they would have gladly offered to their girls...... that is if they'd had any!

Oddly enough, several years down the line, Gordon Bennett was destined to meet its demise and become mixed. Following an unwelcome amalgamation with a nearby boys school and the notorious local girls school situated on the site of the leisure centre and known locally as St. Trinian's, these things might well have come to fruition. The Left-wingers would certainly have been in their element, that is of course, those that would still around, come the amalgamation! In fact, come the amalgamation most of them would have moved on. One in particular, Paul Scobie, was due to finally get his comeuppance and receive the order of the boot, for urinating in petrol tank of the Headmaster's car! He didn't know it at the time, but good fortune was also to smile on

Biggs and he was not destined to witness the future catastrophe.

"Of course we all know the views of the Arch-chauvinist," said Paul Scobie, catching sight of Biggs standing by the door, smiling benignly at them.

Me, an arch-chauvinist? Biggs thought to himself. Surely not!..... That distinction has to be Harry's. He's the arch-chauvinist around here! Now if he had said elitist, I could have gone along with him...... nothing wrong with being elitist. He made no attempt to reply.

There then followed a tirade of verbal diarrhoea, directed at him and his ilk. They were clearly trying to get him to take the bait, but he was having none of it. Another time, he would have gladly joined in the debate and delighted in winding them up, but it was not one of those times. They were starting to give him GBH of the ears, so still smiling benignly, he gave them a little wave and continued on his way to the general office. Laura and Penny made much better company and generally talked far more sense..... most of the time!

The Lefties had never forgiven Biggs for strongly opposing the introduction at the beginning of the school year, of a curriculum-wide IDE! Standing for Inter-Disciplinary Enquiry, this was another buzzword current at the time. It was a hair-brained scheme descending from *on high* and dreamt up by educationalists (whoever they may be). Biggs contempt for educationalists was well known! The initiative, encouraged by the Inspectorate, for whom he had equal contempt, advocated the abolition of demarcation between subjects. The theory was that History, Geography, French and any other subject they could get their hands on, would cease to exist as separate entities. These subjects would be taught within a topic based mishmash of IDE. The Historians and the Geographers jumped on the bandwagon and managed after much cajoling to rope in the reluctant Frenchies as associates. The Scientists and Mathematicians sensibly would have nothing to do with it. At the eleventh hour the Frogs saw the light and pulled out, leaving the Historians and Geographers to get on with it alone. They had been having joint discussions on a regular basis over a period of some months. The venue for these discussions usually turned out to be G19, the public hostelry next to the Lower School. However in March the previous year the Headmaster, having second thoughts about the hair-brained scheme, said that he would be attending their next meeting for a progress report. The intention had been to start IDE at the beginning of the current school year. Having second thoughts about meeting in the pub, they arranged to meet one evening after school in one of the Lower School classrooms. On hearing of this, Biggs went along to the selected classroom before the meeting and wrote in large letters on the blackboard, for all to see when they arrived, 'BEWARE THE IDES OF MARCH!' To his credit, the Headmaster found it rather amusing, but the Geographers and Historians suffered a sense of humour failure of mega proportions. Biggs never admitted writing the warning, but everyone assumed that it was him.

IDE started in September at the beginning of the school year with the new intake of anklebiters. The idea was that it would be extended in mixed ability groups each year until the whole of the Lower School was involved. The kids would then revert to taking *proper* subjects in the Upper School, leading to their public examinations. English, Maths and Science having turned their backs on the scheme sensibility continued setting in ability groups from the Second Year upwards.

As one of the new intake, Christopher's brother Steven was among the first group of anklebiters to be caught in the IDE mishmash and naturally Christopher got to hear about it.

"What's all this load of old cobblers my brother's being taught, Sir?" he asked, looking up from his work in the middle of a Maths lesson. He was meant to be working his way through a batch of simultaneous equations!

"Cobblers!" Biggs queried.

"You know, all this IDE stuff."

"Oh that! ...... So you think it's a load of old cobblers do you?"

"Yes, I do and so does my mum. Why can't they have proper lessons, like we did in our first year here. You know, Sir...... History and Geography..... Proper lessons..... Not all this IDE cobblers. My brother's nearly as brainy as me, but he's not going to learn much doing that, is he, Sir?"

"We'll skip over the bit about you being brainy, shall we and concentrate on the cobblers. Well Christopher, for once we're in agreement. Of course, how much he learns is largely in his hands. If he's as brainy as you say, he'll probably learn in spite of it, but I that agree he would be better off doing proper subjects as you put it. I was against it from the start." Then seeing an opportunity to possibly scupper the whole thing in the near future, he continued, "Of course, you could suggest to your mother that she raises the matter with the Headmaster. He's not one hundred percent behind the scheme. If enough parents did that, it might just have an effect. They could also bring it up with the PTA. They seem to have a great deal of clout, these days and I've heard a whisper that one or two of them aren't too impressed either."

"I might just do that, Sir."

Becoming aware that the rest of the class had stopped work and were listening with great interest to the conversation, he began having second thoughts about what he'd just suggested. He got enough stick as it was, for opposing virtually every new educational initiative foisted on them and he had no desire to be blamed for a parental uprising, so he added. "But you didn't hear it from me......Okay." Then looking at the rest of the class, hoping that they had all got the message. "And that goes for the rest of you...... Okay!"

"Okay, Sir, they all confirmed, nodding their agreement.

Biggs was pleased at the genuine concern expressed by Christopher for his brother's education and smiled inwardly, thinking to himself, From the mouths of babes and sucklings!

The trouble with political ideals in education is that the kids pay no heed to them. Most children survive the day living from one hour to the next. Their behaviour and attitude to what is forced into their sculls is largely determined by such irrelevancies as the day of the week, the strength of the wind and which side of the bed they got out. The only overriding factors are parental support and the strength of will of their teachers, who must also provide constructive and interesting material for them to consume. If either factor is missing, life becomes difficult. If both are missing it becomes bloody nigh impossible. Either way, you can't ram political correctness down the throats of young adolescence.

IDE was destined to last a further three years before being finally relegated to the dustbin, along with the numerous other hair-brained initiatives that had in the past been foisted on them. Unfortunately before its final relegation, many boys were to suffer its consequences and there was a marked deterioration in the subsequent public examination performance of these lads in History and Geography.

Oddly enough the wheel was to turn full circle a decade and a half later, the emphasis being for primary schools to concentrate on teaching the three Rs and learning their tables.

CHAPTER 19

ON A WING AND A PRAYER.   Laura had been given a new magazine assignment on 'Private Flying' and she was looking a little apprehensive. It was clear that she was going to need a lot of help. Laura was a water-baby and had written an article about scuba diving a couple of terms earlier. It was her favourite pastime and she was a bit of an expert on the subject. About flying, she knew next to nothing. She asked Biggs for help, hoping that he would be willing to provide sufficient background information to enable her to write the article!

Now one of the things that was generally known by the staff and by most of boys, was that Biggs was rather knowledgeable on flying. He had a Private Pilot's Licence for light aircraft and for seaplanes. A licence to fly light aircraft maybe uncommon enough, but a licence which also covers seaplanes is rare in the UK, there being so few locations for their operation. Seaplanes were Biggs favourite form of flying.

Outside school Biggs lived for flying! He flew Tiger Moths with the Tiger Club, which at the time was based at Redhill aerodrome. He flew seaplanes. He flew gliders. He instructed on gliders. He even owned a half-share in a two-seat Piper Cub which he kept at Rochester Airport.

It was the second aircraft that he'd owned, his first being an Auster J1/N Alpha, which he purchased for one thousand pounds back in 1968. The aircraft had been stored unused in a barn for ten years and had been in mint condition at the time of purchase, with the minimum of flying hours. His friend, Gerry Fuller, had been toying with the idea of going in with him on the deal, but at first he had reservations. The price seemed too low and he wanted to know what he would be letting himself in for.

Having decided to go ahead with the purchase, regardless, Biggs collected the Auster, G-AKJU from Blackbush aerodrome, and flew it to the Royal Air Force Station at West Malling, where it was to be temporarily based. On seeing the condition of the aircraft, parked outside the hangar and looking immaculate in its new silver paint job and with a brand new three year certificate of air worthiness, Gerry threw his reservations to the wind and readily agreed to go into partnership. He promptly wrote Biggs a cheque for five hundred pounds for a half share.

They'd enjoyed many a happy hours together in that Auster and during the course of the next three years, had flown it across the channel on day-trips to France on numerous occasions. They always used the light aircraft corridor between Dungeness and Cap Gris-Nez, the rule being that all crossings had to be made at 3500 feet or below 1000 feet. Reasoning that the more air you could put between yourself and the deep briny, the better, Biggs always insisted on crossing at the higher option. Gerry Fuller usually suggested crossing at the lower option, with a view to saving time and fuel, but Biggs was steadfast in his refusal, a steadfastness that was eventually to prove a lifesaver! They usually landed at Berck-sur-Mer or Le Touquet and would have lunch before returning. Apart from their regular weekend day trips, they had also flown all over the continent on various holidays. Lausanne, in Switzerland was always their favourite destination, but that old Auster had taken them to Holland and Belgium many times and *just the once* to Spain!

They'd had an unfortunate experience in Spain, at Barcelona airport on their first long flying holiday together after acquiring the aircraft. They'd set out from Rochester airport, their new base for the Auster, rather optimistically heading for the Canary Islands. After clearing UK Customs at Lympne and French Customs at Le Touquet, they'd headed for the South of France, spending their first night at Rouen and the second at Niort. They always stayed a good quality hotel and, having got through the day on a sandwich, they made a point of having a pleasant evening meal and a continental breakfast in their room the following morning.

It was necessary to clear French Customs once again before crossing into Spain, so the just after ten o'clock on the morning of their third day they flew to Perpignan, a Customs airport. Flight plan having been filed and formalities over, they crossed the Spanish border heading for Barcelona, their next Customs airport. Up to then everything had gone smoothly and they'd been really enjoying the trip. But at Barcelona, things were to change for the worse!

Their first inkling that things weren't going quite as planned, was when they tried to establish radio contact with Barcelona Airport. They had filed a flight plan and were on time, so they should have been expected. But despite being able to clearly hear other radio communications in a mixture of Spanish and English, Barcelona steadfastly refused to answer them, that is until the were about four miles from the airport. Neither Biggs nor his mate Gerry could speak Spanish, but then that shouldn't have been a problem, since all International air traffic communication *has* to be in English. Unfortunately the version of English used by the Spanish controllers appeared to be of the pigeon variety! They had to be asked to repeat *everything*! But eventually they established that they'd been cleared to their final approach to the active runway. They called 'finals' and received acknowledgment from the tower. Using their call-sign, Golf, Juliet-Uniform, Barcelona added information regarding wind speed and direction, which only served to confirm in the minds of the two intrepid aviators that they had been cleared to land. However, what they hadn't accounted for was that a KLM Boeing 707 had also been cleared to land on the same runway at the same time! Without realizing it, they had been forced to jockey for position on the approach with the Boeing.... and won! After touchdown, just as they were clearing the runway the Boeing gave way and with a thunderous roar overshot some fifty or so feet above their heads. Of course the Spaniards weren't too pleased and for that matter, neither was the captain of the Boeing. Fortunately he was annoyed, not at Biggs or his mate Gerry Fuller, but at the Spanish air traffic controllers! Although he had been cleared to land himself, he had also heard the clearance given to the Auster some moments earlier and had elected to overshoot rather than risk a collision on the runway.

The Auster was impounded for twenty-four hours until the air traffic tape recordings could be played. The tapes finally proved that they *had* clearly been given permission to land. The tapes also revealed that some ten seconds later, the Boeing, which at the time was some distance from the airfield on a long final approach, had also been given permission to land! What the Spanish controllers had failed to take into consideration when being so free with their landing permission, was that an Auster flies just a tad slower than a Boeing and they had wrongly assumed that it would have cleared the runway before the arrival of the Boeing. It hadn't!

The aircraft was released from house arrest the following day, but so as not to lose face, the Spanish authorities imposed a fine of five hundred pesetas on the Captain of the Auster, namely Biggs. A mere five hundred pesetas for an incident that could have so easily turned into an horrendous tragedy. The mind boggles! Such a ridiculous fine, the sort you would expect to get for a minor road traffic offence, simply confirmed in the minds of Biggs and his partner Gerry, that they were in the right all along! But they also reflected that had things gone differently, they could so easily have been just as dead as if they'd been wrong! Biggs wrote in block capitals in his flying log book against the entry for that flight, NEVER AGAIN!

Since continuing to the Canary Islands would have meant returning back through Barcelona a week later, they decided to amend their plans and fly back to Perpignan. The next ten days they spent flying round France, dropping in at numerous small airfields, sometimes staying the night, before eventually flying back to the UK. It had certainly been an exciting holiday! The printed Five-hundred Peseta Fine, Biggs had framed and it hung in his office at school.

The Auster was taken across the channel on numerous further occasions, before that one never to be forgotten day, when it decided to give them a fright! In the summer of 1970, whilst on their way to Lausanne on holiday, its engine started playing up, just as the were approaching mid-channel. Prior to the incident, they had flown between them in that Auster for over two hundred hours and in all that time its engine had never once faltered. When crossing to France, the time actually spent over water was little more than twenty minutes, but the law of sod had decreed that the one time that the engine was to falter, it would be slap-bang in the middle of the English Channel! Unable to maintain height, they'd been forced to make a PAN call and return to Lympne Airport. All the while keeping an eye open for a suitable field for an emergency landing, they just made it back to the airfield, losing some 3000 feet on the way. They arrived with just sufficient height to clear the airfield hedge and land on the grass. An airfield fire engine, crash truck and ambulance were standing-by at the side of the runway, but thankfully they weren't needed.

A PAN call is a priority radio message, one below MAYDAY, which of course declares a full emergency. Neither Biggs nor his mate Gerry knew what the initials PAN stood for, although Gerry suspected that they might stand for Priority Air Navigation. Biggs always insisted that they stood for Panic And Nausea!

"Told you so," Biggs said smugly to Gerry, after their emergency landing at Lympne! He was referring to the fact that they had attempted to cross the channel at 3500 feet as usual. Gerry had once again tried to convince him to cross just below 1000 feet to save time and fuel, but as always, he had refused. Had they crossed as Gerry had wished, they would have ended up in the drink! Not wishing to ruin the holiday, they left the Auster at Lympne to be repaired and continued to Lausanne the following day in a borrowed a four-seat Rallye Commodore.

They'd had that Auster almost three years and had enjoyed many happy hours together in it. But after that mid-channel hiccup, they both lost confidence in it and although they continued to fly it regularly, it was never taken across the channel again! After enjoying the luxury of flying round Europe in a modern span-can with all its modern navigational aids, they eventually and somewhat reluctantly, decided to sell it. It was purchased in 1971 by a gliding club and fitted with a tow hook for use as a as a glider tug. It was crashed beyond repair within the first week of operation! Had they kept it, that Auster would have eventually been worth a small fortune!

In fact outside school, Biggs lived for flying. Teaching was his means of supporting his addiction. The addiction was flying. It was for this reason that he had been dubbed with his nickname, Biggs! Biggs was short for Biggles! It was a nickname that he had acquired at his previous school and which had somehow transferred with him to Gordon Bennett. He liked the nickname. If a nickname was to be foisted on one, it seems sensible to have a nickname that one liked! In fact, the transfer he had cleverly engineered himself shortly after his arrival, by letting slip in the appropriate quarters. It spread round school like wildfire and had stuck with him ever since, albeit in its abridged form. But he liked the abridged version even more than the original.

Having held a commission in the Royal Air Force Volunteer Reserve for some time, Biggs was also a part-time gliding instructor at RAF West Malling. It was in this capacity that he occasionally came into contact with some of their senior boys, who were members of the local Air Training Corps squadron. At the age of sixteen they were able to attend gliding courses, either at weekends or on week-duration courses in the school holidays. They would on completion of their course reach a sufficient standard to fly solo.

From time to time, Biggs would come across one or two of their younger boys, who were also members of the local squadron, attending for air experience flights in gliders. They were always surprised at seeing him in uniform for the first time and seizing an opportunity to enhance his image, he always made sure that they flew with him. Seeing a glider doing some aerobatics one fine Sunday morning, one young lad on his second flight with him asked if they could do some. Biggs was happy to oblige and after completing one loop, at the top of the second, the lad shrieked with delight, a shriek that could be heard clearly from the ground. After landing he'd said, "That was brilliant, Sir! Why don't you give up the day-job? That was much more fun than being in school." A nice idea, thought Biggs, but it didn't pay the bills. As a Reserve Officer, apart from expenses, his weekends were unpaid. He was paid when attending full-time courses in the summer holiday and he did at one time think of giving up teaching and becoming a regular full-time instructor with the RAF Reserve, but he had always resisted the temptation, reasoning that flying full-time might take the edge off the enjoyment. He had also come to like his dual roll, the one complementing the other.

When not flying gliders or the Tiger Moth, he could usually to be found flying the tug aircraft at a local gliding club or the Sea Tiger on the lakes just outside Rye. The Sea Tiger was a Tiger Moth that had been converted to a seaplane by having its wheels replaced by floats. Flying the glider tug was free, but the Sea Tiger was very expensive and it was only available during the summer months. In the winter it exchanged its floats for a pair of wheels and returned to Redhill.

Flying light aircraft in the United States of America is only a fraction of the cost of that in the UK, which is one of the reasons for Biggs frequent trips to Florida. There was an airfield and seaplane base alongside an adjoining lake to Lake Marianna where he had spent his summer holiday. The holder of an American pilot's licence, issued on the basis of his UK licence, he frequently availed himself of their facilities.

Biggs first interest in flying had been aroused after joining the Air Training Corps Squadron attached to his school. He had his first flight in a Chipmunk. At the age of sixteen, he attended a gliding course at the Royal Air Force Station at Hawkinge in Kent, now long since closed and replaced by a housing estate. He completed five solo flights and some years later went on to gain his International Silver Gliding badge.

After leaving school his ambition had been to join the RAF as a pilot. Teaching was very much a second choice career. However, becoming slightly myopic shortly after reaching the age of seventeen, he needed to wear glasses. A career as a fighter pilot having been scuppered, he decided to go to university and become a teacher instead. Fortunately, wearing spectacles did not prevent him from private flying or flying with the RAF Reserve as a gliding instructor.

Flying was the love of his life and nothing was allowed to get in its way. This had on more than one occasion brought him in conflict with the Headmaster, since he would let no weekend school event interfere with his flying activities. When confronted on one occasion by the Headmaster, when he refused to attend a weekend conference, he explained that he would be instructing at West Malling and that his attendance was indispensable. The Headmaster made it clear in no uncertain terms, that if he wanted to progress further up the promotional ladder, he should learn where his loyalties needed to be. Having no desire to progress further up the ladder, he'd smugly replied, "It's for the greater good." Infuriated by this reply, His Majesty flew into little short of a tantrum and ranted on about the *proverbial* hitting the fan! He was definitely not a happy little soldier!

Biggs on the other hand, always endeavoured to be a happy little airman and on the weekend in question, he'd sent one of their Sixth Form boys on his first solo in a glider. Naturally the boy felt ten feet tall! The young fledgling had been told by Biggs to let the Headmaster know of his accomplishment, thus reinforcing, *the greater good*. His Majesty grudgingly complemented the lad on his achievement, but the incident only served infuriate him even further and from that moment, there were few matters on which they saw eye-to-eye.

Apart from his nephew, Andrew Jones, the only members of staff at Gordon Bennett who had ever flown with Biggs were Tom Bayne and Malcolm Rowe. In the Summer of 1974, they had flown from West Malling in the Rallye Commodore to Le Touquet, first calling in at Lympne to clear Customs. Malcolm's young wife and former pupil had accompanied them on the trip. It had been a glorious day, towards the end of the Summer term. After having lunch in Le Touquet, a walk round the town and a stroll along the beach, they had returned to West Malling, again calling in at Lympne to clear Customs. Tom had flown with Biggs a couple of months earlier, but it was the first time that Malcolm had flown in a light aircraft. Malcolm's wife, Barbara had also flown once before and together with Tom, she had been instrumental in convincing Malcolm to go on the jaunt. He had at first been somewhat reluctant, expressing the view that in his opinion, if God had meant man to fly, he would have provided him with a pair of wings and a built-in parachute! In the event he thoroughly enjoyed the trip.

Biggs nephew, Andrew had also flown with him on a number of occasions. He was the only member of staff at Gordon Bennett to have flown with him in a seaplane. On one particular occasion in the Summer of 1981, they had been flying in the Sea Tiger, G-AIVW from Castle Water lakes, near Rye. They had decided to fly along the coast towards Hastings to give the holiday makers a touch of the spectacular by flying low over the sea, just off the beach.

On their way to Hastings, Biggs had spotted a small speck in the distance, about two miles out to sea. Deciding to investigate they discovered that the speck turned out to be a small boy, who had obviously been carried far out to sea by the strong current, in a tiny dingy. The sea was quite choppy and the lad seemed to have lost his paddle. He was waving frantically for help. Biggs radioed to Lympne Airport for assistance, indicating that the boy needed rescuing. However, some fifteen minutes later, there appeared to be no sign of help forthcoming, despite Lympne air traffic control having said that they would alert the Lifeboat Service. They decided that the best thing to do was to try to expedite matters by alerting the inshore lifeboat themselves. They flew back to Hastings, flying low over the sea past the inshore dingy lifeboat on the beach, waggling their wings to attract the attention of the crew. At the same time gesturing with a hand signal that they would like the dingy crew to follow the Sea Tiger, they returned to the now panic-stricken boy. They stayed with the young lad, circling above him to mark the spot for the lifeboat. Eventually the rescue dingy arrived and picked him up. Their good deed for the day having been done, they returned to Castle Water to polish their halos, after first doing a fly-past along the beach. It had been a most memorable experience.

Back in school, Biggs agreed to help Laura with her article, on the condition that he was mentioned. Several days later, she offered to let him see the final draft.

"I don't get a mention," he complained.

After much cajoling, she finally agreed to amend the article and mention his name.

CHAPTER 20

It was fourth period on a Friday morning and the Express set were enjoying their second single period of the week. They normally had three double periods on Mondays, Wednesdays and Thursdays and two single periods on Tuesdays and Fridays. This was one more than the other Maths sets, the extra period having been purloined from English. Having just come from PE, which invariably consisted of playing basketball in the gym, they usually arrived hot and sticky and not in the most receptive frame of mind. Bearing this in mind, Biggs usually made little attempt to introduce any new material and the period was used to finish off any outstanding work. Every other Friday, the first part of the lesson would be given to an oral test on work covered over the previous two weeks. Since they always marked each others books and called out their marks and since Biggs usually made up the questions as he went along, it involved the minimum of effort on his part. He was all for any form of teaching that involved the minimum of effort! He had switched from teaching science for that very reason, following his appointment as Year Head more than a decade earlier. Maths teaching involved the minimum of preparation and the marking was straightforward, especially since he got the boys to mark most of their own work. It was then simply a case of inspecting their books in class once a fortnight and giving them a grade. He was amazed at first that the boys never took the opportunity to cheat when marking their work, but they never did. Honesty in marking was most definitely regarded as de rigueur Cheating was simply not the done thing!

It was not the week for their Friday test so, as part of their work in calculus, they had been told to finish off some questions on differentiation from their textbooks. They had the uncanny ability to be able to work and talk at the same time and most lessons, when not actually receiving instruction, they were allowed to quietly chatter away amongst themselves. It was a privilege that Biggs did not allowed his other Maths sets, on the basis that he considered them not to have the mental agility to manage the two things at once! But the last period on a Friday morning with his Express Set was special! On Fridays, as a prelude to the winding down of the week, his *elite* were given much more freedom! They all enjoyed Maths on Fridays and Biggs enjoyed listening to them as they chatted away. He found their conversation both interesting and uplifting. It was invariably punctuated with clever put-downs, general insults and innuendo, but it was always good natured. He would occasionally chip in with the odd remark himself, but usually he was content to just listen. Although the whole class were involved in the general banter to a greater or lesser extent, it was normally half a dozed or so boys who did most of the talking, with Christopher and Tony taking centre stage. They were a bit of a double act, often playing the straight-man and funny-man routine. Their roles were reversible, although Christopher usually played the funny-man. They enjoyed playing up to Biggs and to the rest of the class, regarding them as their audience. The topics covered were many and varied and occasionally bordered on the risqué. But provided they did not descend to the lavatorial, Biggs usually did not intervene.

"I see Paul managed to get out of doing PE again today," Tony said. "That's twice now. He skived off last week too!" He was referring to Paul Smith, who was sitting immediately behind Christopher and Tony.

"I've got a sprained ankle," Paul said, by way of explanation. "I twisted it playing football. You know that."

"Yes, but that was two weeks ago, Paul! Methinks you might be dragging it out, just a tad."

"Methinks too," said Christopher.

"Of course, we all know the real reason why he keeps trying to get out of PE and Games," Tony said.

"Really! Why's that Tone?"

"He doesn't like taking a shower afterwards!

"Doesn't he? Why do you reckon that is?..... as if we didn't know!"

"He gets embarrassed, on account of being somewhat underdeveloped in the wedding-tackle department."

"Oh, I wouldn't say that, Tone," Christopher said. "I would have said that he was *massively* underdeveloped in the wedding-tackle department..... In fact I would go as far as to say that he was *spectacularly* underdeveloped." Then becoming aware that Biggs was looking at him with amusement, he whispered to him by way of explanation, but making sure that it was loud enough for Paul to hear, "He's got a small plonker, Sir!"

"No I haven't, Paul said, indignantly. What's this? Have a pop at Paul week!"

"Yup, sure is, Christopher assured him."

"Is this how you go on in the changing rooms?" Biggs asked.

"Of course it is, Sir, Christopher replied. "But then we're all lads together, so what do you expect? It's the nature of the beast! You surely don't expect us to be talking about Barbie dolls or flower arranging?...... Of course, *I* don't have any problem taking a shower, on account of......"

"On account of you being a poser," Tony interrupted.

"Well yes, there is that, I suppose, Tone. But no.... I meant on account of me being spectacularly *overdeveloped* in the wedding-tackle department!"

The class fell about laughing. "You wish!" Tony said.

"Yes, I have that problem too," said Alan Lane, from the back of the room. Up to then Alan had just been listening to the exchanges, but had been taking no part, which was unusual for him, being the class motor-mouth!

"You wish too," said Christopher. "Methinks you might be flattering yourself, just a tad. The only thing that's over developed about you is the size of your gob."

"That's what I said!"

"Huh! Defective ears too!... I said gob, not knob.... Sorry, Sir.... But wethinks Alan's flattering himself! What do youthinks, Sir? Do you think Alan's flattering himself?"

"Yes.... Methinks too," said Biggs, playing straight into Christopher's hand!

"Really, Sir" he exclaimed, looking up from his work, as if in surprise. "And how would *you* know? You don't take Alan for games, so how come you've seen him in the nuddie?"

"We all have! And you too! Don't you remember..... Last year, when we were camping in Wales.... At Lake Bala, when you both went skinny-dipping in the lake."

"Oh, yes! That's right.... I'd forgotten about that."

"Skinny-dipping!" Paul said, with great interest. "I didn't hear about that. Tell me more."

Paul hadn't gone on the trip to Wales and neither had quite a few other members of the class, whose interest was at once aroused.

"Sir, don't tell them," Christopher and Alan pleaded together, but knowing full well that their pleading would be in vain.

"What miss out on a chance to embarrass you both! You must be joking..... It was like this. They made a bet with each other about the name of the nearest star and they asked me to settle it..... And they both lost! They both had to go skinny-dipping in the lake as a forfeit!"

"But you tricked us, Sir," Christopher protested.

"I did no such thing! You tricked yourselves! I asked you quite clearly, if you'd meant the nearest star to the Earth, or the nearest to our solar system. Where's the trick in that? And you both said that you meant nearest to the Earth."

"True," Christopher agreed, reluctantly. ".... but I still reckon you tricked us! You could have explained the difference. You just wanted to see us in the nuddie, didn't you, Sir?.... I bet you enjoyed that."

"Of course I did.... We all did!... Isn't that right, Tony?"

"It sure was, Sir," Tony agreed. "I thought it was hilarious. Are you both going to give us an action replay this year?"

"No, we're not," Alan said, indignantly "Anyway, we're not going to Bala this year, so we couldn't, even if we wanted to."

"That's right," Christopher confirmed. "..... Mind you, Alan.... *you* could give us all a laugh by doing another streak round the school, like you did in the First Year! Don't you remember? We were playing seven-a-side in the playground, because the gym and changing rooms were being painted and the walls were still wet. And we had to get changed in the only available classroom, which was on the top floor. And Mr. Bunting made us run to and from the showers wearing just our towels!"

"I remember that," Tony said. "You tried to whip my towel away, Chris, as we were running down stairs."

"That's right, so I did... And then after showering, someone half-inched Alan's towel, so he had to streak back upstairs to the classroom in the nude..... and we met Mrs. Hickman coming down!

"Yes! I heard about that," Biggs said. "I remember, it was the talk of the staff room at the time."

"Yes, but you haven't heard the best bit, Sir," Tony said. "We had Mrs. Hickman for English next lesson, so Alan had to face her again..... He was well embarrassed."

"That's right," Christopher continued. "And I said to Mrs. Hickman, that it must have been a thrill for her, meeting Alan on the stairs like that, in the nuddie?.... and she said, that she didn't see anything..... because she'd left her magnifying glass at home!.... Alan went as red as a beetroot."

"All right," Alan protested, obviously getting rather uncomfortable. "Don't keep going on about it."

"That was bad, someone nicking your towel!..... Now I wonder who would have done a thing like that?"

"Yes, I wonder?"

"Well, Al, are you going to give us an action replay this year? We'd really appreciate the spectacle, you know."

"No, I'm not!"

"Oh dear! What a spoilsport?..... Mind you, it's probably just as well..... As I recall, it was not a pretty sight."

"Chris, why don't you rearrange these words in to a well known phrase or saying..... Off, sod!"

"Really, Alan! That's not the sort of language we like to hear.... is it, Sir?"

"No it isn't, " Biggs confirmed. "Gentlemen, can we change the subject. I think we've exhausted this one."

"But Sir, it was just getting interesting," Christopher said, then seeing that Biggs was looking at him with displeasure, added, "Oh well, perhaps you're right, Sir..... What shall we talk about now?"

"How about not talking at all?"

"But, Sir... It's Friday! It's our chat-day! You know you enjoy listening to us and we work better when we're chatting!"

"Oh yes! And how does chatting help you to work better?"

"It lubricates our brains, Sir!"

"There's no answer to that, Chris! Just the same, can we just have five minutes with no talk at all, Gentlemen."

"Okay, Sir," said Christopher, checking his watch with the wall clock, which showed 11.58. "No more talking for five minutes, lads. Bossman has decreed it."

"You can cut that out too."

"Sorry, sir." Christopher said, drawing his hand across his mouth, as if zipping it closed.

The class remained silent and a pin could have been heard to drop, the only sounds coming from the scratching of pens. Biggs' mind wandered back to the previous summer, to Lake Bala and their camping expedition in the school minibus to the Welsh mountains. He'd taken a group of Second Year boys with Harry Knight. They had been accompanied by a student teacher completing his final year at college and had been staying at a farm campsite on the quieter eastern side of the lake. Being the penultimate week of term, there were only a few other campers, but they had reserved their usual secluded spot well away from them, at the edge of the lake. It was surrounded by trees and could not easily be overlooked. And yes, Alan and Christopher had both gone skinny-dipping in the lake, as the result of losing a bet with each other! It had been over a totally inconsequential matter, which somehow managed to get blown up out of all proportion! It had been over the name of the nearest star and he'd been expected to settle the matter. The loser had to remove his trunks and swim naked some twenty yards out to a buoy and back again. They'd both shaken hands beforehand in front of everyone and agreed that whoever was wrong, would do the swim and would not try to back out of the commitment. Alan had said that the nearest star was *Alpha Centauri*, at a distance of four and a half light years, while Christopher had insisted that it was *Proxima Centauri* at four and a quarter light years. Of course, they had both fallen into the obvious trap which they should have foreseen and he remembered that he'd taken great pleasure in telling them that they were both wrong. The nearest star to the Earth, is of course our own Sun! Naturally, they both tried to get out of doing the swim, saying that they had meant the nearest to our solar system. That is, they both tried to get out of it, until they were told that the two stars were part of a triple star system, but that the nearest was *Proxima Centauri* by one tenth of a light year. Then Alan, realizing that he would have to do the swim alone, said no, they'd definitely meant nearest to the Earth. A bet was a bet, he'd said to Christopher and they'd shaken hands on it! Not wishing to lose face and after much cajoling from the other boys and of course, from Biggs, Harry Knight and the student, they eventually agreed to honour their commitment. After checking that no other campers were about, they removed their swimming trunks at the water's edge and waded into the lake. As was to be expected, while they were swimming out to the buoy, the other lads hid their trunks, so on return they had to streak through the camp to get to their tents. Half a dozen or so cameras had clicked away, recording the event for posterity! They'd both taken it in good part and neither had seemed in the least embarrassed! Yes, it had been a good trip, Biggs thought to himself and he cursed the Headmaster for not allowing one that year.

At 12.03, Christopher again checked his watch with the wall clock! With a cheeky grin, he gave Biggs a sideways glance, only to witness him shaking his head, but smiling at him in anticipation! Knowing Christopher of old he had clearly foreseen his actions!

"How about taking me up flying, Sir?"

"What?"

"You said change the subject, Sir, so we've changed it to flying."

"You have, you mean!"

"Right, Sir..... Well, how about it?"

"Umm... One day..... maybe!"

That was not the answer that Christopher had expected and he raised both eyebrows in surprise! He had expected at best a spectacular put-down in keeping with Biggs' normal retort to such a question and at worst a straight, no! He certainly hadn't expected a *maybe*! He stared hard at him, looking deep into his eyes, his own eyes slightly screwed. He wasn't being offensive. It was his stare of inquisition that he'd used on him earlier in the year, when he'd worked out the reason for Brenda Hickman's offhand manner, as being due to her time of the month! It was a stare that simply had to discover if Biggs had really meant what he'd just said! Biggs gave him a half, barely discernible wink, just enough for Christopher to think to himself, God, he *does* mean it! Christopher gave him a half wink in return and with his hand close to his chest, so that no one else could see and with his thumb barely protruding above his desk top, he gave a thumbs-up. Silently he mouthed, "Cheers."

The class chatted away for the remaining few minutes of the lesson, but with Christopher taking no part. Despite his earlier involvement in the banter, he had been working hard throughout the lesson and had managed to complete as many questions as the best of those boys who had not spoken. But now, although he was staring intensely into his textbook, it was with unseeing eyes and he had stopped work. He was deep in thought! That half, barely discernible wink that Biggs had given him, had said more than a thousand words of their usual banter and for the first time, he saw him in a new light. They had always got on, but it had always been with the cut and thrust of repartee! Now Biggs had just shown him a kinder, friendlier side to his nature and Christopher was slightly unnerved. He wondered if he could ever again be so cheeky or so cutting with his remarks? Looking up he witnessed Biggs giving him another, but this time more positive wink, and knew at once that he could and that it was business as usual! But they both knew that from that moment, new understanding existed between them!

At 12.15, the pips sounded for lunch.

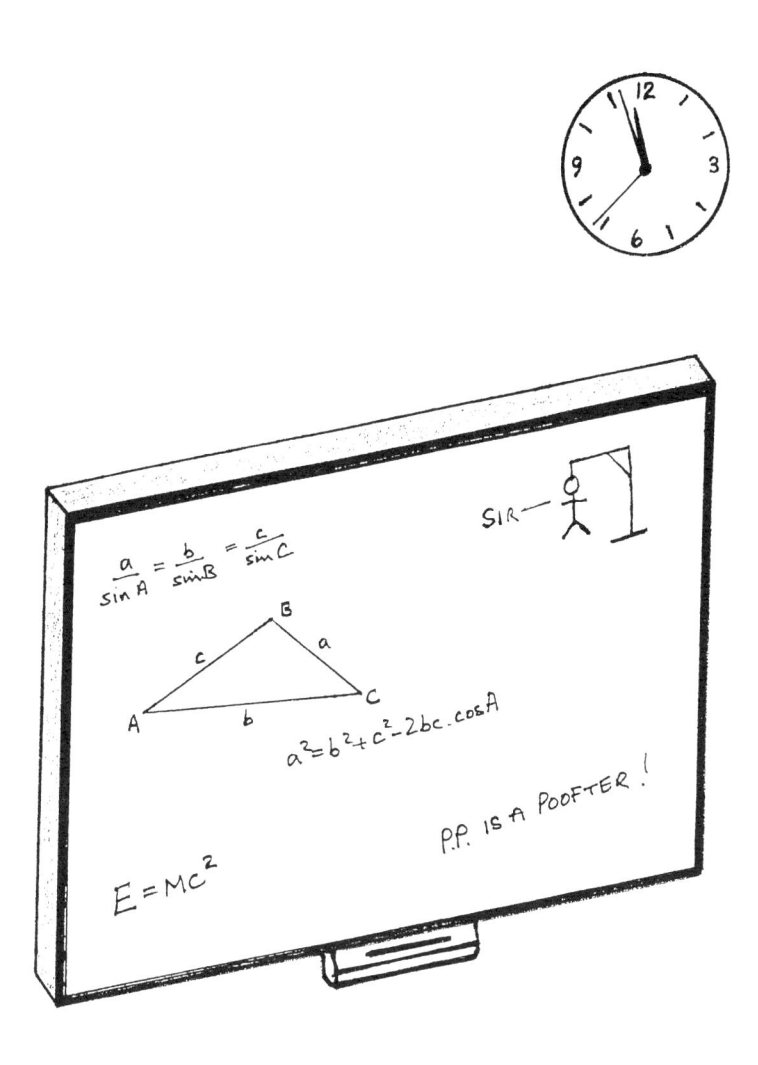

CHAPTER 21

Rumblings were afoot regarding industrial action by the unions in support of the teacher's long outstanding pay claim. It was well overdue and negotiations had been going on for the best part of a year. They were threatening to refuse to cover for absent colleagues, which would have resulted in classes with no teachers being sent home.

The troops became only too aware of the situation, the prospect of being sent home being manner from heaven to their way of thinking.

"Good on you, Sir," said Christopher, one Maths lesson. "We all reckon you deserve a big rise and the only way to be sure of getting it is to go on strike. We're with you all the way."

"What you really mean is you'd quite like a few days off school?"

"We'd be coming out in sympathy, Sir!"

He got enthusiastic support from the rest of the class. Their hopes were dashed, however, when it was explained to them that they would be getting an extra member of staff shortly, as a permanent supply teacher. He would be employed specifically to cover absent teachers, so their chances of being sent home were next to nil.

"That's not fair, Sir," Christopher complained. "Other schools get sent home...... how come they don't have supply teachers?"

"They do," Biggs assured him. "but since we're a split-site school, we're entitled to an extra allocation. In any case, you should be grateful that you aren't likely to be sent home. You wouldn't want to miss any of my pearls of wisdom, would you?"

"I thing we might be prepared to forgo a few pearls, if it meant getting a couple of days off school," Tony suggested. The rest of the class nodded agreement.

"Mr. Hardcastle said that he was casting his pearls before swine," Christopher mused. "......except of course, that he said, 'SWINES! We tried to correct him, but he just did a nutty! Teachers don't like being corrected, do they, Sir."

"I don't mind being corrected when I'm wrong..... but then of course, I'm rarely wrong. Anyway you said that he threw a wobbly!"

"Same difference...... You don't think we're swine, do you, Sir?"

"No, Chris, I don't...... and neither does Mr. Hardcastle ...... It's just that you always manage to rub him up the wrong way and he sometimes overreacts."

"We know! Good eh!"

"He doesn't like it, Chris."

"No, I suppose not," he said, thoughtfully and then adding with a grin "......but, c'est la vie."

"Never mind, c'est la vie! I get all the flack, so would mind you just giving him a break?"

Christopher could see that Biggs was being serious and earnestly pleading for them to behave in Mr. Hardcastle's lessons in future. He looked at Tony, who

175

nodded his agreement. "Okay, Sir. You're on. But remember, we're not all in the same set for Music, so we can't vouch for the rest of the class, but we won't give any more trouble."

"Cheers! I'm sure the rest will follow your lead. They usually do."

The school already had one permanent supply teacher, a Welshman named David Reed, who was engaged mainly on cover. Based in the Upper School, he was rarely seen in the annexe. He used to be a permanent member of staff a few years earlier, but had returned to his native Wales, seeking pastures greener. However, a business venture that he started with a friend apparently ran into trouble, resulting in his return to Gordon Bennett.

The second supply teacher, a Mr. Julian Rockford, was to be based at the Lower School. He was also a former member of staff from a couple of years back, who had decided to try his luck in the big bad world outside school. His line was antiques. Biggs always felt that the name Julian somehow lent itself to being associated with the world of antiques! He had gone into partnership with Martin Steel, a young Chemistry teacher. Martin was still at Gordon Bennett, but taught only part time. Harry Langton went to have a look in their shop once, being a bit of a collector himself. It was closed at the time, but he was able to peer through the window. He said that he knew that beauty was in the eye of the beholder, but if it hadn't said 'J & M Antiques' above the window, he would have described their stock as a load of old junk. The business hadn't been doing too well, so everyone guessed that potential clientele were of a similar opinion.

Julian used to teach English. This was not a shortage subject, but his return made Harry's task of covering for absent staff, much easier. The absent rate always showed a marked increase as Winter approached. Of course it wasn't Winter, but with the approach of the hayfever season, Summer could be almost as bad. Teachers can be a sickly lot at the best of times and there are none more sickly that young teachers, straight out of college. Used to the free and easygoing atmosphere of college or university, many end up physical wrecks at the end of their first week. Biggs recalled the final comment made by his tutor on the last day of his postgraduate year at Teachers' Training College, saying that he would go home at the end of his first day's teaching and sleep the sleep of the just! Being suddenly thrown in at the deep end is bad enough, but having to contend with the myriad of bugs and other nasties coughed, sneezed and squeezed out by hundreds of pubescent kids often comes as one hell of a shock to the immune system of young teachers. They fall foul of anything and everything that's going around. After a year or two they manage to build up an immunity and their absence rate falls. Meanwhile, having full timetables, when they are off sick, they always need lots of cover.

One of the additional advantages of having supply teachers readily available, is that the permanent staff are able to go on courses from time to time, to improve their skills or to acquaint themselves with the latest advances in education. In fact there are two types of teachers; those who teach and those who seem to spend their lives going on courses on how to teach! Biggs was never one for attending courses. Apart from one on visual aids, the only course that he could recall attending during his last twenty years of teaching, was one on Man Management; now there's sexist for you! It lasted for one week and he attended with Malcolm Rowe, albeit reluctantly. They spent most of their time acting out roll play situations and they both found the whole thing quite farcical. It certainly put them both off attending another course. The course was supposed to prepare them for high office, but seeing the way things were heading in education, neither had the slightest desire to attain high office. Neither had they the slightest desire to become a Deputy Head and Headmaster was quite unthinkable. Heads have to eat, drink and sleep education, morning, noon and night. They have to walk a fine line, trying to be all things to all people. This is of course impossible and they usually end up a hindrance to most and the butt of everyone's frustrations. Whatever may be the perceived view of Heads outside their schools, within their walls they are frequently the source of much resentment. Biggs had been appointed Senior Year Head shortly after the course, but preferring the ultimate buck to stop elsewhere he had no desire to progress further.

Needless to say there were teachers who seemed to spend most of their time attending courses; anything to get them out of the classroom and into the eyes of the Inspectorate. Each term the local authority would published a list of courses and seminars available to teachers and one morning Harry Langton pinned up the list for the following term. Shortly afterwards a second unauthorized list appeared along side the authorized version. It read:

COURSES FOR SUMMER TERM. Please apply early in the usual manner.

    Self improvement:
    SI 100   Creative suffering.
    SI 101   Ego gratification through violence.
    SI 102   Whine your way to alienation.

Business and career:
B 101   Teaching opportunities in Albania.
B102   The underachiever's guide to small Headships.
B103   How to become a Rent Boy.

Health and Fitness:
H101   Creative tooth decay.
H102   The joys of Hypochondria.
H103   Suicide and its detriment to your health.
H104   Understanding Nudity.
H105   Skate your way to social ridicule.

Hobbies and Pastimes:
HP 101 Needlecraft for junkies.
HP102   How to convert a wheelchair into a Dune Buggy.

ANON.

Someone wag had penciled in against B103, Peter Partridge and against HP101, Paul Scobie. Later in the day some other member of staff had penciled in, 'Headmaster' against H 105, the significance of which was not apparent at the time, but would become apparent later.

One of the courses on the authorized list also gave cause for much amusement. It was a course for Gay and Lesbian teachers to be held at an address in Great Queen Street!

CHAPTER 22

APRIL FOOL'S DAY. It was the last week of the Spring Term and the Thursday of that week was April Fool's Day! Now boys are not known for the subtlety of their April fool gags, so that week the staff were anticipating the usual round of pathetic attempts. You know the sort of thing: 'Your shoe lace is undone,' 'Why are you wearing odd socks today, Sir?' or to a member of staff driving in, 'Your back wheels are going round forwards.' These were their usual pinnacles of excellence! Now it is a well known in the teaching profession that there is no fool like a boy fool. A teacher saying almost anything with a straight face, will more often than not, be believed. Virtually anything they say can be taken as gospel.

It's not every year that April Fool's day falls during term time, so that year, relying on the mass gullibility of most schoolboys, Harry Langton and Biggs decided that they would beat them at their own game and try to upstage the little perishers. Thinking that the fewer people that knew about it, the better, they decided that apart themselves, only Ian McTaggart and Laura were to be in the know. The four of them were discussing the possibility over a coffee in the general office.

"It shouldn't be too difficult," Ian suggested. "Most of them are gullible enough."

At that moment Christopher Bird entered the office to collect his class register. He obviously caught the tail end of Ian's remark and, inviting himself into the conversation, asked, "Gullible? Whose gullible?"

"You lot are, " Ian replied........"Boys in general."

"We're not gullible," he reacted, quite indignantly.

"Yes you are," Harry assured him. "Say something with a straight face and you'll believe it, no matter how absurd."

"Okay then...... Prove it," Christopher challenged.

"We intend to," Harry said, giving Biggs a sly wink, as he tweaked Christopher's elbow.

"Ouch..... Let go, Sir," Christopher complained. "Your not Mr. Smith..... only he's allowed to do that."

He received a second harder tweak, before being pushed towards the door with the register.

Having been irrevocably committed to pulling off some sort of April Fool stunt, they put their heads together later in the day and after much deliberation, eventually came up with the germ of an idea. A stunt that would require the calling of a special assembly!

Now on the Wednesday of that week, the boys were due to have a medical inspection. Involving most of the Lower School, it would be going on throughout the day and was to feature in the April Fool gag!

"What sort of medical is it?" Tony Roberts asked, during Maths. "Another cough and drop, I suppose?"

"That's right," Biggs confirmed. ".....but without the cough."

"That's bad," Christopher said. ".....but I'm glad you warned us."

"Why?" Biggs asked, somewhat intrigued.

"I can wear my snazzy silk boxer shorts..... Got to impress the nurse, you know!"

"Big thrill," said his mate, Tony. "I wouldn't bother, though...... you've got nothing to impress her with."

"Don't be ridiculous...... She'll be looking at 130 pounds of dynamite."

"That's right," Tony confirmed. ".......with a two inch fuse."

The class roared with laughter. Christopher, having been so cruelly affronted, clearly felt the need to get even, so he gave Tony a hefty thump on the arm. "SIX, if you don't mind," he said, indignantly. "I thought we'd established my credentials in that area?..... Just call me Tripod!"

"Tripod! You must be joking. What good is a tripod that lays in its side?"

"Look who's talking.... Anyway, I'd rather be a Cavalier than a Roundhead."

"Not if you were King Charles I, you wouldn't," Tony retorted.

Thinking that the banter had gone on long enough and that it was getting a bit near the knuckle, Biggs thought that he had better draw it to a close. Had it been their Friday *chat-day* as they called it, he might have let them continue, but it wasn't, so he said, "Come on, Girls ... Let's not be catty, now. It's not Friday you know, so don't take advantage."

Just as he was making his last remark about not being catty, Biggs became aware of someone passing the open door to the classroom..... It was the dragoness, Ms. Lynn Harmon, Chairperson of the Women's Committee and self-appointed guardian of political correctness! He wondered what she was yet again doing in the Lower

School? She obviously overheard the remark and he ended up on the receiving end of an intensive glare. If looks could have killed, he would have dropped dead on the spot, her glare spitting venom faster than a spitfire's guns.

Christopher, clearly aware of Lynn-the-Grins's displeasure on overhearing the remark, waited until he thought she was out of earshot and then whispered to him, "I wouldn't like to be in your shoes, Sir."

"Why not?" Biggs asked, with trepidation.

"She'll probably have you up before their committee in the morning, on a fizzer," he replied, shaking his head and grinning broadly.

"A fizzer!" Biggs queried.

"You know, Sir...... A charge..... I thought you were supposed to be in the RAF. Surely you must know what a fizzer is?"

"I do..... I was just a little surprised that you knew about such things..... In any case, what committee?"

"You know, Sir..... The Women Teachers' group."

"Oh, them...... I wasn't aware that you knew about them."

"You must be joking, Sir," Tony Roberts, piped in. "How many times do we have to tell you? We're pupils.......it's our job to know these thing!"

They obviously had a grapevine far superior to that of the staff! Tony was quite correct, Biggs thought to himself. Understanding the organization and numerous intrigues of the school was all part of the learning process.

In fact, the medical wasn't a cough and drop; it was an eye test and foot inspection, but he always liked to keep them guessing. Harry Langton usually told the kids that they would be getting a jab. That really used to put the frighteners on.

By the end of the day, the plans for the following day's assembly had been finalized. It was to prove to be a memorable occasion.

It was Thursday and April Fool's Day! Since it was not the day for the normal weekly assembly, a special assembly had to be called, which only served to highlight the occasion. Along with the rest of the staff, His Majesty had been kept in the dark. Of course not being a Friday, he would thankfully not be making an appearance. What was to follow would certainly not have met with his approval. The boys entered the hall in the usual way just after nine o'clock. Harry, Ian and Biggs were on the stage with stern faces. Sensing that something was up, the boys entered the hall unusually quietly, obviously wondering what dreadful deed some miscreants had perpetrated.

When the last boy had entered, Harry stepped forward a couple of paces. Following a moments pause, to get their full attention and to highlight his apparent anger, he proceeded to rant and rave about a fictional complaint from the school nurse the previous day. It concerned the extremely poor behaviour of a large number of boys during the medical inspection.

"The behaviour of some boys was appalling," he raved at them. "Most of you were fooling around...... hiding each others shoes and socks and deliberately misreading the eye chart..... We've managed to identify most of the culprits and I will be seeing those boys immediately after this assembly. They can be sure of one thing...... letters will be going home to their parents."

There was a deathly hush from the body the hall, but the looks on the faces of boys indicated that they were confused; clearly none could recall anyone hiding shoes and socks or misreading the eye chart!

Harry continued his tirade. "I am just not prepared to tolerate this sort of behaviour. The nurse was unable to do her job properly, so we end up with the need for a repeat inspection later this morning. This time you're going to get it right and to make sure that you do, we're going to have a dress rehearsal right now..... STAND UP.... ALL OF YOU."

The boys stood.

"Now remove your shoes and stocks and stand on your chairs," Harry continued.

Confusion reined! The kids, thinking, Is he serious, looked around to see what others were doing? The staff, unaware what was going on, were even more confused. Most of them were of the opinion that Harry had finally flipped his lid, but they made various hand gestures to the kids, indicating that they should do as instructed.

"NOW," Harry screamed, as some of the younger boys started to do as they were bid. The rest, albeit hesitantly at first, followed suit and after a few moments the assembled multitude stood with bare feet on their chairs....... all FOUR HUNDRED of them, looking a right load of Charlies....... It was a sight to behold.

"Good. Now we'll practice reading the eye chart....... Mr. Smith, when your ready."

Biggs switched on the overhead projector, which had been made ready before the assembly.

Addressing the boys again, Harry continued, "As Mr. Smith writes a letter and it appears on the screen, I want you to repeat it, clearly and concisely, but without shouting."

Harry gave Biggs the nod and he wrote the first letter, 'A.'

"A," the boys chanted back, in unison.

Biggs had great difficulty in keeping a straight face, but managed to contain himself enough to write the second letter, 'P.'

The boys chanted, "P."

Eying them carefully, looking for a faint glimmer of light, he wrote the third letter, 'R'..... but none seemed to have twigged yet!

"R," came back the reply.

As Biggs wrote the letter, 'I,' and the chant came back, there was a slight faltering in one or two voices, the light clearly beginning to dawn. And as the letter, 'L' appeared on the screen, it became obvious that most of the boys had finally twigged so, no longer able to keep a straight face, he continued writing the remaining letters in quick succession, thus revealing the final message and coup de grace........ 'APRIL FOOLS.'

The assembly was reduced to uproar...... a mixture of disbelief, raucous laughter and annoyance at having been conned so blatantly. The uproar continued for a full two minutes, as Harry, Ian and Biggs congratulated themselves on the success of the operation. Ian, although in with the plan, was unaware how it was to be brought to a conclusion with the use of the overhead projector. He could hardly contain himself, as he rolled about on his chair in hysterics.

"By the way," Harry said, to one of the anklebiters in the front row, "Your wearing odd socks, young man." The lad looked down to be caught yet again!

The boys put on their shoes and socks, still barely able to believe what had just happened. Before things had a chance to get out of hand, it was decided that it would be prudent to cancel any other assembly business and the boys were quickly dismissed. Not a great deal of work was done that morning!

Later in the day, Biggs met Christopher in the corridor. "Remember our conversation about gullibility?" he chided him.

"Yes, Sir." Nice one...... You may have fooled the rest, but you didn't fool me, though."

"Who are you kidding? You were standing bare feet on your chair just like the rest."

"I know, Sir...... but I realized what was going on as soon as were told to take our shoes and socks off...... I just didn't have the nerve to be the odd one out."

Biggs believed him!

The following day was Friday and the last day of term. Despite the previous day's hoax it was decided to hold the normal weekly assembly as usual, although the Headmaster phoned to say that he had to go out and would not be attending. The smug look of satisfaction on the faces of Harry, Ian and Biggs as the boys entered the hall had to be seen to be believed. As a consolation for being conned the previous day the boys were told that as it was the last day of term they would be allowed home half an hour early.

Teenage boys are not normally known for their interest shown in political matters, but when politics are combined with aggression it can a different kettle of fish. The rumblings between Great Britain and Argentina over the Falkland Islands had be going on for some time and it had stirred in the kids a moderate interest. The invasion of the Islands on the last day of term certainly served to concentrate their minds and was to provide a topic of conversation over the Easter holiday. They went home the promised half an hour early, confident in their own minds that the conflict would be resolved in next to no time. The sleeping lion had been aroused!

"Maggie will soon sort out those nasty Argies," Christopher said to Biggs, popping into his office to say good-bye, shortly before departing for the holiday.

"I'm sure she will," Biggs confirmed. He was relaxing in one of his armchairs with a cup of his favorite afternoon brew.

"I smell Lapsang!" Christopher said, eying the teapot.

"Want some?"

"Yes please, Sir."

Biggs poured him a cup and beckoned him to sit in his other armchair." Not wishing to get involved in a discussion on the Falklands, he quickly changed the subject. "What are you going to do with yourself over the holiday.... Run amuck, I suppose?"

"Do you mind, Sir. I never run amuck! In fact I'm going to have to spend a boring week in Norfolk, with my mum and her weird friend! We'll be staying in some sleepy village nobody ever heard of, in the middle of nowhere and whose name I can't even remember."

"Weird?.... What's weird about her?"

"God, she goes in for seances and all that rubbish.... You know, sitting round a table, trying to contact the dead! Did you ever hear of anything so ridiculous?"

"No, not really. So you're not a believer in an afterlife then?"

"No, I'm not. I reckon when you're dead, your dead!... You don't believe in God, do you, Sir?"

Biggs shook his head. "How did you know? I've never mentioned it!"

"I'm not sure. I think it's probably just the impression I've gained since we've known each other."

"Let's not get involved in a theological discussion, Chris. It's too heavy and too late in the term."

"Fair enough.... I just wish that I could look forward to a more exciting holiday. My daft brother gets to spend a week at Scout camp and I get to spend it in Yawnsville, USA. There's no justice, is there?"

"You told me last term, that you'd joined the Sea Cadets? Don't they have a camp at Easter?"

"Yes, but I joined too late and they had no spare places."

"Would your mother have let you go, if they'd had some spare places?"

"Let me? She'd be glad to get shot of me!.... I could have stayed with Tony for the week, except that he'll be away too..... I suppose you'll be off flying or gliding again.... up in the wild blue yonder?"

Biggs nodded, but made no reply! He looked thoughtfully at Christopher for a few moments! He was thinking about the *maybe* that he had given him earlier in the term, when he had jokingly asked to be taken up flying.

"What, Sir?.... What did I say?"

"Nothing..... Would you be interested in something that didn't involve being in Yawnsville, USA over the holiday?... Something more exciting.... and something that could prove quite challenging, even for an extrovert, like you?"

"Would I?.... Just lead me to it!"

"Give me your telephone number..... I might just have a proposition for you!"

Christopher wrote down his phone number on Biggs' jotter. "A proposition? What sort of proposition, Sir?"

"No promises! I need to make a few phone calls! I'll give you a ring tomorrow, about midday, so be at home!"
"I can't wait..... Sounds intriguing!"

CHAPTER 23

SUMMER TERM.

It was Monday morning and they had just returned from the Easter break. Harry Langton had put Biggs down to cover a Third Year Physics class, their regular teacher Mr. Moid being off sick with a dose of the Delhi-belly. At least that was the official story! Reality however, proffered a different version! The Delhi part was genuine enough, but the *belly* part translated to a delayed flight from India, where Mr. Moid had spent his Easter holiday, visiting his long lost relations. Air India had apparently failed to come up with the goods, his flight having been delayed some eight hours. He was due to make a miraculous recovery at two o'clock that afternoon! Meanwhile Biggs had been lumbered with covering his first period. He didn't really mind, since they were *his* Year and he was the obvious person, having been Head of Physics in a previous incarnation, that is before switching from the *academic* to the *pastoral* side of teaching a decade or so earlier.

Looking round the laboratory Biggs at once realized that almost half the boys were also members of his *elite* Express Maths set. He had not taken the group before, but he was not in the least surprised at seeing so many, considering the obvious connection between Mathematics and Physics. Alan Lane and Paul Smith had secreted themselves at the back of the room, presumably hoping not to be noticed. Christopher Bird and his mate Tony Roberts were sitting next to each other as always, at the front. Christopher, not known for hiding his light under a bushel, always liked to sit at the front, where he could take centre stage! And where Christopher went, so went Tony!

Being the first lesson of the term, no work had been set, but as it was only a single period, Biggs thought he would just add-lib.

"What were you doing at the end of last term?" he asked, throwing out a general question.

"Air pressure and its measurement," said Craig Baker. "Oh, and the aneriod and mercury barometers."

Craig had been in Biggs' Set One Maths class in his second year and only just missed making it into the Express set in the Third Year. He was a very hard working lad with a pleasant personality and Biggs would have liked him to have been in the group. Unfortunately he couldn't quite make the grade and would have struggled to keep up. But in the end, given the choice of moving up, it was Craig himself who had said that he wouldn't like to get left behind and that he thought it would be best if he joined the new restructured Set One.

"We also touched on the aircraft altimeter," volunteered Christopher, adding tongue in cheek. "It works on a similar principle to the aneroid barometer, you know."

"Does it now, Christopher?" Biggs had loaned an altimeter to the Science department a couple of years earlier! "Now why didn't I know that?"

"Oh, and we also talked about how an aeroplane flies. Do you know how an aeroplane flies, Sir?" Christopher added, with a knowing smirk!"

"Of course he does," Craig said. "You've got a pilot's licence, haven't you, Sir?"

"Yes, Craig," Biggs confirmed in answer to his question, but he was looking at Christopher! Christopher's observation had been very much tongue-in-cheek and designed to elicit a response that only they would understand! They shared a secret, a secret known only to the two of them..... and possibly Tony, but Biggs wasn't sure if Tony knew!

The *maybe* of the previous term, given to Christopher in answer to his request to be taken flying, had over the holiday, turned into a reality! During the second week of the Easter holiday Christopher's brother Steven had been attending his Scout camp and his mother, despite Christopher's protestations, had decided that she would spend the week with her friend, who lived in a small village in the county of Norfolk. Christopher, not relishing the prospect of spending a boring week in Yawnsville, USA, as he had described it, jumped at the opportunity of spending it with Biggs at the Royal Air Force Station at West Malling on a gliding course! Biggs had been running a course for cadets of the Air Section of the Combined Cadet Force over the holiday period. Christopher had joined the Sea Cadets the previous term and as a member of a Cadet Pre-service Unit, with a bit of string-pulling, he could legitimately be given air experience flights in RAF gliders. But just to make doubly sure that everything was above board, Biggs had asked the Adjutant of one of the local Air Training Corps squadrons to put him on their roll. Being an instructor himself with the Gliding School, he readily agreed.

Although one of the oldest boys in the Third Year, who could easily be taken for a sixteen year old, Christopher was still only fourteen and wasn't old enough to attend a gliding course as a trainee. And not withstanding that the fact that he had been entered on the roll of the local squadron, as a Sea Cadet, he probably wouldn't have been allowed to attend as a trainee anyway. Even Biggs couldn't have pulled that many strings! But that didn't prevent him from attending as an extra pair of hands and general dog's-body! So permission having been given by his mother and the Commanding Officer of his Sea Cadet unit, he set off with Biggs, wearing his Sea Cadet uniform, to spend the week at RAF West Malling as an *honorary* Air Cadet.

Not being able to watch over him all the time because of his other duties, Biggs had been a little concerned at throwing Christopher in at the deep-end, in an unfamiliar surrounding with older lads that he didn't know. He needed someone to keep an eye on him throughout the week, so shortly after arrival, he had been put in the charge of one of the staff cadets, a Cadet Sergeant Craig Jackson, who was to act as his mentor. Jackson was a seventeen year old cadet from a local squadron, on permanent attachment to the Gliding School. He had an outgoing, charismatic personality and was in many ways very similar to Christopher and Biggs knew that they would get on together. Staff cadets were like mini-gods and could be likened to prefects in a school! They were NCO cadets who were members of the various Air Training Corps Units throughout the county, but who also attended most weekends at the gliding school as assistants. Having completed gliding courses themselves to a proficiency standard, completing three solo flights and having proved to be of exceptional ability, they had then gone on to undertake advanced training. Weather permitting, they flew most weekends and quickly managed to build up quite a few hours in the air. They retrieved the gliders with Land Rovers after landing, towing them on a retrieve trolleys, designed specifically for the purpose. They towed out the cables, drove the launch winches and generally bossed the trainee cadets about. Having taken an RAF driving test and having been issued with a driving permit, within the confines of airfield and the RAF Station roads, Ministry of Defence regulations permitted them to drive at the age of sixteen. They of course needed to be seventeen and have a driving licence to take the vehicles onto the public roads. Quite a few were trained to fly to a standard which enabled them to carry other cadets on air experience flights and some eventually went on to become instructors.

  It had been made clear to Christopher that it would be a working holiday and that he would be left very much to his own devices. He would also have to muck in and get on with older cadets on the course, at least two years his senior, most of whom were from public schools throughout the area. It was made very clear to him that as a cadet, he would be subject to RAF rules and discipline and that the regime would be very different from that at school. He would be expected to do exactly as he was told by any instructor or staff cadet without question at all times. He would also be the most junior cadet there and bottom of the pecking order, although he would have equal standing with the trainee CCF cadets on course! In short, if he was told to jump, he would jump and the only question that he could ask was, 'How high, Sir?' In exchange for humping gliders about, helping in the kitchen and generally doing everyone's bidding, he would be given a couple of flights each day in a glider and he might even enjoy himself! If he proved his worth, Biggs told him, he might just get something more, but without saying what! Christopher said that he understood what he was letting himself in for and was quite happy to go through with it! "It'll be a challenge!" he'd said. "I like a challenge." Despite being at least two years younger than the CCF cadets on the course, most of whom came from fee-paying public schools, Biggs felt certain that he would be able to win them over! He had the ability get on with virtually anybody, regardless of age or social background. In the end, his charismatic personality carried him through and he coped admirably. In fact he became somewhat of a mascot with the older cadets!

Royal Air Force West Malling existed on a Care and Maintenance basis with a skeleton staff, there being no regular RAF unit in residence, other than the Gliding School. The school had quite commodious accommodation and provided its instructors, staff cadets and trainees with all facilities on a self-help basis. Meals were provided by the Army and were delivered daily from Maidstone Barracks in sealed containers. But the preparation and washing-up was carried out by the cadets on a daily rota, except that Christopher's name appeared every day! In the evenings he was left with the other lads to fend for himself. The cadets were not allowed to leave the camp, but they had plenty to keep themselves occupied, including television, table-tennis and a full-size snooker table. There was even a Link flying trainer which they were permitted to use under the supervision of a staff cadet. Biggs went to the pub most evenings with the other instructors!

The only slight difficulty Christopher experienced with anyone, was with a cantankerous old civilian instructor, Mr. Roy Roberts. Most of the instructors, Biggs included, were officers commissioned in the Training branch of the Royal Air Force Volunteer Reserve, but there were a few civilian gliding instructors, including Roy. He had a sarcastic streak in him and at times he could be quite cutting with his remarks. He often referred to Christopher as *Navy* and would make such remarks as 'Watch out the Navy's about' or 'I see the Navy's fouled up again.' His stock phrase which he would trot out whenever he was kept waiting was, 'Where are my marmite soldiers?' He would particularly trot it out if kept waiting for his lunch. The trainee cadets on course always served themselves in their own dining room. However, the instructors and staff cadets had a separate dining room and it was the custom for them to be served by the Duty cadets of the day, which always included Christopher. In fact Christopher, knowing that he was to be on duty every day, with a different pair of trainees and not wishing to get lumbered, decided that he would take charge of the dining arrangements and began organizing things to suit himself! He took it upon himself to act as waiter and serve the instructors and staff cadets and he had the other pair cadets doing the washing up! Since it was a different pair of Duty cadets each day and since Christopher was on every day, they just assumed that he was in charge and meekly did as they were told! So notwithstanding the fact that the cadet trainees were all very much his senior, the majority being of NCO rank, in the kitchen the Navy proved to be very much the Senior Service!

For some reason known only to himself, Roy always expected to be among the first to be served and if he wasn't a cry of 'Where are my marmite soldiers,' would ring round the dining room! Of course Christopher was no stranger to sarcasm, but he couldn't quite manage to work Roy out, that is until his mentor Sergeant Craig Jackson explained that Roy's bark was very much worse than his bite and that the only way to deal with him was to give him back as good as he gave! They put their heads together and came up with a plan for Christopher to turn the tables on Roy!

At lunchtime on the third day of the course, Christopher made a point of serving everyone except Roy, who of course demanded as usual, 'Where are my marmite soldiers.'

"We're preparing a special treat for you, Sir," Christopher assured him, as he continued to serve everyone except him! "It won't be too long now."

Roy was obviously getting rather annoyed at being kept waiting, but eventually after everyone else had been served, Christopher ceremoniously brought in his lunch on a covered plate and placed it in front of him.

"Your favourite, Sir," he'd said with a grin, lifting the plate cover to reveal four neatly cut marmite soldiers!

Everyone fell about laughing, including the other cadets, who had left their own dining room and were standing in the doorway. Even Roy, seeing the funny side of it, could barely contain himself.

"That's the trouble with this place," he'd said. "Everyone thinks he's a bleeding comedian!.... Now where's my roast beef?"

"Not until you've eaten your soldiers, Sir," Christopher had forcefully insisted.

Roy obediently ate his marmite soldiers and was eventually served with his proper lunch. With the aid of his mentor, our budding young Sea Cadet had successfully turned the tables on Roy, at the same time greatly enhancing his own image and firmly establishing himself as the camp comedian. From that moment he never looked back!

Christopher received his couple of flights each day with various instructors or staff cadets. He flew a couple of time with Biggs, on one occasion remaining airborne for nearly an hour on thermal up-currents. They'd descended in style doing a series of loops and various other aerobatic maneuvres all to Christopher's delight. But his real reward for his hard work came on the penultimate day of the course, when the *maybe* finally became a reality. He was taken up in the two-seat Piper Cub aircraft, in which Biggs had part ownership. The red and white Cub, G-AXHP was normally based at Rochester Airport, but had been flown into West Malling for the duration of the course. Deciding to give the Army grub a miss for once, they had flown to Stapleford airfield in Essex for lunch. Christopher, having previously been given some basic flying instruction in gliders, was soon able to master the basic maneuvres and fly the Cub himself. They landed at Stapleford and had lunch in the clubhouse restaurant. After their bite to eat, they flew to Rochester airport to refuel and then back to West Malling, returning a couple of hours later. Of course, not having being around to organize the Gliding School dining arrangements, the washing-up had been left undone and Christopher had to contend with it all himself!

"It was brilliant, Sir. That was one the best holidays I've ever had." he'd said at the end of the week. "But that trick you played on us with the donkeys, making us get up at 5.30 in the morning...... that was just wicked!"

The cadets on course, Christopher included, had fallen for the regular prank played on all new trainees on their first day. They always arrived the evening before their flying training was due to commence and it was the custom for the Course Commander, Biggs in this instance, to give them a general briefing. Part of the briefing included information about the donkeys belonging to the local farmer, which were allowed to roam the airfield at night. The first chore each morning was to get up at 5.30, round them up, on behalf of the farmer and give them their first feed of the day! A bale of hay was kept for the purpose in a small shed outside the Gliding School Headquarters. The cadets were always shown the bale of hay and the general area on the airfield where the donkeys were usually to be found. Strangely enough, it was always on the far side of the airfield, well away from the Gliding School, involving a long walk! Come rain or shine, at 5.30 am on the first day of each course, the gullible young cadets were always to be found scouring the airfield, in a forlorn attempt at rounding-up those nonexistent donkeys..... donkeys that were simply a figment of someone's hyperactive imagination!

"They always fall for it," Biggs had said. "It works every time."

Christopher had thoroughly enjoyed his week as an honorary Air Cadet. He had worked hard throughout the week and had got his just reward. He hinted that he wouldn't mind doing it again sometime, if the opportunity arose. He got another *maybe* from Biggs! But he was told not to talk about his flying exploits with him in the Cub. It was not to made general knowledge, there possibly being unwelcome overtones back at school. Christopher understood that the Scobies and Partridges on the staff wouldn't understand and that it was probably best to keep quiet about it.

"Can't I even tell Tony?" he'd asked. "He won't blab and I don't usually keep things from him."

"I'm not sure! You can talk about the gliding course and flying in a glider. After all, you are a cadet and that was a legitimate activity, but for the time being I'd rather you didn't mention about flying with me in the Cub."

"Okay, Sir. My lips are sealed. I won't tell my pain-in-the-butt brother either. If I do he'll spread it all over the school."

Back in the laboratory!

"Well, since Christopher seems to know so much about flying, I think we might prevail on him to give us a little talk on the matter, don't you think, boys?"

The class readily agreed and Christopher came smiling to the blackboard, to give an impromptu talk. He drew a series of diagrams showing airflow and cross-sections of aircraft wings and explained with the proficiency of an expert, how an aeroplane flew. He talked about lift and drag even managed to correctly answer a battery of questions from the rest of the class. His talk lasted to the end of the lesson.

"Do I get paid for that, Sir? How about fifteen minutes of your pay. I think that's about how long my talk lasted."

"Spherical objects!" Biggs retorted.

"Really, Sir! Not the most aerodynamic of shapes. I think a plonker would be more suitable! It's shaped more like an aerofoil!"

The class burst out laughing.

"Chris, you're impossible!"

"I know, Sir! I always try to be..... I take it that was a *no* then.... regarding the pay I mean!" Biggs just smiled benignly at him. "Oh well, never mind, Sir. I don't mind doing your job for you!"

"Surely it was worth at least a couple of tuck shop vouchers, Sir," Tony said, siding with his friend. "The boy done good!"

Biggs conceded the point and gave Christopher a couple of vouchers from his briefcase.

"Cheers, Sir," and then rather more quietly, "Oh, and thanks again for, you-know-what!" He gave one of his vouchers to Tony.

"What did you mean by you-know-what, Chris," Tony asked, having overheard his remark to Biggs.

Christopher simply tapped his nose with his forefinger indicating that it was a secret. "Later!" he said.

The task force was on its way and television pictures of the fleet heading for the South Atlantic towards the Falkland Islands only served to confirm in the minds of the kids that the conflict would soon be resolved. How they cheered when the Belgrano was sunk by a single torpedo fired by our brave boys under to ocean in HMS Conqueror. How they booed when HMS Sheffield was sunk by those nasty Argies and their devilish exocets. The conflict was to go on for a while yet and was to provide a daily topic of conversation, but nothing shook their confidence that in the end, that Great Britain would emerge victorious. Of course there were members of staff with far Left tendencies who thought that we should have tried to resolve the conflict by negotiation and that Mrs. Thatcher was nothing less than a warmongering female Winston Churchill. Naturally the Lefties' views got short shrift with the kids who regarded them as little short of fifth columnists. Peter Partridge, one of the foremost advocates of appeasement, was dubbed by the boys, Lord Haw Haw. Behind his back as he proceeded round the school could be heard the muffled whispers, "Argentina calling, Argentina calling."

CHAPTER 24

It was in Harry's office that Biggs had one day arranged a meeting with Ian McTaggart and Mike Gladstone to discuss the annual mini-marathon. Harry had said that he would look in if he was not too busy. Pigs might fly, Biggs thought to himself! Being too busy was the one thing that Harry avoided like the plague! Some ten minutes after the meeting was due to start, he had still not appeared. Laura said that she had not seen him all morning, but that he had left a message saying that if he was late, they should start without him.

The mini-marathon was a sponsored run held annually to raise money for the school and for some deserving charity. It covered a six mile course in the district. Although the whole school was involved, the greatest enthusiasm was always with the younger boys in the Lower School and it was Biggs' lot to organize it. The previous year the school had raised nearly two thousand pounds and paid for the training of a guide dog for the blind. As a reward the boys were taken on heavily subsidized day trips at the end of the Summer term. They agreed to have the same reward again, but to try to find another deserving charity, perhaps something nearer home?

Just as they had finished their deliberations, Harry burst in to the room and sprawled on his chaise longue, his face beaming with delight. They awaited with anticipation, expecting some world shattering news.

"I've just come from a meeting with the Head," he said. ".... and guess what?..... To encourage the kids in the mini-marathon, he intends letting them run in fancy dress and he says that he will be doing the course himself........ ON ROLLER SKATES!" They all fell about laughing. The thought of the Headmaster on roller skates was just too ludicrous for words and so out of character. It was then that Mike Gladstone recalled the list of unauthorized courses published by some wag at the end of the previous term. It was against H 105, 'Skate your was to social ridicule,' that someone had penciled in 'Headmaster!!'

His Majesty did not intend gracing the Lower School with his presence on the first Friday morning assembly of the term, so it was decided to use the time to brief the boys on the mini-marathon. It usually turned out to be an enjoyable day and the vast majority boys were always keen to take part, although it was sometimes necessary to get their enthusiasm aroused. A show of hands indicated that sponsor forms, issued a couple of days earlier, were filling up nicely. Asking if there were any questions, produced the usual deluge of inane rubbish and irrelevance that should have been expected. However, one boy, known for his general apathy and lethargy on such occasions, asked if they *had* to take part?

"Of course you don't," Harry assured him, in a loud voice, exaggerating his broad Scots accent. "..... but if you don't, then a week next Thursday, I'll be making you an offer you can't refuse."

The boys giggled in amusement. Harry had obviously been watching a recent television repeat of 'The Godfather.'

Later that morning, Biggs received a summons to attend the Headmaster's office. His Majesty wanted to be briefed on the preparation for the mini-marathon. Malcolm Rowe, from the Upper School was also in attendance. Malcolm would be looking after things at his end, thus reliving Biggs of some of the burden of the organization.

Biggs outlined what had been done so far and His Majesty seemed satisfied. He confirmed that he would be allowing fancy dress and that he would be taking part on roller skates, himself. Biggs tried to ascertain his prowess on skates, but he would give nothing away.

Returning to the Lower School and pausing outside the staff room on his way to the general office, he became aware of a somewhat heated discussion taking place. Several members of staff were debating the merits of running in the mini-marathon. Peter Partridge, their gay English teacher, had apparently said that he intended running and he was trying to get a Alan Howlett to accompany him. Alan, strongly opposed to the idea, was making it very clear to all concerned that he was having none of it.

"I have no intention of making a fool of myself in front of everyone," he protested. "I'll leave that to you."

"Making a fool of yourself! But that doesn't usually bother you," Peter retorted, sarcastically.

It was a remark hardly designed to encourage Alan to participate and one which simply served to strengthen his resolve. Although in his mid-twenties, Alan was wasn't exactly built for running and most members of staff had a great deal sympathy with him at the time. Being somewhat horizontally challenged, the standing joke with the kids was that he had to use two sets of scales to weigh himself, one for each foot.

"Running in fancy dress as well, are you?" he added contemptuously.

"I'm thinking about it," Peter replied.

"What will you be going as.... a fairy?" interjected Jimmy Bunting, second-in-charge of the PE. department

The staff giggled, but a couple of the *wets* mildly rebuked him. An unkind remark perhaps, but then if Peter would insist on wearing his 'GAY RIGHTS' badge round the school, what was he to expect? Biggs had no wish to get embroiled in the discussion, so left them to continue with their bitching.

The Headmaster had on more than one occasion, challenged Peter regarding the wearing of his badge. He backed down, however, when Peter threatened to take the matter up with his union. It was a time when the unions were quite militant and most Heads tried to avoid conflict with them. Mr. Martin's problem was solved, however, when he got unwitting support from an unexpected quarter.

Most of the boys seemed to have strong views on the subject of homosexuality and had themselves raised with Peter the question of his badge wearing. Peter had always been quite open about it and willing to discuss the matter with them, but he always insisted that it was his right to advertise his sexual orientation if he so chose. But this cut no ice with the kids and since the recent dubbing with his new nickname, Lord Haw Haw, he had not been flavour of the month. He arrived one day to find that most of his Forth Year English class were wearing home made badges on their lapels which read, 'STRAIGHT.' They were adamant in their refusal to remove them, maintaining that it was their right to express their sexual orientation, if they so chose. Peter got in a bit of a state and took the matter up with the Headmaster. He got little satisfaction, however........ 'Sauce for the goose,' was Mr. Martin's wry response. Shortly after the incident Peter stopped wearing his badge!

The day before the mini-marathon, Harry took Laura to the local cash-and-carry in the minibus to obtain bulk quantities of refreshments. Biggs had intended going himself, but unfortunately he had been put down to cover a class of mathematically challenged kids and Harry didn't think much of his suggestion that he should take the class for him. They weren't the easiest group to deal with and Harry only ever put himself down to cover *nice* classes! In fact he had deliberately put Biggs down to cover the class, so that he could go to the cash-and-carry himself, at the same time giving himself a legitimate excuse for being away from school for some considerable time on personal business!

THE BIG DAY. Gordon Bennett's very own mini-marathon. With a gentle breeze in the air and not a cloud in the sky, it was a glorious summer morning and ideal for the run. Nearly seven hundred boys were due to take part, nearly four hundred of those from the Lower School. There were of course, the usual ragbag of sprained ankles, wheezers and skivers, all with sick notes from their mummies or daddies!

The senior boys, although following more or less the same course, were due to start and finish at the Upper School. A phone call to Malcolm Rowe confirmed that everything was in hand at his end. The response from some of the senior boys had been less than enthusiastic and apparently one or two arms had to be metaphorically twisted. At least Malcolm Rowe said that the twisting was metaphorical, but at Gordon Bennett nothing could be taken for granted. Looking back on it, Biggs could sympathize with them to some extent. It was after all, their fourth or fifth run and the novelty must have been wearing a bit thin.

In the Lower school there was still a great deal of enthusiasm and the boys were obviously entering into the spirit of things. After changing into their running kit in their tutor rooms, they assembled in the gym, one year group at a time, ready for departure. Most intended running in their PE kit, although quite a few sported track suits, all with designer labels of course. About twenty boys were wearing fancy dress, with a motley assortment of costumes ranging from Vicars and Tarts to Superman and Robin Hood.

Christopher Bird had a little trouble struggling into his Batman costume, while his kid brother, dressed as Robin, watched in amusement. The costume was a bit on the tight side and it bulged in embarrassing places, somewhat belying his mate Tony's earlier remark about having a two inch fuse! Either that or he had undergone a rapid bout of puberty during the Easter holidays! Boys are notoriously unconcerned about making fools of themselves on such occasions. At other times they would break a leg rather than stand out from the crowd.

PC Brian Stevens, dressed in his police track suit, intended joining them for the run and was able to keep an eye on things from the aspect of road safety. Paul Scobie obviously intended running as a hippie, so he had no need to get changed. Two other members of staff had the courage to wear fancy dress. Peter Partridge, dressed in drag, was certainly not lacking in bravado considering his sexual persuasion. However, Peter had not managed to convince Alan Howlett, their horizontally challenged friend, to run. Brenda Hickman was dressed as a witch! She was carrying a broomstick, but she assured everyone that she did not intend cheating by flying round the course. Everyone waited with anticipation for the Headmaster to make an appearance on his roller skates. He eventually arrived without them, just before the start of the run, to wish the boys good luck. He said that he intended starting from the Upper School with the senior boys. Only a couple of the seniors had seen fit to wear fancy dress! They were obviously of an age when such frivolity would have done no favour to their street credibility.

By ten o'clock staff, posted to strategic locations as marshals, were in place and everyone was ready to start the run. The boys were sent off in groups of ten at two minute intervals. The younger boys were dispatched first, with the Hippie, the Drag Act and the Witch to keep an eye on them. Steven Bird was allowed to depart later with his brother, Christopher, since it was obviously sensible to keep Batman and Robin together. Members of the public and the children from the local primary school opposite, turned out to give them a cheer. The press photographer from the local rag was there to record the start for posterity.

The whole operation went smoothly and by ten to eleven the last group of athletic Third year boys were finally dispatched. Laura had the refreshments ready for the runners on their return and Penny had the first aid box on standby. Thankfully it wasn't needed. The first group were not due back for some time, so there was a little time to relax and obviously time for a nice cup of coffee.

Harry Langton and Biggs had planned to drive round the course in the school minibus to look for stragglers and to take some photographs. It was a sure bet that neither had planned to run and that they would end up giving themselves an easy task! It wasn't possible to cover the entire course since part of it passed through a local park, but they stuck to the route as far as possible.

The boys were spread out quite nicely in small groups. The last group sent off had already overtaken quite a few of the early starters and one or two of the less athletic boys had slowed to a walking pace. It was generally looking good, however and Harry snapped away with the camera, paying special attention to the boys in fancy dress.

They passed their aging Head of PE and Games, Gordon Marshall, going like the clappers. He was well passed sixty and must have been just about one of the oldest PE teachers still on the active list. Most PE teachers resort to teaching other subjects as they enter their fifties and it's certainly time for them to consider a career move when the kids start outperforming them. The Hippie, having given up taking PE and Games while still in his thirties, was clearly an exception. Gordon, however, was very fit and ran for the local Harriers. The previous year he had run in the London Marathon, so Gordon Bennett's six mile course would have been little more than a gentle amble for him.

Finally they spotted the Headmaster, on his roller skates. Much to their surprise he was doing rather well! Gliding effortlessly along with his hands behind his back, he looked quite proficient. He must have spent hours practicing at the roller disco! They wondered what other hitherto undiscovered talents he possessed? Harry took some photographs of him for public display, or possible blackmail at a later date.

They arrived back at school just in time to meet the first group of boys home, being provided with refreshments. Most were exhausted, but all said that they had enjoyed the run. The last group returned just after midday. Sponsor forms were signed and returned to the boys and after a shower and an early lunch, they were allowed home.

A mixture of elation and relief usually follows the completion of a major event such as the mini-marathon. Elation, because it was generally regarded as an outstanding success and relief, because so many things that could have gone wrong, didn't go wrong. The staff congratulated themselves on a job well done. It was obviously time to visit G19, so they all adjourned for a well earned nogging and cauliflower cheese.

The Headmaster took the assembly the next day and congratulated the boys on their participation and enthusiasm. Prizes were to be awarded to the boys collecting the most sponsor money and also for the best fancy dress. The sponsor prizes were to be awarded at a later date, after the money had been collected. Getting people to sponsor a major event is usually quite easy, but collecting the money afterwards can sometimes prove to be more difficult.

The prize for the best fancy dress went jointly to Christopher and Steven Bird for their Batman and Robin combination. They each received a £5 record token. Steven was full of himself, but rather surprisingly, Christopher was mildly embarrassed when collecting his prize. Biggs had never seen him embarrassed before! They both got a cheer from the assembly.

"It has been decided that a special prize should be awarded to the member of staff in the best fancy dress," the Headmaster said. "It was a difficult decision, but after careful consideration, the winner is Mrs. Hickman, for her witches costume."

The boys cheered loudly as she came forward to collect her prize, a giant box of chocolates...... and a broomstick. Biggs thought the prize should have gone to Peter Partridge, the drag act, for his bravado. It was not to be, however, undesirable overtones possibly being raised!

On the Monday following the mini-marathon, Laura started collecting the sponsor money. The boys had been told to bring it to the office during morning registration throughout the week. There was a queue of boys waiting outside the office with the first 'pips' yet to sound.

"How much?" Ian McTaggart asked the first boy.

"Fifteen pounds," he replied.

Ian patted him on the head and looked at the second boy in the queue.

"Fifty-seven pounds and there's more to come," he ventured.

"FIFTY-SEVEN POUNDS," Ian said, incredulity in his voice.

He nodded, his face beaming as Ian led him into the office. Laura was still putting on her morning face, but looked up smiling.

"This young man has a small fortune for you, Mrs. Clayton."

Still smiling, she took the envelope containing the money. Harry, standing by the connecting door to his office and overhearing the conversation took the boy by the arm and led him into his office. He emerged a few moments later with a small bag of sweets. Harry always had a few bags at the ready to offer deserving boys. The boy's name was Timothy Warmer. A small and cheerful looking Second year boy, he was rather overwhelmed by the praise showered on him from all directions.

"Do you realize that if every boy did as well as you, we would raise over thirty thousand pounds," Harry said.

A nice thought, but unfortunately Timothy's gallant effort was to be more than offset by the many who would manage to collect only a pound or two. The one or two pounders would invariably drag out the collection as long as possible, hoping that it would eventually be forgotten and they would be able to keep some of it. There is a sort of inverse Parkinson's law which pertains to the collecting of sponsor money by schoolboys, something along the lines:-

'The time required for collection expands as the amount to be collected diminishes.'

By the end of the morning thirty-five boys had managed to bring in over four hundred pounds between them and it was looking good. However, just before lunch Laura phoned the Upper School to find out how much they had collected...... just over twenty pounds!

"Typical," said Harry, contemptuously. "...... and I bet they think that they are doing a marvelous job."

The final total at the end of the following week was just over three thousand pounds, well up on the previous year. The Upper School's twenty pounds had risen to over eight hundred pounds and Timothy Warmer's fifty-seven pounds had risen to over one hundred. About twenty Lower School boys had each managed to raise in excess of fifty pounds, which was a splendid effort on their part. However, there was no getting away from the mathematics of it. Those twenty boys had between them raised approximately one third of the total amount raised and more than the entire Upper School! As previously stated, that meant that an awful lot of boys had managed to collect only a pound or two each. There must be a moral there somewhere?

It was decided that part of the money collected should be given to the local Toy Library. Laura, wandering round her local supermarket one day, got talking to the lady who ran it, a Mrs. Betty Harmon. Fortunately she was no relation to Gordon Bennett's own Ms. Lynn-the-Grin Harmon. The thought of having two of them in the school at the same time would have been a situation too dire to be contemplated. It seemed a worthwhile cause, providing a bank of toys for circulation to severely disabled children. They received a small grant from the local council, but relied largely on donations and were apparently always in need of additional funds. Laura told Betty that the school would make a worthwhile donation to them, if she would agree to come and talk to the boys about their work. She readily agreed to the suggestion and arrangements were made for her to give her talk a couple of weeks later, at a morning assembly.

Betty arrived just after nine o'clock on the appointed day. She seemed a little apprehensive at first, so Laura gave her a cup of coffee to calm her nerves. It was easy to understand her apprehension. The thought of having to contend with four hundred staring faces first thing in the morning was enough to give anyone the jitters. Having long since overcome the jitters himself, Biggs only reaction to the staring faces was, 'God, what the hell am I doing here?'

Harry Langton took the assembly and introduced Betty to the assembled multitude. After a somewhat hesitant start, she quickly got into her stride and, with the aid of some specially adapted demonstration toys, gave a very interesting talk. The boys listened attentively and gave her a round of applause when she finished.

A young anklebiter presented Betty with a cheque for five hundred pounds. She appeared to be rather taken aback by the amount, but quickly recovered her composure and thanked the boys for their generous donation and for their effort in raising the money. After the assembly they learnt that the Toy Library were only expecting something in the order of fifty pounds, hence Betty's surprise at the size of the cheque. They all polished their halos!

The previous year a donation had been made towards the training of a guide dog for the blind. A visually handicapped lady had given a very interesting talk and demonstration with her dog. A photograph of a German shepherd, named Cindy, for whose training the school paid, hung outside the general office and served as a constant reminder to the boys of their generous gift. When making charitable donations to worthwhile causes, it was always thought desirable for the boys to be able to see something tangible for their effort. That always seemed preferable to sending money to some national charity, where any contribution would be little more than a drop in the ocean.

The Falklands war had continued a pace with no let up in the interest shown by the boys. With the taking of Port Stanley, the final victory and surrender of the Argentineans, came euphoria. Understandably the boys regarded Mrs. Thatcher as the best thing since sliced bread. She was the epitome of everything great in Great Britain and no amount of attempted indoctrination to the contrary by the Lefties was able to convince them otherwise. Of course ever since an age when they had become politically aware she had been Tory Leader. She had been Prime Minster for three years and was destined to remain so long after they were due to leave school. They may not have been able to name many other government ministers, but they certainly knew who the Prime Minster was. The Iron Lady was as much a heroine in the eyes of Biggs as she was in the eyes of the boys. Of course as far as the Lefties were concerned, this put him on the far Right of Attila the Hun. But he had little regard for their views and simply didn't care what they thought of him. In fact throughout much of the conflict with Argentina, he took great delight in winding them up at the slightest opportunity. On his office desk he had a small union flag.

CHAPTER 25

RAFFLES. Since the start of the term Biggs had been vaguely aware that loose change, normally kept in the left hand pocket of his jacket, had been noticeable by its scarcity. The jacket usually hung over the back of a chair in his office. The door was often left open and it occurred to him that an opportunist could have been entering and rifling his pockets! This theory clearly needed putting to the test, so he set about devising a stratagem for catching the culprit.

"Fill the pocket with paint," Ian McTaggart suggested, very much tongue in cheek.

It was the sort of zany remark that everyone had come to expect from him, the mentality of his anklebiters clearly rubbing off. He may have been joking, but it gave Biggs an idea; a false pocket, filled not with paint, but gentian violet! Gentian violet is a harmless vegetable dye obtainable from most chemists. Once in contact with the skin, it leaves a deep violet stain that is very difficult to wash off. Biggs asked Laura looked for a suitable strong plastic bag to make a false inner lining to the pocket. Meanwhile, he purchased the dye from the chemist across the road. The bag was carefully taped inside the pocket. Some loose change as bait, together with a liberal quantity of the violet dye was placed inside. With the jacket in its usual position, draped over the back of the chair, the trap was set. 'Come into my parlour said the spider to the fly.'

Biggs had to go to the Upper School third period to take a Fifth Year group for Maths. This meant that he would be away from the annexe for the rest of the morning, giving the thief time to operate. They were not his regular Maths class, but he had taken them the previous year and their regular teacher, Harry Knight, was going to be away for several weeks following a minor operation. They were quite a pleasant group and Biggs volunteered to take them, on the strict understanding that he would not be required to cover any other absent teachers while Harry Knight was away. Taking them had the additional benefit of getting him out of the Lower School for a while. In the Upper School, he always had a respite from having to deal with the shortcomings of others.

Harry and Biggs had always got on together, both sharing a sensible no-nonsense approach to the teaching of Mathematics. They had one other thing in common, namely flying. Although he no longer flew, Harry had been an RAF pilot during the Second World War. He had apparently spent most his war flying over the North Atlantic ocean hunting for German U-boats. His proud boast was that for the entire duration of the conflict, he hadn't spotted a single enemy submarine, let alone sink one! For the previous four years they had together taken groups of boys to the Welsh mountains, always camping at Lake Bala, the last occasion being when Alan and Christopher had skinny-dipped in the lake. It was because of Harry's impending operation that they had decided to give the trip a miss that year.

Returning to the annexe just after the start of the lunch break, he went straight to his office to examine his coat and sure enough, the change was missing. The next step was to find the culprit without raising his suspicion and before he had a chance to scrub off the dye. The majority of the boys had school lunch, so Biggs guessed that the best chance would be in the dining hall, when most of the boys would be together. Trying not to make it look too obvious, he casually wandered round the dining hall with Ian McTaggart looking for the telltale signs. The culprit was soon found, stuffing chocolate pudding into his mouth. Both hands were deeply stained with the violet dye. It was Nicholas Walton. He had joined the school the previous year, having been given the order of the boot from his previous school for being an out-and-out little sod. Known as Nick-the-Dip, he was Gordon Bennett's very own Raffles. He was hauled from the dining hall, protesting his innocents, his mouth still full of chocolate pudding.

It was not the first time that Biggs had been the victim of Nick-the-Dip and he cursed himself for not suspecting him earlier. The previous year he had mislaid his pocket calculator and he suspected that it had been stolen. It was an expensive scientific model in a simulated leather case. Some weeks later when covering a Maths lesson for an absent colleague, he spotted Nick using a similar calculator. An examination of it confirmed his suspicion. The boy vehemently denied stealing it, maintaining that his mother had bought it for his birthday. Not believing a word he said, Biggs took the calculator from him and excluded him from school until such time as he could see his mother. Mrs. Walton came to the school in high dudgeon a couple of days later with her miscreant offspring. She confirmed that she had most certainly bought the calculator for his birthday. He was a truthful boy and he should have been believed! She accused Biggs of picking on her little darling because he was popular! When she had finished her diatribe, Biggs leaned forward without saying a word, holding up the calculator with the back of it facing her. He slowly pushed it upwards out of it's case, to reveal printed on the back, STOLEN FROM MR. SMITH. She went as red as a beetroot! She then turned her anger on her now not-so-little-darling and gave him a clip round the ear. She accused him of showing her up and of not even being clever with it! He was suspended for two weeks.

He had been suspected on several occasions of rifling the pockets of other boys in the changing rooms. He always vehemently denied the accusations and managed to cover his tracks well. Getting proof had always proved difficult and he'd invariably managed to get away with it. He clearly hadn't reckoned with Inspector Biggs on this occasion, however. Nothing concentrates the mind like being a victim of crime, albeit petty theft and stealing his loose change was Nick the Dip's undoing. In fact it proved to be his nemesis! Since Biggs was the victim, he thought it best for Harry Langton dealt with the little sod. Harry said that considering his previous record, the matter was too serious and referred him to the Headmaster. After initially denying the whole thing, despite the evidence of the dye, he finally confessed and asked for a whole string of other offences to be taken into consideration! They were and he was expelled!

Nick-the-Dip apart, there was very little pilfering at Gordon Bennett and belongings left lying around were usually handed in. Nick's expulsion certainly served to concentrate the minds of any would-be light fingers. No doubt a number of boys must have been aware of Nick's activities, but the jump from not stealing themselves, to grassing on others who do, is a big one. In any school, grassing on fellow pupils is just not the done thing. Of course Biggs' elite Maths Set had a special dispensation to grass on each other, but then they were a law unto themselves!

CHAPTER 26

COVER LESSONS. Having to cover lessons for absent members of staff is not the favorite pass-time of the average teacher. However, forfeiting non-contact time, otherwise known as free periods, has become an unfortunate necessity. Most teachers without additional responsibility at the secondary level, expect to get an average of one free period each day. They have also come to expect that they are likely lose a couple of them each week on cover. Secondary teachers are one up on Primary teachers, however, who get very little non-contact time.

Because senior staff have additional responsibilities they are in the fortunate situation of having a great deal more non-contact time then the average teacher. Of course much of this is taken up with organizing things, or at least pretending to organize things, seeing kids and parents and generally dealing the shortcomings of others. None the less it does give them a greater freedom to control their daily destiny. Having an office into which they can retreat is another great boon. Being able to shut out the world, even for a short time can be a great stress reliever. In short, rank has its privileges.

Harry Langton, normally responsible for cover, generally saw to it that Biggs did his fair share. In fact, Biggs always reckoned that he ended up doing more than his fair share. However, since he was to a large degree, able to organize his time to suit his own convenience, he was in a position to avoid doing cover on occasion. Bearing in mind that parents are notorious for not turning up on time for an appointment, Biggs usually arranged to see them in the middle of a double free period. This had a twofold advantage. Firstly, it allowed for a degree of latitude either way when they were not on time. Secondly and much more importantly, it meant that he couldn't be used for cover either period. "Sorry, Harry," he would say. "...... got to see a parent this morning." Harry Langton would then have to scurry off and find some other poor sod to do the cover.

It is usual for Primary school teachers to take their charges for the majority of their subjects and for this reason, they are generally thought to be all-knowing by their little darlings. However, at the secondary level there is much more specialization and the kids, who have now ceased to be little darlings, tend to compartmentalize their teachers into subject areas. Since having different teachers for different subjects is the norm, the notion that a teacher might be knowledgeable outside their own subject area, is at first a virtual nonstarter. However, after a couple of terms in their new school, the realization that this is not the case can be quite an eye-opener.

In case of Biggs, although generally regarded as a Maths teacher, his original qualifications were in Science, his specialty being Physics. Since only science teachers were normally allowed to cover classes in a laboratory, he was sometimes called upon to cover a science lesson. This avoided the need to find a spare classroom for the cover. He quite enjoyed taking the odd lesson, much as he had enjoyed taking Mr. Moid's Third Year Physics class on the first day of term. It gave him the opportunity to keep his hand in and to astound the kids with the extent of his scientific knowledge. He would sometimes ignored the work currently in hand and pick some topic at random that he thought would be of interest. Now most kids recognize the connection between Mathematics and Science, so it did not come as much of a surprise to them that a Maths teacher could have knowledge of things, scientific. History teachers on the other hand, were generally regarded by the kids as scientific illiterates, which for the most part they were. Of course, the Historians were one up on the Games teachers, who were generally regarded as just being illiterate. Receiving an end-of-year report from them, neatly written and without spelling mistakes often came as another eye-opener!

Having to cover a First Year Science lesson just after morning break on one particular occasion, Biggs wandered along to the laboratory to meet his class. He arrived to find them quietly lined up in an orderly fashion outside the laboratory...... A pleasing sight, he thought. He instantly recognized one of the boys as being Steven Bird, Christopher's brother. Obviously aware of the special understanding existing between his brother and Biggs, Steven regarded the meeting of eyes as an invitation to speak.

"Is that right that you've got an aeroplane, Sir?"

"Who told you that, Steven?"

"My brother, but it's not true, is it, Sir?"

"Why would Christopher tell you an untruth?"

"Because he's a porky teller. He does it all the time." Steven replied. "He also said that Mr. Langton used to be a British secret agent in MI5..... now that can't be true, can it, Sir?"

"Ah, I'm afraid that information is classified and can only be given out on a need to know basis......"

"AND WE DON'T NEED TO KNOW," the rest of the class chanted, before he had a chance to finish.

"You've got it."

As he let them into the laboratory using his master key, he mused to himself that Christopher had obviously been true to his word and told nobody about their flying exploit in his Piper Cub during the Easter holiday. Even his kid brother seemed not know about it! When the boys were seated he checked the class list for absentees. Biggs knew quite a few of them by name and quickly realized that one boy in particular, Gary Saunders, was noticeable by his absence. In fact, Gary was always noticeable! He had the dubious distinction of being the smallest boy in the school, but conversely, his lack of stature always made him stand out. It would of course be politically correct these days to say that he was vertically challenged, but the boys just referred to him as 'short-arse.'

"Where's Gary?" Biggs asked.

"Don't know, Sir," volunteered one of his classmates. "He was here before break."

Shortly after Biggs started talking to them, there was a timid knock on the door, which opened to reveal the sheepish face of Gary peering into the room. Obviously confused at seeing Biggs instead of his regular teacher, he looked round the room at his classmates to make sure that he had come to the right place.

"You're late. Where have you been?" Biggs asked him, as he approached his desk.

"I'm sorry, Sir," he said, sheepishly, "but I got carried away, Sir."

Now it's funny what can go through one's mind following such a remark. Biggs' immediate reaction was to think that Gary had been involved in some engaging activity and had become so engrossed that he had forgotten the time. But what activity, he couldn't think? It certainly never occurred to him to put any literal interpretation to Gary's reply and the rest of the class seemed as bemused as him.

"Carried away?......... What do you mean, you got carried away?"

"One of the boys from the Upper School picked me up and ran off with me, Sir," Gary replied, still with his sheepish expression.

Howls of laughter went round the class. It obviously hadn't occurred to them either, to put any literal interpretation to his excuse for being late.

"Who was it? Did he hurt you?" Biggs asked, now feeling some sympathy for the lad.

"No, Sir. He didn't hurt me," Gary confirmed. "I don't know who he was, but he was very big. He was quite friendly about it, though. He let me go at the end of the road and I ran back. I think he just did it for a joke!"

Biggs concluded from Gary's description of the kidnapper, that it was Andrew Bolton, returning to the Upper School after his music lesson with Mr. Hardcastle. He may have had the IQ of a daffodil, but he was certainly not without a sense of humour and it was the zany of sort thing he would do. Gary did not seem in the least put out by his experience, so bearing in mind that Andrew wouldn't be down for another week, the matter was left to ride.

Thinking back to the fact that Steven seemed not to know about Christopher's flight with him in the Cub, he reasoned that their mother must have lived up to her name and kept mum too! He wondered how much Steven did know? Collaring him after the lesson, he asked, "Is that right you went away with the Scouts over Easter, Steven?"

"Yes, Sir. How did you know I was in the Scouts?"

"Christopher told me. What did he do while you were away? Did he go to Norfolk with your mother to stay with her friend?"

"You seem to know an awful lot about what we do, Sir? I suppose he told you about that too?"

"We have no secrets between us..... Well, did he?"

"But..... you must know the answer to that, Sir. He said that he went to an RAF camp with you!" Steven looked suspiciously at Biggs!

"Oh yes, so he did! What else did he tell you?"

"He said that he enjoyed himself and that you took him up in a glider, Sir!"

"Nothing else?"

"No, Sir." What else is there?" He clearly couldn't understand why he was being subjected to an inquisition and suspected that he was being kept in the dark about something!

"Nothing, Steven," Biggs assured him, hoping to allay his suspicion. "I was just wondering how much Christopher told you about the camp, that's all?"

"Oh, right, Sir.... I'd better go, or I'll be late for my next lesson."

CHAPTER 27

A TOUCH OF THE VERNACULAR. No matter how well children may be taught English in school and no matter how many times they may be corrected regarding the grammatical construction of their sentences, they will always adopt the language of their peers. Ordinary everyday words with clearly defined meanings, are attributed with new meanings and the use of the oxymoron is legion. Schoolboy jargon transcends the playground, enters the classroom and all aspects of their life. It is general understood by the majority of adults, who of course were children once themselves. We are all aware that the accepted meaning of words can change over the generations, but unfortunately the newly adopted meanings often preclude the use of these words as was originally intended. When Biggs was a schoolboy, homosexuals were generally known as 'Fairies,' 'Pansies,' or 'Nancy boys.' Otherwise they would be referred to as being 'Camp' or 'Fruity.' 'Gay' simply meant happy or cheerful, while it's rather more derogatory counterpart, 'Queer' had little connotation other than peculiar or strange. Who would now take these words to mean anything other than homosexual? The new meanings of these words have not just entered our language, they have taken over and their use clearly cannot be regarded as slang.

Schoolboy slang is more temporary and not generally adopted by the rest of society. There are of course a few exceptions, a typical example being the use or rather misuse of 'Wicked.' Although defined as meaning evil or sinful, it is usually attributed by kids and a good many adults, to things that are good. At Gordon Bennett, things that were very good or brilliant were often referred to as 'Well Wicked.'

One wet Monday during the midday break, Christopher and his mate Tony were passing Biggs' office, having just finished their lunch. Seeing his door ajar and realizing that it wasn't very nice outside, they thought that it would be a good idea to invite themselves in for a coffee. When not on duty, Biggs usually spent his lunchtime with Laura in the general office or with Harry Langton, but Laura was in a grumpy mood, having started yet another diet and Harry was off roving somewhere. He rarely went to the staff room at lunchtime for fear of being descended upon by hoards of over demanding staff, expecting him to solve their myriad of petty problems. In no mood to put up with Laura's grumps, he decided that he would prefer his own company. He was relaxing in his armchair, thinking back to his last Summer holiday in Florida at Lake Marianna. Of course it wouldn't be too long before he would be back there again and he was looking forward to gently splashing down on the lake in the Piper seaplane again. He knew that he was wishing his life away, instead of living for the moment, but the trouble was that the moments seemed so uninspiring The future looked forbidding and he wondered where his life was going? He had no desire to become a Headmaster or even a Deputy Head, but the thought of remaining in his present roll for the next twenty or so years was just too mind numbing to contemplate. Had he perhaps taken a wrong turning at some stage in his life? He wasn't sure, but at that moment he wished that he could have been somewhere else! He was not looking forward to the week ahead and was feeling a bit low.

"Want some company?" Christopher asked, giving a cursory knock on the door and opening it slightly.

Looking up and seeing Christopher and Tony peering round his door, grinning like a pair of Cheshire cats, Biggs at once brightened up. Yes, he thought to himself, he would like some company. He knew it wasn't very nice out and that they were hoping to scrounge a cup of coffee, but that did not detract from the fact that they had sought out *his* company. They saw a enough of him in their Maths lessons and in Games, so he regarded it as pleasing that they should be seeking his company at other times.

"Why, if it isn't the Mr. Men! Yes, come in .... both of you. Shut the door and keep the plebs out."

"The Mr. Men!" Tony queried.

"Yes, that's right..... Mr. Smooth and Mr. Sidekick!"

"Do you mind, Sir. I'm not just Chris's sidekick, you know!" Tony said, indignantly.

"Now there's an overreaction, if ever I heard one! I didn't say that you were, Tony.... Of course, you realize that you rather walked into your own trap, by reacting as you did!"

"How do you mean, Sir?"

"You see the thing is, Tone," Christopher said, at once realizing the significance of Biggs' remark and before he had a chance to reply. "Sir didn't say *which* of us was Mr. Sidekick. You just *assumed* that you were! I think that our friend Sigmund might have had something to say about that, don't you, Tone?"

"Knickers!"

"In fact I think he would have said that you were revealing some sort of personality complex! What do you think, Sir?"

"Don't bring me into it, gentlemen..... Although, you did rather overreact, Tony, so I do think there might have been a bit of a Freudian slip hiding in there somewhere."

"I'd say it was a dead giveaway, Sir.... You also assumed, Tone, that *I* was Mr. Smooth, which of course is perfectly understandable!"

"Shut up, Chris," Tony said laughingly, unable to think of a suitable reply.

"Shut up!.... What a comeback?" Christopher said, rather rubbing it in. "Then there was the knickers, of course!.... I must remember to enter them in my book of witty repartees! They might come in useful one day, should I ever find myself arguing with a moron."

This is definitely better than suffering Laura's grumps, Biggs thought to himself! Tony just smiled, shaking his head. He knew that he had lost the battle of words with his friend.

"I don't know how you've put up with him all these years, Tony? Has he always been like it?"

"Always, Sir."

"So we've established that your not Mr. Sidekick, Tony. So who *do* you see yourself as then?"

"Mr. Charisma!"

Christopher fell about laughing! "Dream on, my son!"

"I suppose you'd both like a cup of coffee, gentlemen?"

"Yes please," said Tony. Christopher eagerly nodded agreement.

"Help yourself...... Milk's in the fridge."

"You've got your own coffee machine now!" Tony observed, rather surprised. "I thought you used the one in the office?"

"I do.... did, but it's always running out and I seem to be the only one who bothered to recharge it these days. Anyway it's nice to be independent and not have to rely on other people."

"So that you can offer a cup to your guests.... like us," Christopher suggested, with a grin, pouring out two cups for Tony and himself. "Do you want a refill, Sir?"

"Yes please..... Guests!"

"You invited us in, so that makes us your guests, doesn't it?"

"Yes ...... I suppose it does, although I think it might be truer to say that you invited yourselves in?. Anyway did you both have a good weekend? I suppose you were both hanging-out together, as always?

"What are you implying, Sir?" Tony said, with a smirk, taking the bait again. "We don't live in each other's pockets, you know!"

"Oh, I thought you did!..... Implying?... I was making no implication, Tony!"

"What he means, Sir," Christopher said, laughingly, ".... is no, we're not gay and no, we're not *coming-out*. But he's too embarrassed to say it." Christopher was clearly not in the least embarrassed to say such things.

"Chris, your impossible!" Tony said, turning a little red around the cheeks.

"I try to be!"

"Gentlemen, you do me an injustice! Nothing was further from my mind."

Christopher was as straight as a die, but his philosophy had always been, live and let live. He was certainly not in the least homophobic and, unlike many of his peers, he was prepared to act in a friendly manner towards anyone, which ever way they swung! Tony on the other hand, although by no means a homophobe, was a little more circumspect in his attitude to homosexuality!

"Anyway, Sir, in answer to your question, I had a well boring weekend," Christopher continued, passing Biggs his coffee and offering him a chocolate biscuit. "I had to look after my soppy cousin. She can be a right pain in the butt..... I suppose you were off flying somewhere again, Sir?"

"Yes, I was and I wish I still was."

"I wish I could go flying, Tony said. "It must be well wicked."

Biggs glanced at Christopher, who gave him a wink and the merest shake of the head, indicating that true to his word, he hadn't told his best friend about his flight in the Piper Cub some weeks earlier.

Biggs smiled. "I like your use of oxymorons."

"Oxywhats?" Tony said, somewhat bemused.

"Oxymorons...... Two opposites added together to reinforce one of them."

"Ah! .....you mean like *well wicked*?" Christopher said, catching on at once.

"That's right ..... and the other one you just used."

"*Well boring*!... Got it..... Oxymorons..... Must remember that.... I'll just trip it out casually, when we next have English with Mrs. Hickman..... She'll be well dumbfounded!"

Biggs smiled. "Of course, you realize that in your case, the stress has to be on the second half of the word!"

"So you think that we're a pair of morons, do you, Sir? ..... That's no way to treat your guests. We could take offence, you know..... except we know you don't really think that..... You don't, do you, Sir?"

"You know the answer to that, Chris. If I did, you wouldn't be here now. Drink your coffee and offer me another biscuit."

Apart from staid old English teachers like Malcolm Rowe, most members of staff wouldn't dream of correcting the kids in their unwitting use of oxymorons. Most of them regarded there use as quite acceptable and would occasionally lapse into the vernacular themselves.

Going into a classroom on one occasion while 'mock' exams were in full swing, the Harry Langton had been somewhat amused to find that a class tutor had written on the blackboard his interpretation of the marking scheme. A list read as follows:-

0%	to	19%	-	Disaster area.
20%	to	39%	-	Disappointing.
40%	to	59%	-	Middling.
60%	to	79%	-	Wicked.
80%	to	99%	-	Well Wicked
		100%	-	Impossible.

Usually the high-jacking of a word lasts for a couple of terms before another takes over, although 'Wicked' now seems to have entered into the permanent vocabulary of most schoolboys and quite a few adults. At least it's not as bad (or is it good?) as an earlier misuse of '*Bad*,' the meaning of which was completely reversed and taken to mean '*Good*.' At one stage there was the ridiculous situation of things that were very good or brilliant, being referred to as being '*Bad Good*,' an oxymoron to end all oxymorons. Fortunately this particular variation lasted for only a short time and the word reverted to its proper meaning. However, it was then usually attributed to things that were not liked or unpopular. It would be used in excess and with great emphasis, unpopular things being referred to as 'BAAD.'

From time to time various phrases would be in vogue. They would enter the kid's thesaurus of popular phrases. After excessive use, they would eventually be dropped, only to be revived at a later date. Examples that come to mind are:-

'We don't wish to know that.'	- On hearing something to their detriment.
'We must know these things.'	- When information was not forthcoming.
'Mega-overload.'	- Too much information forthcoming.
'Mega-masses'	- A very large amount.
'Trust me, I'm a pupil.'	- When teachers doubted them.

Teachers losing their cool when the kids misbehaved would be referred to as, 'Doing a nutty,' 'Throwing a wobbly,' 'Going Ape,' or 'Going spare.' The derivation of 'doing a nutty' or 'going ape' seems pretty obvious. 'Throwing a wobbly' is less obvious, but probably refers to a teacher being likened to lump of clay going horribly wrong on a potter's wheel. The derivation of 'going spare' remains a mystery!

Boys are notorious for the insults and abuses that they seem prepared to hurl at each other. But there is of course, an etiquette which always has to be observed! It's quite acceptable to insult one's friends and near acquaintances, but enemies should not be insulted, unless they are smaller..... that is if you want to avoid a punch-up! The use of surnames outside the public school sector is not common and most boys address each other by their first names, a nickname or just 'Hey, you!' A plethora of abusive nicknames would always abound, usually emphasizing some facial feature or some other bodily shortcoming. At the more acceptable end of the scale would be such names as lofty, shorty and four-eyes. At the less acceptable end would be such names as dick-head, jug-ears, dragon-breath and the most insulting of all ...... wanker! The brighter element at Gordon Bennett always regarded it as clever to make use of euphemistic substitutes for sexual organs. Thus, *Balls* would be referred to by the more refined mathematicians as *Spherical objects*, an observation originally made by Biggs to a boy who had been spouting him a load of crap!

Boys have been known to divide themselves into Cavaliers and Roundheads. On this side of the pond, the Cavaliers are generally in the majority, that is of course, unless the school has a large predominance of Jewish boys. On the American side of the pond, the roundheads are usually predominant. Of course, such a division would not be possible in a girl's school, since they would not have the wherewithal to make the distinction! No doubt this distinction would be of more than a passing interest to girls in a co-educational establishment, investigations presumably taking place behind the bike sheds!

Of course, kids will always dream up nicknames for their teachers. These can be equally as abusive as those they seem prepared hurl at each other. Fortunately they usually have the common courtesy to use them behind their backs. To their faces, they are generally respectful, although on one occasion Biggs was addressed by one young anklebiter as Mr. Biggs. The young lad actually thought that it was his name! There was some doubt as to whether or not he thought his first name was Ronnie!

The staff are much more circumspect in their method of addressing each other. Unless the are drinking buddies or colleagues in the same department, 'Mister' is the normally accepted form, particularly in larger schools. Although oddly enough, Harry Langton was usually known as Harry, by all but the most junior members of staff. He rarely used the first names of his subordinates, however and he usually addressed them as 'Mister.' But it was hardly a term of respect for another colleague, since he had the annoying knack of stressing Mister in such a way that it could be taken as a put-down. Most of us are familiar with the way in which 'Sir,' can be used in a similar manner!

Malcolm Rowe related in G19 one evening, how he had been stopped for speeding earlier in the week. He obviously hadn't been using his rear view mirror, that is until he had been awakened by the *blues and twos* of the police car behind. He pulled over to the side of the road and waited apprehensively for what seemed an eternity. A radio check on his car having been completed, he was eventually approached from behind by one of the white-capped traffic officers (the worst kind to be stopped by). The very large and imposing figure of the officer proceeded to wander round Malcolm's car, without saying a word, as though it had a couple of hours to kill. Then after checking his tax disc, it eventually spoke, saying sarcastically, "Good afternoon, *SIR* ..... Motoring a bit, weren't we?"

Malcolm, apparently having lost touch with reality and the seriousness of his predicament, had replied, "Good afternoon, *SIR*.... Strutting a bit, weren't we?" A piercing glare from the officer, indicating that he lacked even the slightest excuse for a sense of humour, finally brought Malcolm back to reality, causing him to adopted a more sensible and deferential stance. From then on it was a classic case of, Yes Sir, No Sir, Three bags full, Sir. It obviously paid off, since he was let off with a warning.

CHAPTER 28

CRIME AND PUNISHMENT. At Gordon Bennett they always endeavoured to make the punishment fit the crime. This was in fact very fitting, since most of the staff regarded the goings-on as a bit of a comic opera. In any school, not only is it essential for justice to be done and seen to be done, it has to be seen as fair in the eyes of the kids. Kids in general and teenage boys in particular, are not adverse to being punished, as long as they see the punishment as fair....... 'It's a fair cop, Sir!'

Several years earlier the use of the cane had been abandoned as the antepenultimate deterrent. As with any school, the ultimate deterrent was expulsion, with exclusion or suspension as the penultimate.

The decision to abandon the cane was made unilaterally, by the Headmaster of the time, a Mr. William Rayner. The staff were very much taken aback by his sudden edict, which came completely out of the blue. At the first staff meeting following his appointment, he informed them of his intention to abandon its use there and then. There had been no consultation with the staff and to say the least, they were not best pleased. At the time there was a move afoot to end the use of corporal punishment in schools and presumably he had jumped on the band wagon to secure his appointment as Headmaster. This had been a very hypercritical act on his part, since at his previous school he had been known as 'Caner Rayner.' Virtually his last act as Deputy Head was to cane a boy for stamping on a daffodil in the school grounds! It wouldn't have been so bad if he hadn't announced in morning assembly that the cane was to be no more! It would have been far better to have just let its use die a natural death and he was advised in the strongest possible terms not to make the announcement. The protestations of the staff fell on deaf ears, however and he insisted that it was best to be 'up-front' with the kids. As a Headmaster he was next to useless and being up-front with the kids failed to get him their respect. Fortunately he only remained at Gordon Bennett for a couple of years, before moving to pastures greener, leaving them with the legacy of being a non-caning school. He moved to leafy Surrey to become Headmaster of a larger school in an up-market area. Apparently he made no attempt to abandon the cane at his new school!

The use of corporal punishment at Gordon Bennett had always been minimal, but it had always been there as a deterrent. There wasn't any noticeable deterioration in the behaviour of the kids following its abandonment, but it posed the problem of what to put in its place? Corporal punishment once abandoned is very difficult to reinstate! Of course there were the old chestnuts, such as detentions and impositions and for some time there was a noticeable increase in the number of exclusions. There were also a few rather unusual, if not bizarre forms of punishment which came to light.

Biggs had to see a parent who arrived without appointment one morning, complaining that the previous day her son had been made to drink salt water as a punishment! He found it difficult to keep a straight face and didn't really see what she was complaining about, or for that matter, what he was expected to do about it? He told the mother that it was the first that he'd heard of the incident, but that he would look into the matter and get back to her. She seemed well enough satisfied and left. Of course when it came to punishments, Biggs was no stranger to bizarre himself! He recalled the incident of soap-licking with young Timothy Warmer earlier in the year. He'd had no comeback, so presumably Timothy hadn't gone whingeing to his parents about it!

The teacher responsible for administering the salt water punishment was their notorious Mr. Ho Wong, who taught the lad Biology. Boris Ho Wong was Head of Science and normally based in the Upper School. He came to the annexe twice weekly to teach a Second Year group. Further investigation revealed that the salt water incident was true. It was given because the boy had refused to believe that the tongue recognized only four tastes, namely, *sweet*, *sour*, *bitter* and *salt* and that other taste sensations came from reinforcements, to the larger extent from the sense of smell and to a lesser extent, from sight! Biggs got back to the mother the following day saying that it wasn't really a punishment, but simply a taste-test and that her son must have got the wrong end of the stick! She actually believed him and gave her son a ticking-off for wasting her time and making her look a fool!

Boris kept a number of variations on the Chinese water torture up his sleeve. On one occasion the previous term, a parent had complained to Harry Langton that Boris had kept her son in during morning break as a punishment. Apparently he had been made to count the number of drips from a dripping tap in the laboratory. He had to log each one individually and note the time of drip as indicated on a stop-clock. His final task, given as an additional homework imposition, had been to display his results graphically on a Drip/Time graph! The punishment, given because the boy had been squirting water at one of his classmates, seemed eminently suitable and Harry said as much to the mother.

Biggs was never an advocate of *lines* or written impositions as punishments, since these frequently served to put the wrongdoer off writing altogether. There were also the professional line-writers and essay-writers to contend with, boys who for a negotiable fee would undertake to complete impositions on behalf of their clients. Essays always demanded a higher fee than lines, since they required a degree of mental activity, a commodity often in short supply. One ingenious line-writer went so far as tape three pens together so that he could increase his productivity by writing three lines at a time. It was always advisable to check a boy's handwriting, before accepting an imposition as being genuine!

Detentions were a necessity, but had the disadvantage of keeping in the teacher as well as the miscreants. There was for a time at Gordon Bennett, a formal detention class each evening with volunteer teachers on a detention duty rota. Only those teachers volunteering their service were allowed to make use of the facility. But it was only too easy for size of the class to become unmanageable and there was a clear application of Parkinson's Law, in that the number of detainees always seemed to expand to fill the available places. Two or three miscreants together are manageable, but twenty of the sods can be a different kettle of fish. It introduced more problems than it solved and was eventually scrapped. Biggs never used the facility, since he thought that it tended to divorce the punishment from the crime in the eyes of the kids. He also regarded it as an easy cop-out for ineffective teachers.

Always in favour of the short sharp shock, he usually relied on elbow tweaking and press-ups for minor misdemeanors, but he was not adverse to the occasional rapping of knuckles with a ruler. Of course nowadays in the present political climate, many would regard the rapper, guilty of an assault and the rapped of having his human rights violated. Such ideas counted for nothing at the time. Of course, it always paid to know which boys would be prepared to accept having their knuckles rapped for a minor transgression and which were likely to complain to their parents. What worked for one boy would not necessarily be suitable for another. Also, a boy might well accept from one teacher, what he would not be prepared to accept from another! Between rapper and rapped there has to be a rapport!

Biggs had cause to rap Christopher over the knuckles one Maths lesson, when he came close to overstepping the limit of his agreed latitude in repartee. As always, he was sitting next to his mate Tony Roberts. Their desks were immediately in front of Biggs' desk, so they were both in knuckle-rapping range without him having to get up. Naturally he accepted the reprimand without complaint and at once apologized for his indiscretion. However, a few moments later and very much tongue in cheek, he said with a slight smirk, "Of course, you know that I could tell my mum that you hit me, Sir."

"Umm...... yes...... you could," mused Biggs. "...... but you won't!"

"How do you know, Sir?" Christopher demanded.

"Because you're not that sort of boy...... who goes running to his parents, complaining at the least little thing. In any case, you know that it wouldn't be in your interest!"

"How do you mean, Sir?"

"I let you get away with too many things..... doing and saying things that I would normally jump on if other boys did or said them..... You know that it wouldn't be in your interest to rock the boat Apart from that your mother would probably give you a clip round the ear for being cheeky."

Christopher's smirk changed to a broad grin, as his mate Tony shook his head, saying, "You've really got us sussed, haven't you, Sir?"

"You can bet your life on it, gentlemen!"

Between the rapper and rapped, there has to be a rapport!

Knuckle rapping, elbow tweaking and press-ups aside, for more serious offences there was....... *The Run*! Biggs got the idea from reading an article about a well known Scottish Public School, in which the boys would be given a number of laps of the school field to complete in their PE kit. The boys were not supervised, but simply on trust to complete their punishment. The idea transposed well to Gordon Bennett. Anklebiters were required to complete a set number of laps of the playground, while the older boys would have to lap the school field. A variation for the older boys would be to run to a nearby park and obtain some useless piece of information from a particular notice in the park. Biggs rarely stayed to watch the boys complete their punishment and he would sometimes make a point of making sure that they saw him leave while they were still in the middle of their run. However, first thing the following morning, they always had to report to him that they had completed their task. The boys thought that he would always be able detect a lie, so they never did lie! Biggs was not sure that he always could, but the important thing was that the kids thought that he could and that's what counted! Of course they had no way of knowing if they were being watched or if another teacher had been asked to keep an eye on them. It was all a game of bluff! If the boys turned up with their PE kit ready to complete their run and the offence was minor, Biggs would occasionally let them off, or substitute press-ups instead. A willingness to do their punishment without complaint, he regarded as very much in their favour. As a special dispensation, Christopher did not to have to report the following morning after a run! The dispensation was given simply on the grounds that he *was* Christopher and as such would not dream of trying to pull a fast-one! His mate Tony had a partial dispensation, in that he didn't have to report if he'd suffered the same punishment as Christopher and they did their run together.

Another weapon in Biggs' armory was that of the *Confessional*. He got the idea from the first school at which he taught after leaving college. It was a Catholic boy's school in North Kent. Now long since closed and replaced by a housing estate, it was originally run by a band of Brothers, the Headmaster being a notorious Brother Dominic. Caner Rayner wouldn't have been able to hold a candle to Brother Dominic! Apparently thrashings were common place, even for minor offences. The Brothers had been replaced by lay teachers a couple of years before Biggs joined the school, but most the older boys still had cause to remembered them. Although all the boys at the school were Catholic, about a third of the staff, including Biggs, were not.

Friday was confession day! At eleven o'clock the confession bell would ring and any boys who wished, would get up, without so much as a by-your-leave and walk out of their lessons. They would then go the church adjoining the school to confess their sins! Usually three of four boys in each class would avail themselves of the opportunity. Of course, it was always the little sods and trouble makers who would endeavour to purge themselves, so that they could embark on their next round of mischief with a clear conscience.

Not being a Catholic, Biggs was not privy to the secrets of the confessional, but he had seen enough television to get a good idea of what went on. Deciding to give it a try at Gordon Bennett, he was surprised at first how effective it proved to be. It was most effective with boys who were prepared to play the game and, as with the knuckle-rapping, with whom it was possible to have a rapport. If he suspected that they had transgressed in some way, but had no proof, they would be summoned to a *Confessional* in his office. Of course the majority of kids not being Catholic, it had at first been necessary to explain to them how it worked what was required of them. But they soon got the hang of it and after a while it was only necessary for him to say, 'Confession time.'

It always worked best if there were two or three transgressors together and preferably friends. That way each boy would see that the others came clean. A lone confessor was more likely to try to hide the truth. Again it was a game of bluff, since they had no way of knowing how much he knew. They always knew, however, that any punishment visited on them would be much more severe if they lied or tried to cover up their wrongdoing. Boys guilty of the offence under investigation would invariably confess.

If they were not guilty, confusion would be apparent, but in an attempt to wipe the slate clean, they would search through their collective memory banks and download a whole list of other things that weren't known about!

Occasionally, when in a devilish mood, Biggs would summon two or three likely characters to a confessional when no offence was under investigation, purely on the basis that they were likely to have done something untoward since their last confession. It never failed to uncover some misdemeanor or other. To obtain absolution the boys would have to complete their metaphorical Hail Marys, usually in the form of a run. Thus purged of their sins, they were free to embark on another series of transgressions before their next confessional.

Needless to say Christopher and his mates were occasional attendees at these sessions. Being very astute, Christopher quickly realized that it was all a game of bluff, but knowing that he was allowed to get away with a great deal and not wishing to rock the boat, he always went along with it and played the game. He said as much a couple of years later. Although he could at times be cheeky, he was rarely guilty of any serious wrongdoing and as time went on he had to attend fewer and fewer sessions.

Harry Langton was known for devising some bizarre forms of punishment. Biggs wandered along to his office one day after school for a chat and hoping to scrounge a glass of sherry. He was somewhat surprised to find a Second Year boy wearing a dog collar and lead, tied to Harry's door handle! It was an uncommon sight, even by Gordon Bennett's standards!

A number of anklebiters were standing in line to attention, obviously in trouble. Brenda Hickman was their English teacher and she was standing next to Harry while he remonstrated with the little monsters. The Second year boy had been put on 'hold' by Harry, while he dealt with the anklebiters. Biggs whispered to the lad, asking him if he was in trouble? He said that he was, but 'Only a little bit.' Untying the knot he led him off saying, 'WALKIES,' in the fashion of a well known lady dog trainer, who had been on television earlier that week. Not surprisingly, Harry's young anklebiters were reduced to hysterics. Brenda Hickman tried unsuccessfully to stifle a giggle and Harry just stared in amazement. Biggs returned about thirty seconds later and retied his lead. The lad responded well to the command, 'SIT,' much to the further amusement of Brenda and her anklebiters. Harry feigned not to be amused..... at least Biggs assumed that he was feigning. He reasoned that any teacher who would go the trouble of attaching a dog's collar and lead to a boy and then tie him to his door handle, could hardly be expected to be taken seriously! Just in case Harry wasn't though, he thought that it would be prudent to forgo the chat and the sherry and make a quick exit.

CHAPTER 29

THEIR JUST REWARD. The teacher's pay claim had been settled at last. It was long overdue, the negotiations having been going on for almost a year. They all looked forward to getting a sizable lump sum in back pay. On the down side, there were rumours in the educational press of future job cuts. Everyone hoped that they were only rumours! However a group of highly amused teachers were one day gathered round the staff room notice board, to which some wag had pinned a large notice. It read:-

Following the possibility of teaching staff cuts recently outlined in the press, the following suggestions for suitable alternative employment are offered.:-

Harry Langton	-	Reporter for Skivers Weekly.
Ray Smith (Biggs)	-	Kamikaze pilot.
Alan Howlett	-	Sumo wrestler.
Lynn Harmon	-	Page three girl.
Boris Ho Wong	-	Lord High Executioner.
Paul Scobie	-	Editor of Hippie Weekly.
Peter Partridge	-	Rent Boy.
Jimmy Bunting	-	Ship's Fog horn.
Don Royston	-	The invisible man.
Headmaster	-	Teaching.

Anon.

Conspicuous by his absence and everybody's guess for Anon was Ian McTaggart.

The news regarding the pay rise had obviously reached the troops. During a Maths lesson one morning, shortly after the announcement of the settlement, Christopher asked, "What are you going to do with all that extra money, Sir."

"What extra money?"

"You know, Sir," chipped in Alan Lane, from the back of the room. "..... your pay rise..... how much do you get now?"

"Not nearly enough," he assured them. "I've told you before...... all teachers are over worked and under paid."

"You must be joking," Alan continued. "Over paid and under worked is more like it..... and look at all the holidays they get...... and they get paid for them."

"Doesn't your dad get paid for his holidays, Alan?"

"Yes, but he doesn't get THIRTEEN weeks!"

"Anyway, holidays have nothing to do with it," Biggs said. "We need them to recover from the trauma of teaching you lot throughout the year."

"I suppose you'll be buying another new car," Alan continued, undaunted.

"He needs to buy himself a new squash racquet," Christopher, said. "It might improve his game. I always have to throw away a couple of points each time we play, so as to make a game of it."

"Ouch. Let go, Sir.... that's my racquet arm," he pleaded, cringing helplessly on floor, following a mega session of elbow tweaking.

The end of term was in sight, just a few short weeks away. The public examinations were over and many Fifth and Sixth Formers would soon be leaving. Having enjoyed, or in some cases suffered the protective custody of school for more than a decade, they were about to embark on the next stage of their lives in the big bad world outside school. Those returning next year, either to commence or continue their A-Level studies, would have to suffer the final few weeks, along with the rest of the school. The internal mini-exams were also over and the end of year reports were being prepared. In short the school year was coming to a close, the long summer holidays were beckoning and there was an air if expectancy abroad!

"So when are we having our day out, Sir?" Tony asked.

"Day out?" Biggs queried, but knowing full well to what Tony was referring.

"Our Express Set day out," Christopher said, apparently having now fully recovered from his session of elbow-tweaking. "You know...... for working so hard and for being so brilliant. Just think of all that extra homework we've been doing. Mega-masses of it....... and without complaining." Biggs raised both eyebrows. "Well, without complaining too much........ In fact hardly complaining at all."

Biggs smiled. He had taken them for a day out the previous year when they had been in Second Year Set One Maths. It had been their reward for working hard throughout the year and for doing masses of extra homework. They had caught a train to Otford and gone on a hike through the Shoreham valley to Eynsford. He remembered having a nice pub lunch in the village of Shoreham with Ray Dennard while they amused themselves playing football. Later when they finally arrived at Eynsford, they had paddled in the river by the ford. Thirteen years old and the brightest kids in the school, but they hadn't been too old to paddle in the river and make fools of themselves! He remembered how they had been fooling around and splashing each other with water and how Alan Lane, having been pushed over by Tony, ended up sitting in the stream. It had been less than a foot deep, but he still had to go home on the train with a wet backside! It was the third year running that he had taken a number of different groups on the *Shoreham walk*, as he always referred to it. And this year?..... yes, they had worked even harder and Christopher was right..... they *had* done masses of extra homework, mostly without complaint. And to cap it all, without exception, they had performed brilliantly in their end of year examination. He had no doubt in his mind that his protégé would sail through their 'mocks' and their O-Levels the following year. He knew that he would be taking them and that it was in his interest to keep them sweet! But he was sure that they wouldn't settle for another hike through the countryside this time. After all they were a year older and were sure to have greater expectations.

"Fair enough...... Where do you want to go?"

"MARGATE," they all chanted in unison. They had clearly discussed the matter amongst themselves beforehand!

"Okay. But there's no money available to subsidize it, so it means paying the full cost yourselves and the chance of getting a coach at this late stage is nil. It'll mean going by train...... Still want to go?"

"YES," came back the unanimous reply.

They arranged to go on the Thursday of the following week. It was necessary to have two teachers with twenty-five boys, so he asked Ray Dennard if he wanted to accompany them again. Ray didn't need much convincing that a day trip to Margate was infinitely better than another day in school, so he readily agreed.

One or two of the more objectionable members of staff, finding out that Biggs was taking his *elite* out for the day registered their disapproval. There were *official* days-out for each tutor group and the details of these were to be published in the weekly bulletin, but the Margate trip was extra and very much *unofficial*. He was endevouring to keep it low profile and he told the boys not to broadcast the trip, but that didn't stop some of the staff from finding out. It only took a careless word, overheard by some other boys, for the information to become common knowledge.

"That sod Bird gave me a load of lip this morning," Paul Scobie said. "When I asked him why *they* should have the privilege of having a 'jolly' to Margate, he said it wasn't a jolly, it was a maths project! And then when I queried that, he said that they were going to count the bikini tops on the beach as part of their work in statistics."

"Really! That was very imaginative of him!" Biggs said. "What's it got to do with you, anyway? You don't take Bird, so why were you accosting him round the school and asking about their trip. *I'm* the one you should be asking. And as for his answer, I told them to say it was a Maths project, if some busybody started giving them the third-degree." The bikini tops were of course Christopher's idea!

"Typical," snorted the Hippie. "Then his sidekick Roberts said that they had to estimate bust size for each bikini and find the ratio of bikinis to one-piece bathing costumes." Biggs smiled inwardly to himself. He could just imagine Tony and Christopher attempting to wind-up the

Hippie by saying such things. "They're all too full of themselves..... and you let them get away with bloody murder."

Biggs knew that he let them get away with a great deal, but couldn't be bothered to reply. He just shook his head and smiled, thinking to himself, if you didn't like the answer, you shouldn't have asked the question!

They arranged to meet at the railway station just after 9 am in time to catch the 9.20 train to Margate. The cost of the trip had been kept to a minimum by traveling after 9 am, when it was a lot cheaper. Biggs and Ray Dennard left their cars at school and walked to the station. They arrived to be met with a greeting of "Here comes *Two-Ray!*" They both smiled. They had met with the same greeting the previous year when they had met at the station before embarking on their hike through the Shoreham valley. There were two twin lads in the Third Year, named Michael and David Shea. They were identical twins and very difficult to tell apart, so when they were together, the boys simply referred to them as *Two-Shea. Two-Ray*, I like it, Biggs thought to himself. Casual dress was the order of the day and the boys had been told that they could wear what they liked, providing they didn't come looking like a load of scruffs. Quite a few of the boys wore shorts and Biggs sported his silk Hawaiian shirt. Christopher and Tony wore baseball caps, Christopher wearing his backwards!

"How do you *increase* your intelligence by ten percent," Biggs asked, throwing out a general question, but looking at Tony.

"Don't know, Sir. How?" Christopher asked on behalf of them all.

"Wear a baseball cap, of course!.... And how do you *decrease* your intelligence by ninety percent?" He was now looking straight at Christopher!

"Yes, we know, Sir," Christopher said with a grin, obviously anticipating the answer.

"WEAR IT BACKWARDS!" the rest chanted.

"That's the trouble with this Maths set," Christopher said. "Everyone thinks he's a bleeding comedian!" He had obviously remembered the remark made by Roy Roberts, following the incident with the marmite soldiers at West Malling!

It was a glorious Summer's day. The train journey was uneventful, but the boys were in a bubbly mood and obviously excited at the prospect of their day out in Margate. One group played cards, while the rest chatted away merrily, telling the odd corny joke.

"Did you hear the one about the kid who complained to his mother that a man with no arms had made an improper suggestion to him?" Alan Lane asked.

"No, but I'm sure you're going to tells us," Tony said.

"His mother told him not to worry about it..... He was 'armless!"

"God! Now where have I heard that one before," Ray Dennard remarked

"I don't think that was a very nice joke, Alan?" Christopher said. ".... making jokes about people with no arms! In fact, I think it was not nice at all. It was a very *armist* joke. ..... What do you think, Sir?"

This isn't the Christopher that I know, Biggs thought to himself. He's got to be leading up to topping Alan with a better joke!

"It wasn't even very funny, Alan" Christopher continued, without waiting for a reply. "In fact, it was nowhere near as funny as what happened to the man with no legs."

I knew it, Biggs thought to himself. Here it comes!

"What happened to him?" Tony asked, playing the straight man.

"Oh, he was arrested by the Old Bill for arsing about!"

The compartment roared with laughter.

"That was a very *legist* joke, Christopher," Biggs said. "Hit him for me, Tony."

Tony thumped down hard on Christopher's knee with his knuckle, giving him a painful dead-leg. They may have been best friends, but Tony wasn't going to miss out on a chance to cause his friend a little discomfort!

"Sorry, Sir," Christopher said laughingly, but holding his knee. ".... but I just couldn't resist it." He continued to hold his knee and roll about on his seat, rather overplayed the agony routine. "That hurt, Sir."

"You should be an actor, Chris," Biggs said. "In fact, I think you deserve an Oscar for that performance!"

Christopher made no attempt to get back at Tony for giving him his dead-leg. Tony had only been doing as he'd been bid, even if he had enjoyed it. He knew that he would have done the same in his position.

The train pulled into the station just before eleven o'clock and they set off for Dreamland. Biggs had no intention of following them around all day, so after being briefed as to their behaviour, the boys were left to enjoy themselves. It was obviously time for the two Rays to adjourn to a local public hostelry for a well earned nogging.

They would all be meeting up at 3.45 p.m. for the return journey.

After sufficient oesophagal lubrication they thought that they had better return to the fun-fare to check that everything was in order and the lads were not getting into any mischief. Biggs knew that they wouldn't be. He knew that they wouldn't dream of doing anything to cause him embarrassment, but it was his duty to check and anyway he wanted to have a go on a few rides himself.

Christopher, Tony and Alan were just about to go on the Big Dipper and on seeing the two Rays, challenged them to join them on the ride. Ray Dennard declined saying that he had a gippy tummy, a white lie, but Biggs knew that he couldn't refuse without being called chicken. The boys would have delighted in making cluck-clucking noises all the way home on the train and he wasn't going to have that. He climbed aboard, sitting next to Christopher and immediately behind Tony and Alan. The car climbed tortuously up the steep incline before descending into its routine of sick-making twists and turns, pulling G-forces that he wouldn't have dreamed of pulling in the Tiger Moth. They were pushed hard into their seats and were battered from side to side and the ride seemed to go on for an eternity. But eventually and much to Biggs' relief, they finally slid into the station. As they came to a halt, Christopher looked at him to check his reaction, probably hoping to see him turning a sickly shade of green.

Biggs hadn't enjoyed the ride, in fact he'd hated it, but he couldn't let Christopher see that, so turning to him he said with a bemused look, "When's it going to start then?"

"Nice one, Sir."

After a gentle turn on the Big Wheel, the two Rays left the boys to it and went in search of a good licensed restaurant. They found a suitable one overlooking the sea and partook of a fish and chips lunch, washed down with two pints of lager. During a turn along the promenade after their meal, they encountered several of their lads chatting up a group of girls and doing battle with sticks of candy floss. Christopher, Tony and Alan had also left the fun-fair and were leaning on the promenade railings looking down at the beach, probably counting bikini tops.

"What's the ratio, then?" Biggs asked.

The boys at first looked puzzled by the question, but eventually the penny dropped!

"You've been talking to Mr. Scobie, haven't you, Sir," Christopher said with a grin. Then plucking a figure out of the blue, ".... I reckon it's about seventy to twenty-nine, in favour of bikinis."

"Twenty-nine? What happened to the odd one?"

"Nudies. Well at least semi-nudies," Christopher said, pointing to a young lady in the distance, sunbathing topless. "Does that count as a one or two-piece?"

"A half-piece," Biggs said, then looking at Ray Dennard, "Wouldn't it be nice if some appreciative lads thought that it might be a good idea to buy their teachers an ice cream for taking them out for the day."

"Yes, that would be a nice gesture, wouldn't it?" Ray concurred.

"What?" Alan demanded. You've had a day out as well! You've only been doing your job and you've spent most of the time in the pub, so why should we buy you an ice cream?" Alan wasn't noted for his generous nature.

Alan received a thump on the arm from Christopher. "Don't be so mean, Alan," he rebuked him. "I suppose you'd rather be back in school? ..... Just ignore him, Sir. He's just an old meany!... I'll get them."

He returned a few minutes later holding four 99s, one for himself and Tony and one each for the two Rays. He declined Biggs' offer to pay for them.

"It's my treat, Sir. We're not all as tightfisted as Alan."

"Where's mine?" Alan demanded.

"Spherical objects," Christopher said.

It was almost time to return, so after wandering back to the Dreamland entrance where they had all arranged to meet, they set off for the station. They arrived back home just after halve past five. It had been an enjoyable day. Biggs had subsidized the trip to the tune of one pound per head out of his own pocket, without telling the boys. But he knew that it had been money well spent.

With little more than a week to go before the end of the school year, the pace was beginning to slow and in not a great deal of work was being done. Even Biggs had stopped setting homework to his Express set, for which they were very grateful. They knew that he would be taking them in their fourth year, at the end of which they would be sitting their O-Levels. They also knew that they would be getting mega-masses of extra homework, so they were grateful for the respite.

Biggs was due swap places with Malcolm Rowe and move to the Upper School as Senior Year Head, thus retaining responsibility for his current Third Year boys, who were of course shortly to become Forth Year's. He was pleased about that. He wouldn't have relished the thought of handing them over to Malcolm and then taking over the new Second Year himself He had always preferred teaching older boys and had in many ways regretted moving from the

Upper School. He had only done so to secure his post as Senior Year Head. He'd been appointed a couple of years earlier at the same time as Malcolm Rowe. At the time, they were both based in the Upper School and both had wanted to remain there. In the end it came to a flip of a coin to decide who would move to the Lower School and he'd lost! But the agreement had been that they would swap places after a couple of years. Now he was shortly to be returning and the future was looking brighter. Even the dragoness, Ms. Lynn Harmon would be leaving at the end of term, so he knew that he would not have to contend with her sexist machinations. Lynn-the-Grin had finally decided that the male chauvinists pigs at Gordon Bennett were beyond redemption and she had decided to try her luck at St. Trinian's. There had been great jubilation amongst the male staff on hearing the news. All in all, things were looking up and after the long Summer holiday, part of which he intended spending in his beloved America, he thought that he might even be able to look forward to the start of the new school year.

CHAPTER 30

"I don't believe it!" Biggs said. "You jammy sod, Chris! You couldn't repeat that in a month of Sundays."

"Easy-peasy...... and there's me thinking you were a big hero! But there's nothing to this flying lark, is there? It's kid's stuff."

It was the middle of August, two years on and Christopher was sixteen, going on seventeen. He had left school with a string O-Levels, all straight 'A's and had joined the Navy. He was at home on his first leave after starting his basic training.

Since his first flight in a glider at West Malling, when he had become an honorary Air Cadet and since his flight with Biggs to Stapleford in the Piper Cub, he had really caught the flying bug. He'd since attended five further gliding courses in the school holidays, as a helper and general dog's body and had received some serious flying training in gliders and in the Cub. Having transferred from the Sea Cadets to the Air Training Corps and entered on the permanent roll of the local squadron, he began attending most weekends at RAF West Malling as a sort of unofficial staff cadet. He was finally sent solo by Biggs in a glider, shortly after his sixteenth birthday.

He had been at a loose end and kicking his heels at home when the phone rang.

"Hello, Chris."

"Hello, Sir. How's it going?"

"It's going fine..... Do you remember some while back, you said that you would like to fly in a Tiger Moth and I said that if you kept your nose clean, I might take you up one day. Well are you still on for it?"

"The Tiger! You bet, Sir!..... Am I just?"

"Okay. We'll be flying a Tiger Club aircraft at Redhill, so you'll need to get another letter of permission from your mother, since you're still under eighteen. Oh, and you will need a jumper and a warm jacket. It may be summer and I know it's been warm recently, but it can still get quite cold at altitude. We'll be open to the elements and it will be a bit draftier than a glider."

"Brilliant, Sir. You've just made my day!"

"I'm pleased to hear it."

They arranged to go a couple of days later, when the forecast promised good weather. Biggs picked up Christopher from his home and they set off for Redhill aerodrome in the Trans Am. Redhill was a grass airfield, with two landing strips and the home of the Tiger Club. Christopher had flown once before from Redhill with Biggs in a Super Cub.

"I've been looking forward to this ever since you phoned, Sir."

"Come on, Chris, what's with the Sir? School's out! You don't have to call me Sir anymore..... It's Ray, okay.

"Right.... Got it.... How's it going, Ray?"

"Well.... I've just got this twit to take flying in a Tiger Moth, but apart from that, it's going fine."

They arrived at the airfield just before eleven o'clock. It was a glorious Summer's day. With a gentle breeze, good visibility and barely a cloud in the sky, it was a perfect day for flying. Biggs showed Christopher round the hangar. It was packed tightly with a myriad of light aircraft, some club owned and some privately owned. There were Tiger Moths and their look-alike Stamps. There were four-seat and two-seat Jodels. There were two-seat Condors and tiny single seat Turbulents all, painted a bright yellow. The common factor was that they were all tail-draggers. The Tiger Club didn't go in for modern nose-wheeled aircraft.

"Do you fly them all?" Christopher asked.

"No, not all. Many are privately owned. But I fly the Tigers, the Jodels, the Condors and the Turbulents. Oh, and of course the Super Cub which we flew in last time.... I do a lot of glider towing in that."

"Which one's ours?"

"It's outside waiting for us." Biggs pointed to a red and silver Tiger Moth, G-ACDC, parked on the grass outside the hangar. "But first you've got to sign a blood chit!"

"Blood chit?"

"Don't worry. It doesn't mean you've got to give blood. It's the temporary membership card that you filled last time. You have to join the club as a passenger member to make it legal."

Christopher signed the card and Biggs attached to it the letter of permission from his mother, required because he was under eighteen years of age.

"Well, Chris, once again you've just become a temporary member of the World's most exclusive and most famous flying club. Would you like to know who some of your fellow members are?"

"Who? Anyone important?.... apart from you, of course!"

Biggs showed Christopher a small book listing the members of the club. The members were listed alphabetically and he pointed to two names on separate pages...... HRH The Prince of Wales and the HRH The Duke of Edinburgh.

"Coor!"

"Well, if you ever meet either them in the future, you'll have a topic of conversation, won't you? You'll be able to say that you were members of the same club! There aren't many people who can say that, you know."

Christopher thumbed through the book and smiled when he found Biggs' name. What do the dates mean?... 1974 in your case.

"The year of election to membership of the club."

"And what do the letters G/C, G/T and S against your name stand for."

"Glider pilot, Tug pilot and Seaplane pilot."

"And the lads back at school thought they knew you! But they didn't know diddly, did they?"

Biggs smiled. "You knew more than most!.... Come on. Let's meet the Tiger.

They wandered out to the Tiger Moth. Although Christopher had seen Tigers before, it was the first time that he had been up close to one. He followed Biggs round the aircraft as he did the external checks.

"It looks a bit flimsy, all wires and fabric?"

"It may be all wires and fabric, as you put it, but don't let that fool you. It's incredibly strong and much stronger than many modern spam-cans!"

"It's got a tow hook, I see?"

"It sure has."

"Can they all tow gliders?"

"All the Tigers can."

"How about the others?"

"The Super Cub and the Condor have hooks. Oh, and I believe the big Jodel has, but I've never flown that."

When the external checks were completed, Christopher put on his World War II helmet and after strapping him into the front cockpit, Biggs went through the instrumentation and the working of the intercom.

"Why am I in the front seat? I thought I would be in the back."

"No. The pilot always flies from the back of a Tiger."

"I like the notice," Christopher said, pointing to a small brass plaque which read, 'AIRCRAFT BITE FOOLS.'

"It's to remind pilots that, no matter how experienced they might be, if they are foolish and mistreat the aircraft, they might well end up with their own set of wings.... or possibly horns! There's an old flying saying: There are *old* pilots and there are *bold* pilots, but there are very few *old bold* pilots!"

"I like it."

After strapping himself in and completing his startup checks, Biggs asked the mechanic to swing the propeller.

"Sucking in! Switches OFF."

"Switches OFF." Biggs confirmed.

The mechanic swung the propeller a few times to suck in fuel.

"Switches ON."

"Switches ON. CONTACT."

As the propeller was swung one more time, the engine roared into life. Although quite loud, the engine noise was not deafening and to a large extent it was deadened by the headsets. It was allowed to run for a few minutes at a fast idle in order to reach it's working temperature, then after completing further engine checks, Biggs signaled for the chocks to be removed from the wheels and they taxied to the holding point ready for take-off. Takeoff checks having been completed, Biggs taxied onto the grass runway.

"Ready, Chris?"

"Ready."

Biggs opened the throttle fully and they roared down the grass strip, getting airborne after only a short distance. The Tiger climbed rapidly and on reaching 500 feet they turned left, so as to stay clear of the Gatwick control zone. They headed for the North Downs ridge and the M25 motorway.

"Well! What do you think of it so far?"

"Fantastic!"

Climbing steadily all the time and keeping to the right of the M23 motorway, they eventually turned East and followed the M25 towards Sevenoaks.

"Put your hands and feet on the controls, Chris and follow me through."

Having flown several times before with Biggs in his Piper Cub, once in the Super Cup and many times in a glider, Christopher was quite familiar with the action of the controls. But the sensitivity varies from aircraft to aircraft and, so Biggs demonstrated their action again, as if he was a novice, as he had done many times before to countless other student pilots. Then followed a series of gentle turns, with Christopher following through on the controls and getting the feel of the aircraft. He quickly got the hang of it and Biggs could feel him starting to initiate the control movements himself.

"Okay, Chris. You have control. My hands are off."

"What.... You want me to fly it?"

"There's nobody else here! Just keep it straight ahead. Look at the nose and try to keep it in the same position on the horizon with a gentle stick pressure...... Good. Now try a gentle turn to the left. Ease it in gently, with stick and rudder together. Remember the stick is very sensitive. Treat it like your dick!...... Oh, I don't know though! You need to treat it gently and not play with it!"

"Do you mind, Ray..... I always treat it gently!"

"I'm pleased to hear it. And how about playing with it?"

"No comment!" Christopher giggled, through the intercom. "Let's just say that I always treat it gently!"

"In that case, do the same with the stick."

Christopher pushed the stick gently to the left and with the help with a touch of left rudder, the Tiger obediently went into its turn.

"Okay. That's good. Now centralize the controls and a slight back pressure on the stick to prevent the nose from dropping. Good..... Now ease out of the turn by pushing the other way and releasing the back pressure on the stick. You need to push a bit harder coming out of a turn. Watch the nose on the horizon..... Okay that was good. Now just try some gentle manoeuvres yourself to get the feel of it."

Christopher successfully executed a series of gentle turns to the right and to the left, confirming in Biggs' mind what he already knew, that Christopher had excellent coordination and was a natural pilot! He had flown with him enough times to know that was a natural, but the jump from a glider to a Tiger Moth could well be compared to that from a push bike to an Trans Am! He encouraged

Christopher to do steeper and steeper turns without letting the nose of the aircraft drop. He even managed to coordinate the actions of the stick, throttle and rudder pedals smoothly, with the precision of an expert, so that the Tiger flew cleanly into and out of the turns without losing height. Yes, Biggs thought to himself, Christopher was a natural pilot.

"Okay Chris. That was great. I have control..... Let's make it a bit more exciting! How about some aerobatics?"

"Yes please."

After a steep clearing turn to check that no other aircraft were about, Biggs increased the throttle and put the aircraft into a fairly steep dive. Then opening the throttle fully, he pulled steadily back on the stick and the Tiger pulled up into a loop. As they went over the top, Biggs closed the throttle and for a brief moment it fell silent. But that momentary silence was rapidly replaced by an increasing rush of air as Tiger entered the descent phase of its vertical circle and the ground loomed up in front of them, Finally leveling out, Biggs thought that he had better check Christopher's reaction before continuing further.

"Well?"

"Fantastic..... Let's do in again."

They completed a second loop.... and a third, followed by a couple of stall-turns and a steep turn pulling quite a bit of G-force and finishing with a final loop, all to Christopher's delight.

"Okay, Chris. You have control.... Take us back.!

"Back? Which way's back? I'm lost!"

"Steer 260."

"Right... 260. Christopher gently turned the Tiger onto 260 degrees. "That's almost due West, isn't it?"

"Very good. Who taught you maths? Well make a navigator out of you, yet."

"I don't want to be a navigator. I'll just settle for being a pilot."

"In a light aircraft, you have to be both..... But for now just concentrate on the flying..... Don't let your nose drop."

"Sorry."

As they approached the airfield, Biggs directed Christopher into joining a left hand circuit and resisted the temptation to take over the controls until the were about to turn onto their final approach.

"Okay, Chris. I have control, but follow me through for the landing."

After turning finals they did a glide approach ending with a gentle three point landing. Brilliant, Biggs thought to himself... It wouldn't have done to let Christopher see me do a bouncy landing! The Tiger was very forgiving, but it could be a bugger to do a perfect three-pointer every time. After taxing back to the hangar they climbed out of the Tiger and Christopher offered Biggs his hand "Thanks Ray. That was fantastic! I'll never forget it."

"It's not over yet, Chris. You really got the hang of that! I was really impressed. The Tiger is not an easy aircraft to handle at the best of times, even for an experienced pilot. You have to have one hundred hours as first pilot before you can join the Tiger Club and then undergo a series of check flights before you are let loose on the Tiger..... And you got the hang of it straight away! Yes, I really was impressed. We'll do a couple of circuits in the Condor. I want to see what you can really do!"

The Condor was a side-by-side two-seater and was more suitable for instructing, since it was easier for the instructor to monitor the actions of the pupil. They climbed aboard and after completing their checks which Biggs talked Christopher through, they taxied to the runway and took off. With Christopher following through on the controls, he talked him round the circuit. Although Christopher did not speak, he was making a mental note of Biggs' every action and where on the circuit each action was performed. They did the first circuit with touch-and-go landing. As they climbed out on a second circuit Biggs could feel Christopher initiating each control movement as he talked him through, so he removed his hands and feet completely and let him get on with it, only flowing him through on the controls for the final touchdown.

"Okay, taxi to the holding point."

Christopher taxied the Condor to the holding point ready for a third circuit.

"Do your takeoff checks...... out loud."

"Throttle friction set... Trim set.... Mixture rich.... Carburetor heat, off.... Fuel on..... Flaps, one notch.... Gauges: Altimeter set to zero; Gyro, set.... Flying gauges okay: Engine temperature in the green; oil pressure in the green.... Engine gauges okay... Harnesses secure... Hatches locked..... Magneto check?"

"No need, we've done two already.... Check the approach is clear."

"Approach clear."

"Line up on the runway."

After checking a second time that the approach was clear, Christopher taxied to the end of the grass strip.

"Okay, Chris. It's all yours...... Fly me a circuit."

Christopher lined up on the strip and opened the throttle fully. They roared down the strip and on reaching sixty mph, he gently eased back on the stick and lifted the

Condor off the ground. He continued a gentle climb and at 200 feet he raised the flaps. At 500 feet he turned 90 degrees onto a left hand circuit. He continued climbing to 1000 feet, leveled out and adjusted his elevator trim to relieve himself of all stick pressure. He then turned another 90 degrees to the left to fly downwind, parallel to the strip. Without being told, he did his downwind checks out loud. "Brakes off.... Mixture rich.... Carb. Heat set cold.... Fuel on." Then with a cheeky grin, he added, "Undercarriage.... no greens, but down and welded!"

Biggs burst out laughing! "Smart arse!"

Christopher continued flying downwind and then turned 90 degrees to the left onto his base leg. He eased back on the throttle and pulled one notch of flaps. At 500 feet he turned finals, pulled full flaps and adjusted the elevator trim to maintain a steady sixty-five mph descent. As the aircraft approached the ground, he gently closed the throttle and eased back on the stick, completing the most gentle of landings. Up to that moment, apart from his 'smart arse' observation, Biggs had not said a word and had not once touched the controls!

"I don't believe it! You jammy sod, Chris. You couldn't repeat that in a month of Sundays."

"Easy-peasy...... and there's me thinking you were a big hero! But there's nothing to this flying lark, is there? It's kid's stuff."

"Okay, clever Dick..... Let's see an action replay.... Do it again."

Christopher taxied back to the holding point of the grass runway. He did his take-off checks out loud and took-off for another circuit. Without saying another word, he completed it as competently as the first, making another superbly gentle landing. He turned to face Biggs, with a smile of satisfaction. "Easy-peasy."

"Show-off...... Put it there, Chris," Biggs said, offering him his hand. "You shouldn't have joined the Navy. You should have joined the RAF as a pilot. You're a natural. I've been teaching people to fly for over ten years and in all that time, I've never met anyone take to it so easily!.... Well, you might as well finish the job. Take us back to the hangar."

"Thanks Ray. That was brilliant." Christopher taxied back to the hangar, parking next to the Tiger Moth, G-ACDC, that they had flown earlier.

After a coffee in the clubhouse, Christopher treated Biggs to a Pub lunch of scampi and chips, before being taken home. He invited him in for a coffee and chin-wag.

"That was the best day out I've ever had. I'll never forget it. Thanks for everything, Ray..... and I don't just mean today's flying...... That was out of this world. I do mean *everything*. The gliding and all the other times you've taken me up. In fact the past five years at school..... They've been great!"

"What about the knuckle-rappings, the elbow-tweaking and the put-downs? Were they great too?"

"Of course they were! They were all part of it. I wouldn't have missed any of it. And look at all the scrapes you got me out of with other teachers, when I couldn't keep my big mouth shut."

"Yes, I'll give you that. There were quite a few of those."

You've been much more than just my teacher and Year Head. You've been more like a friend.... How come we got on so well, right from the start?"

"I can tell you the answer to that, Chris. I've never said this before, but you were exactly like me, when I was at school, many moons ago. In fact we could have been dead-ringers for each other!"

"Dead-ringers, eh. I should have guessed. But you don't mean in terms of looks, do you?"

"That's right. I don't mean in terms of looks. After all, I was much more handsome!"

"Dream on! You couldn't have been. I'm an Adonis!"

"Now whose dreaming?... No, I mean in terms of temperament and general attitude to authority. I had a glib tongue, just like you and I was cheeky, without going over the top, just like you. In fact, thinking back on it, I've probably been reliving my own schooldays through you."

"You mean a sort of reincarnation?"

"In a way, I suppose, except that you have to be dead to be reincarnated."

"Oh, yes, so you do."

"Do you remember what you said when we first met? You were in the Second Year and I asked you if your name was Christopher Bird?"

"Yes, I do as it goes..... I said, I do have that privilege, Sir.... Any other teacher would have thrown a wobbly, but you just burst out laughing!"

"That's right, so I did. And the reason that I found it so funny was because when I was about your age, a new teacher to my school had asked me the same question.... except of course that he asked me if my name was Ray Smith.... and I gave him exactly the same answer!"

"Great minds think alike, eh.... Anyway, thanks again for everything. It's been great five years. I've enjoyed every minute."

"It was no big deal, Chris."

"Oh, yes it was! Don't sell yourself short. It was a very big deal!.... Anyway, how about keeping in touch?"

"Good idea, Chris," Biggs said, as they shook hands. "Let's do that. Good luck with the Navy. Write and let me know how you get on. You've got my phone number and you know where I live, so let's meet up and go for a drink when you get some leave."

They did.

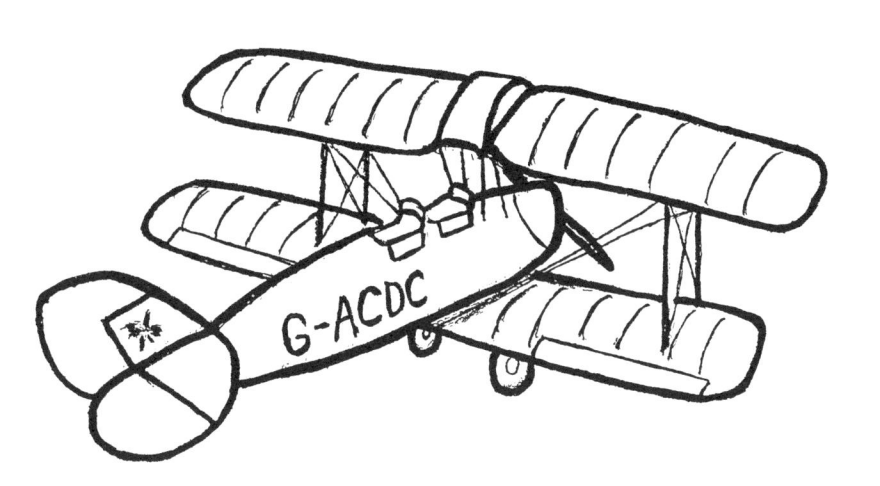

* * *

Christopher stands guard

Time out from gliding - The Piper Club at Rochester

Biggs' playtime